John DeChancie

CASTLE
MURDERS

Castle #??

D0051720

Was it the Royal Scribe?
In the library?
With a broadax?

FOUL PLAY

Dalton looked the body over. "No bruises. No blood. Look at that jewelry. A thief wouldn't leave those. I suppose we could rule out foul play."

Thaxton scratched his chin thoughtfully. Then he said, "Let's turn him over."

"Should we touch the body?"

"We can always put him back. Get his legs."

They shifted the body to its side, then gently rolled it over.

Thaxton's eyebrows rose. "Hello, hello, what's this?"

A small rent in the fabric of the gown, a dark stain surrounding it, was located between the shoulder blades at a spot to the left of the middle of the back.

"Then again, foul play just might be the ticket."

Praise for
CASTLE MURDERS

**Don't miss the other books
in the outrageous *Castle Perilous* series
by John DeChancie!**

Ace Books by John DeChancie

CASTLE PERILOUS
CASTLE FOR RENT
CASTLE KIDNAPPED
CASTLE WAR!
CASTLE MURDERS

The Skyway Trilogy

STARRIGGER
RED LIMIT FREEWAY
PARADOX ALLEY

CASTLE MURDERS

John DeChancie

ACE BOOKS, NEW YORK

This book is an Ace original edition,
and has never been previously published.

CASTLE MURDERS

An Ace Book / published by arrangement with
the author

PRINTING HISTORY
Ace edition / May 1991

ISBN: 0-441-09273-X

Ace Books are published by The Berkley Publishing Group,
200 Madison Avenue, New York, New York 10016.
The name "ACE" and the "A" logo
are trademarks belonging to Charter Communications, Inc.

PRINTED IN THE UNITED STATES OF AMERICA

10 9 8 7 6 5 4 3 2 1

This book is dedicated to
Beth, Bettie, Bev, Cally (Cassy), Debbie, Deno,
Jan, Jo, Kay, Leigh, Pamela, Romana, Sarah,
Stephanie, Aaron, Bill, Brian, Brion, Bud, DDB,
Grant, Irv, Jim, Joel, Jon, Lawrence, Nicolai, Patrick,
Pete, Roy, Scott, Smokey, Steve, Stu, Tim, Tom,
Walt, and the rest of the stalwart contributors
to the Science Fiction Echo—part of a
worldwide nexus called
FidoNet—cybernauts all.
:-)

And this huge Castle, standing here sublime,
I love to see the look with which it braves,
—Cased in the unfeeling armour of old time—
The lightning, the fierce wind, and trampling waves.

—Wordsworth

THE EIDOLONS OF THE KING
PREFACE TO THE CASTLE EDITION

ORDINARILY AN INTRODUCTION OR PROLEGOMENON is expected to
shed some light on the material it prefaces or introduces,
enough so that the reader may find his way through an
unfamiliar literary landscape. In the present case, however,
this prefatory note to the work now known as *The Eidolons of
the King: Tales of Castle Perilous* can serve only to delimit
areas of shadow that shroud the work in mystery.

Particularly obscure is the question of its origin and authorship. To say that its provenance is mysterious is to put it
mildly. To put the matter simply: the original paperbound
volumes of the books of *The Eidolons*—cheap pulp paper,
hastily glued bindings, garish covers and all—were found one
day in the castle library, having been shelved among finely
wrought leatherbound tomes of bardic sagas and epic poetry.
No one knows who put them there.

Would that this were the only mystery! The deeper and more
fundamental question, of course, is: Who wrote these books
and how did their author come by his intimate knowledge of
Castle Perilous? to say nothing of his apparent clairvoyance in

producing these accounts of the storm of recent events that have raged round it.

Castle Perilous! At its very mention the heart skips a beat. For the benefit of the reader and especially for those castle Guests who seek a general orientation within these pages, it might do well to pause here and describe what the name evokes for we who make the castle our home.

For the castle itself is a mystery. Its very existence maintained from second to second by a transmutational spell laid long ago on a great demon, Castle Perilous is a magical construction. Its huge bulk—far more than what mortal hands could amass piling stone upon stone—bestrides a citadel commanding the bleak Plains of Baranthe in the Western Pale. The castle is a world in itself; but far more than that, it contains countless worlds.

Some explication is needed. As would any structure of its size, Perilous has innumerable doors and windows; but the anomaly is that some of these are portals to other worlds. Pass through any of the castle's "aspects," as they are called, and you cross into a strange new cosmos. There are exactly 144,000 aspects in the castle. Any resident or Guest of the castle can describe the sensation of wonder engendered when, after traversing gloomy hallways, one goes through an archway or alcove and steps out onto a vast savannah where herds of animals graze—or into a deep forest limned in cathedral light—or onto a desolate plain whereon sits a domed city under an alien sun.

But let us return to the controversy surrounding the authorship of *The Eidolons*.

Who is the man whose name is emblazoned (immodestly so, if I might add) across the covers of these "paperbacks"? Where does he live? As the language of these works is contemporary (if quasi-grammatical) English with lapses into pseudo-Elizabethan cant, one might well conclude that the author hails from the castle aspect known as Earth. But, truth be told, a thorough search of the appropriate reference volumes has failed to produce any mention of either the author or his works. Moreover, no trace can be found of the publisher whose name and address is printed on the verso of the title page! (There are attendant minor mysteries, of which we should make passing mention. The author's surname, for instance. What nationality is it? English, via Anglo-Norman? French? Anglicized Italian? The name is very possibly a pseudonym. And who are the individuals whose fawning endorsements are bruited on and about the cover? Presumably approving critics or admiring colleagues of the author, and we would be forced to conclude one or the other or both, were it not for the fact that no trace can be found of these people either. Phantoms all! Then there is the matter of the cover "art." What sort of deranged soul could . . . ? But let us set these relatively trivial matters aside.)

What, then, are we to make of all this? The only conjecture to acquire any currency has it that *The Eidolons* originated in a world that is a variant of Earth and one in which the castle is a fiction, not the reality we know. Here we tread disputed ground, for some hold that there are more than 144,000 universes. In fact, there may be an infinite number of them, of which the assortment provided by the castle is only a random and constantly shifting sample. Be that as it may, the conjecture that these books were generated in some backwater universe does not explain how they came to the castle, nor how they were written. Indeed, it makes the issue all the more obscure, for how could a stranger to the castle, a stranger even to the universe in which the castle exists, have produced these highly romanticized but essentially accurate accounts, even to describing the intimate thoughts and sometimes inexplicable actions of the master of Castle Perilous, Incarnadine, King by the grace of the gods and Lord of the Western Pale?

We can dismiss out of hand the notion that His Majesty penned *The Eidolons*, for he has categorically denied it.

Who then? A Guest? If so, why the secrecy? What is he (or she) hiding?

I have no answers to these questions, but, as Royal Librarian, I can here offer a somewhat different explanation for the origin of *The Eidolons*.

The castle's library is an enigma in itself. Not a day goes by when the library staff is not surprised by finding some new wonder on its shelves, books that were not even suspected to exist. Marvelous books, strange books—even dangerous books. (One such describes the construction of a weapon so terrible that I cannot bring myself to describe its intended effects. Another provides schematics for an infernal device which, from what can be made of it, is intended for the express purpose of trapping a god. Which deity is to be bagged is not specified. Needless to say, these and other dismaying oddities have been sequestered in the Closed Stacks, where, if I have anything to say in the matter, they will remain indefinitely.) Where do these books come from? Not even Lord Incarnadine can say. He himself has added very few books to the collection. Thus, I am not beyond imagining that the library itself has magically generated *The Eidolons*. How? I know not. Why has it chosen to do so in such a peculiar idiom? I cannot fathom it. But the works exist, and that is enough for me. Their significance and importance cannot be questioned.

You hold in your hand a new edition of *The Eidolons*, painstakingly set in movable type from the originals, printed on vellum stock, and bound in fine-grained leather with gilt lettering and filigree. The text is faithfully reproduced without editorial emendation or gloss.

Read *The Eidolons* and wonder, taking with a grain of salt its melodramatic excesses. Written in an uneven style by turns breezy, serviceable, and sesquipedalian, these tales hew close to all the conventions of the popular romance, and are consequently guilty of the faults and foibles that go along with such fare. But minor narrative flaws can be ignored, as can the occasional textual solecism. (In the first volume, "portfolio" is used where "folio" is meant. A typo, or the result of the author's ignorance? We will charitably opt for the former, as "folio" does appear elsewhere.) It is the story, after all, that is of prime interest.

Above all, read the castle tales and enjoy them. The magic casements open; the perilous seas and all of Creation lie before you. . . .

—Osmirik, Royal Scribe and Librarian

FOREWORD
TO THE FIFTH VOLUME

ENIGMA UPON ENIGMA!

Initially only four volumes of the Castle Edition of *The Eidolons* were planned, for the simple reason that only four original paperbacks were found. Now, a fifth penny dreadful (Really—how long are these cheap books expected to last?— surely no more than a fortnight!) has appeared in its rightful place on the shelf next to its kin.

Curiously, the "Preface" to the first edition was reproduced in this new volume, thereby giving new life to the "inside job" theory of authorship. You may well imagine my chagrin at finding myself quoted on the back cover. "Read the castle tales and enjoy!", indeed.*

But what is absolutely mystifying . . . there are no words to express the emotion . . . is that this very "Foreword" appeared as well—paradoxically so, for I had not even begun to write it!

Yet here it is, written in an uncanny imitation of my own

---

*Why the vaguely Yiddish usage? Incidentally, even this footnote appears in the original.

style, complete with expressions of my astonishment at finding it.

I will not begin an attempt at explanation. The librarian proposes, the library disposes!

Read on.

—Osmirik, Ryl. Scrb. & Lbrn.

ABELARD, SOUTH DAKOTA

IT WAS A STARK AND DORMY NIGHT.

The campus was quiet. Northeastern State University wasn't the liveliest of schools, and it was Monday night, and it was snowing again, the wind howling out of the plains. Nothing to do but stay in the dorm and study.

There was enough on Melanie McDaniel's study agenda. Deadlines were approaching: a paper for Philosophy 101 on Aristotle's *Ethics* was due in three days, and one on Conrad's *Nostromo*, for English 125 (20th Century British Novels), had been due three days *ago*. There was a calculus test tomorrow. Other stuff. But Melanie didn't feel much like studying. She didn't feel much like doing anything but fiddling on her computer.

Fiddling was what it was. Melanie was on-line via modem to the campus's computer bulletin board system, or "BBS." Through it she was plugged into a worldwide network of amateur computer users called the CyberNet. The Net was a forum, a meeting place, for people who liked to gab about anything and everything. The discussions were grouped into topic-areas, with subjects ranging from current events to "Star

Trek" to computer software. Melanie posted messages in many
areas, but she particularly like Woman Talk: The National
Women's Forum, a cross between a slumber party and a
backroom political caucus.

The cathode-ray tube of Melanie's IBM clone displayed:

To: Melanie McDaniel
From: Cindy Thayer   Msg 256
Subject: Men again!

I second the emotion. Men are congenitally polygamous, as in Higgamus Piggamus. When WE'RE that way,
we're "sluts." You can't win, kid. Sorry you lost him. But
there are a lot of fish in that sea—except that they're
all kind of slimy and scaly. Keep your chin up. Bye!
                                                   Cindy

—

Origin: The Boardinghouse: Cooperstown, NY (1:398/
276.9)

She looked out the window. Icy snowflakes ticked against
the glass. Abelard was completely blotted out. Nothing was
visible except an outside light in the quadrangle, a yellow halo
in the darkness. She thought about Chad and about how the last
thing he had said to her was that he needed "space" and that the
relationship wasn't going anywhere and that he needed to be
free of commitments in order to concentrate on getting through
a tough term on his way to his economics degree. Maybe when
he was through grad school and had his MBA he'd be ready for
a serious relationship.

Yeah? So then what was he doing now, impaled as he was on
the claws of Nadine Borkowski? She was into him deep. He'd
even cut his hair and sold his BMW motorcycle. *She* wasn't
about to ride on the back of that thing, so what did he need it
for? Yes, Nadine. Anything you say, Nadine.

Chad wasn't polygamous. He was just dumb. Dumb to fall
for that domineering, scheming, lowborn, vile, deceitful . . .

She took a deep breath. So what? She'd lost him, and that was that. Did she still love him? Of course; he was terrifically good-looking and a lot of fun. But someone else had snared him, and Melanie was history. Life goes on.

Yes, she was still in love with him.

Melanie typed at the keyboard, telling the BBS to search for messages with the name McDaniel in the "To:" line. A pair popped up, and she keyed in the digits for the first one.

To: Melanie McDaniel
From: Fran DiMiro
Subject: Abortion

The Fundamentalists aren't going to change tactics now. Sure, some recent court decisions have been going their way, but

Melanie squelched the message. Another go-around on the abortion issue. She wasn't in the mood for serious discussion right now. Besides, she didn't know how she felt about the issue any more. For years she had harbored the suspicion, unspoken and even unrealized until very recently, that if she were indeed ever faced with the decision of whether to have an abortion, she wouldn't be able to go through with it. Not because of moral qualms, but general queasiness.

Well, now she was faced with it. She was almost sure she was pregnant with Chad's baby. You don't miss two periods and put it down to the whims of nature. Not if you knew your diaphragm had slipped off on at least one occasion. There was an outside chance that the missed periods were due to something else, but . . .

An abortion? She just didn't think she could go through with it. Funny how you could intellectually believe in a thing and not be able to accept it emotionally.

Without logging off the system, she left the desk and lay down on the bed to cry quietly for a while.

When she was done she got up and sat back down at the computer. She hoped The Blues weren't returning: her depression. She had suffered with it off and on since her early teens, and had once been prescribed medication for it. Now, what with Chad and the pregnancy, a bad bout of The Blues was a danger.

Drying her eyes, she punched in the other message number.

To: Melanie McDaniel
From: Linda Barclay   Msg 287
Subject: Boyfriends

Melanie smiled. She liked Linda and had been exchanging messages with her for several months over the private channel of the system. Linda knew everything about Chad and about Chad's straying off to Nadine. Melanie had been very open, spilling everything but the pregnancy. That was still top secret.

The body of Linda's message read:

You sounded pretty down in your last post. Did something new happen? I mean something BAD new? If so, tell me about it. Don't stew. I know you've heard it all before, but it isn't the end of the world when your boyfriend dumps you. Life goes on. Doesn't help, does it? Okay, but talk about it. It might stop hurting just a little bit. Post back soon. See ya.

—

Origin: The Castle BBS (1:897/675)

Melanie gave the computer instructions to boot up the wherewithal to post a message. The process was the computerized equivalent of writing a note on a piece of paper and thumbtacking it to a cork bulletin board, except that it was done with electrons, not paper and metal and cork.

To: Linda Barclay
From: Melanie McDaniel
Subject: Life

You're right, I'm not feeling very good. Its like what's outside tonight, just snow swrling around and darkness and lonliness. Sometimes i think i just want

everything to go dark forever, and no more Melanie. I
guess im in a pretty bad way. Hell. Damn. Know any
good fourletter words? You cant say the F word on
the Net or the moderator will come around and wjs

Her eyes filled with tears and she was blinded. By the time
she'd dabbed her face dry with a tissue she saw that she had
inadvertently hit Control-s. The message had been "Saved"
and posted on the system. Well, she'd just kill it and start all
over again—but then she shrugged. What the hell. Leave it.
She didn't feel like BBSing any more tonight.

She was about to log off, when she noticed something
blinking in the upper left corner of the screen. It was a prompt,
and it read PRESS "R" TO READ INCOMING MESSAGE.
She'd never seen anything like it before. Was the System
Operator trying to talk to her on-line?

She hit R and the message spilled across the screen at 2400
bits per second.

To: Melanie McDaniel
From: Linda Barclay   Pvt Msg
Subject: Worried

No, you don't sound at all good. Something did
happen. Tell me about it. Post back immediately. I can
talk to you on-line. Please answer!

—Linda

—

Origin: The Castle BBS

Melanie was puzzled. All this time she had assumed that
Linda was posting from a BBS far away in another city. It took
days, sometimes weeks for a message on the CyberNet to
negotiate the maze of interconnecting phone lines and reach its
intended recipient, and the same length of time for an answer
to get back. The Net was not a direct-communication system.
That would cost a lot of money, and the Net was a nonprofit
system. A bulletin board didn't work like that. It was slow;
however, it was cheap.

But Linda was answering a message that Melanie had just

posted minutes ago. That was impossible, if Melanie understood the way the Net operated. The only way it could happen was if Linda were sitting at the terminal of the university's BBS computer over in the Student Union, just a block away.

But the message's Origin line had read "The Castle BBS," not the "Eagle's Eyrie," the name of the university system. Melanie had never noticed a location tag for The Castle, but it had to be outside the university.

At the SELECT: prompt she hit R for "Reply" and TO: LINDA BARCLAY came up automatically. For "Subject" she hit the RETURN key and the computer reproduced Linda's subject line: WORRIED. She began typing the body of the message.

I was surprised to get your message. Are you somehow patched through the Eagle's Eyrie? How did you get my message so quickly? Anyway, I'm sorry about that last post. Was feeling pretty rocky. But I'm okay n

Suddenly the keyboard froze. She vainly jabbed random keys and hit RETURN, but nothing happened. Then:

CHAT: start
Hi, Melanie! Thought I'd break in and talk on-line. Your message did worry me. How are you really feeling?

On the screen, the cursor had moved to a blank line. Melanie was puzzled. She typed:

Linda? Is that you?

Yeah, it's me. Want to tell me what's going on inside your head?

How are you doing this? Are you on the university system?

No, but I'm using a modem you wouldn't believe. It can do almost anything. I'm on a direct line to your computer.

Wow, that really neat. I can't understand it, but its great. Anyway, your right, I'm pretty down. But Ill be alright.

Excuse me if I don't believe that. You're really sound depressed. You're not thinking of doing something silly, are you?

Melanie thought about. She was indeed thinking of doing something. But what she typed was:

No, I"ll be alreight. Excuse my typing

You're putting up a good front, but aren't you having suicidal thoughts?

Melanie sighed. No use to hide it.

Okay your right. How did you know?

How? Because I've been there myself. But I sense something else wrong, something major. Care to tell me?

Well, there is something. Jeez, I don't know.

Are you pregnant?

Melanie was amazed.

Linda, do you have a cristal ball? Yeah, you guessed it. I'm preggy.

That's "crystal." I don't need one to know who the daddy is, do I? The dork.

Chads not a dork. He's immature and needs someone to tell him what to do and be a mother to him. I wasnt ready to do that.

Sorry. Have you told him?

No. Why complicate his life? It was my fault anyway.

It takes two to tango, kid. Well, have you thought about what you're going to do about it?

If your talking about abortion, I think ive pretty much ruled that out.

So, you either keep the baby or give it up.

I havent even begun to think aobut that. I guess Ill have to drop out of school.

Not necessarily, but you might want to do that just to get yourself together.

Yeah, Im so behind. I haven't done a thing all term. I might flunk out.

Ever thought about getting away for a while, away from everything, just to clear your head?

I'd love to be somewhere else, anywhere else. The Virgin Islands maybe. Hah! Great place for a woman in my condition. Sun, sand. Blue water. I'd love it.

Well, I can't give you the Virgin Islands exactly. But you're welcome to come stay with us at the castle.

What's the castle?

It's just what it sounds like. I live with a lot of people in a huge castle. It's fun. We'd love to have you.

Where is it?

Very near to you. In fact, you wouldn't believe how close it is. Want to hop over for a visit?

Sounds inviting. Maybe I'll take you up on it someday.

Why not now? We can come pick you up.

Melanie thought it over. What the heck. What else was she doing that was so important?

Tonite? Well . . . OK. Yeah, if it's not too much trouble. Want me to wait outside the dorm? Im in Haberman Hall. Are you going to send a car? Hey. You guys aren't terrorists or anything, are you?

Yeah, we hijack castles. We have a fix on you right now. You don't have to do anything. Just a sec.

The cursor blinked at her silently. She sat and waited for half a minute, then keyed:

Linda, are you still there?

Yep. Melanie, go to your closet and open the door.

Melanie frowned.

Huh?

Just go look in your closet. You'll be surprised.

Well, if you say so. This is really

Melanie didn't know what to say. She got up and went to the closet of the small dorm room and put her hand on the doorknob. Was this some practical joke, some jape designed to make her feel foolish? If so, it wasn't very funny, and it didn't seem like a thing Linda would do. But what else could it be?

She turned the knob and opened the door.

The closet was full of her roommate's junk, just as before. No change.

So it was a joke after all. Melanie didn't understand.

Then she saw light coming from the rear of the closet and suddenly noticed that it looked as if the back wall had been torn out. Light was coming through from what she presumed was the room next door.

"Melanie?"

It was a woman's voice, and one she didn't recognize.

"Who is it?"

"It's me, Linda. Can we clear some of this junk out of the way?"

Melanie shoved aside her roommate's four winter coats—one of which was fox fur and very expensive—and revealed a smiling face.

"Hi! Melanie? I'm Linda."

Linda was pretty and blond and had large blue eyes. Her teeth were very white and even.

"Hi," Melanie said. "You were right next door all the time?"

"Not exactly. Is all this stuff yours?"

"No. My roommate ran off to Peru with a guy, an archeologist. She left all her stuff."

"So you have the place to yourself, eh? Great. Want to come through?"

"Uh . . . okay."

Melanie shoved the tangle of clothes to one side and made an opening for herself, which she slipped through, ducking under the low shelf. She stumbled on a guitar case, and Linda helped her out the other side.

What was on the other side was not another dorm room. It was an immense chamber with a vaulted ceiling, filled with strange and wondrous things. The place looked like something out of a Frankenstein movie. Melanie's gaze was torn between the huge machines resembling electrical transformers along the far wall and an arrangement of even stranger components in the middle of the floor.

"That's the computer I've been working with," Linda said, pointing to the latter grouping. "It's a mainframe."

"A mainframe?"

"Yeah, but it's different from your average computer. Works by magic."

"Magic?"

"Yeah. Come over and meet Jeremy. He's our computer whiz."

Linda led Melanie across the floor and around a U-shaped wall of instruments. Seated at a terminal in the middle was a thin young man in blue tights and a red tunic—he looked no more than sixteen years old.

Jeremy looked over his shoulder. "You want to hold the portal, or can we let it float?"

Linda turned to Melanie. "Are you going to stay with us for a while? We can call the portal back any time."

"Uh, sure. Yeah, I'll stay."

"Break the spell, Jeremy."

"Sure thing."

Jeremy jabbed at the keypad, looked at the screen, then sat back and swiveled around. "It's broken."

Melanie looked back at the wall. The opening was gone, replaced by dark stone. She turned back to Linda, who, she now noticed, was dressed in black tights, pointed shoes, and an orange and white striped doublct. She looked like she was dressed to play Hamlet.

"Linda, where are we?"

Linda smiled brightly. "Welcome to Castle Perilous."

Castle—Queen's Dining Hall

THE DISCUSSION HAD SOMEHOW GOTTEN SIDETRACKED onto music, having started out on the question of whether new inductees would benefit by a proposed formal orientation session. The upshot was "No," and that had been the end of the matter.

"Myself, I like classical," said the man everyone called Monsieur DuQuesne as he picked at a plate of clams in Mornay sauce. He was small and round-faced and wore old-fashioned round glasses. He was always dressed for the opera: white tie and tails. He was sociable, but no one knew much about him because he rarely spoke of himself.

"So do I," Deena Williams said.

DuQuesne was mildly surprised. "You do?"

"Yeah. What's the matter? Don't you think my kind can like that stuff?"

"It's not that. You've never said anything before."

"Well, I do. Oh, I like the kind you can dance to, all right, but I think classical's good too."

"Who's your favorite composer?"

"I listen to it, but I don't know much about it. I kind of liked that thing you were playin' when I came to get you for lunch."

"That was the *Peer Gynt Suite*, by Edvard Grieg."

"Grieg, huh?"

The dining hall was full. The Earth portal had been wandering lately and there were many new people from all over the world. Consequently, the table bore dishes representing many different kinds of cuisine.

Tall, curly-haired Gene Ferraro was sampling something he thought might be Balinese: rice, nuts, and vegetables in a ginger sauce. He chewed thoughtfully. Malaysian? Anyway, it wasn't bad, if you liked that sort of stuff. He swallowed.

"Edvard Grieg," he said, "was as fat as a pieg."

Deena Williams looked at him. "You say somethin'?"

A man called Thaxton, light-haired and distinguished, was seated to Gene's right. "He certainly did. He said that Edvard Grieg was as fat as a pieg."

"I heard him. 'Pieg'? What the hell's that?"

Thin, balding, and middle-aged, Cleve Dalton was on Gene's left. "There's a term for that sort of rhyme, but it escapes me."

"It's called 'cheating,' " Thaxton said.

"What brought on that bit of verse, Gene?" Dalton asked.

"Nothing. It just suddenly occurred to me that Edvard Grieg was —"

"Et cetera, et cetera," Thaxton said. "Well, go on, man. Finish it."

"Finish what?"

"The clerihew."

Deena looked offended. "Cleri-what?"

Thaxton said, "At Balliol we used to improvise them at table."

"Balli-*what*?"

"Oxford."

A man in Nigerian tribal dress seated next to Deena said, "We used to do limericks at Trinity."

Thaxton said, "I shouldn't be surprised at anything they do in Cambridge." He turned to Gene. "Well?"

Gene regard the stone-ribbed ceiling for a moment. Then, stumped, he took another bite.

"You don't start a clerihew without finishing it."

"Oh, I do it all the time," Dalton said. "Music? Let's see. Uh, okay. How about this: Gustav Mahler / liked to jump and holler."

Thaxton frowned. "It's all very well to start something. Well, I suppose I'll have to do your dirty work." He took another bite of Steak Diane and chewed thoughtfully.

"Right. I've got it." He got up and recited:

> "Gustav Mahler
> Liked to jump and hahler.
> He wrote to perfection
> The tune *Resurrection*."

Dalton scowled. "Not what you'd call inspired."

Thaxton sat down. "You can do better, I suppose?"

"Maybe."

Many of the diners were in costume. Not all were medieval, some shading into the Renaissance and beyond. Gene was dressed in something out of Dumas or Edmund Rostand. On the table in front of him, a wide-brimmed hat blossomed with a white plume. He had taken to training with a rapier lately and had become quite the proficient fencer. He was good with almost any kind of sword. He was in fact the castle's best blade-wielder, dazzling swordsmanship being his particular magical stock in trade.

Suddenly goosed by the Muse, he sat up straight. He blurted:

> "Edvard Grieg
> Was as fat as a pieg.
> He wrote *Peer Gynt*.
> I sure wish he dynt."

Groans around the table.

Dalton picked up the plate with a roast chicken on it and set it in front of Gene. "For that, you win the pullet surprise."

Thaxton said, "For *that*, you ought to be taken out and shot."

"One bullet through the head, please. Quick and clean. Except for a little blood and brains on the ground."

"Very little brains, I'm afraid."

"Hey, I'm eatin'," Deena complained.

DuQuesne said, "What are you up to these days, Gene? You're dressed fit to kill, and something tells me that should be taken literally."

"Snowclaw and I are staging a revolution in Arcadia."

"I don't believe I know that aspect."

"Keep, west wing, right next to the chapel."

"Human world?"

"Yeah."

"What do they make of Snowclaw?"

"Sheila tricks him out to look human. She's good at that."

Thaxton said, "I've never understood why that beast doesn't hang about with his own kind."

"I don't recall ever seeing Snowclaw's kind in the castle," DuQuesne said.

"Well, with the other nonhumans, then."

Gene said, "Snowy's always said that he basically likes the way humans smell. Reminds him of rotting blubber. He happens to like rotting blubber."

"Where do the nonhumans hang out?" Deena wanted to know.

"They have their own dining hall," DuQuesne said. "Haven't you ever been there?"

"No. Where is it?"

"North forebuilding, near the Hall of the Kings."

"The Hall of the Mountain Kings, perhaps?" Thaxton said slyly.

DuQuesne ignored him. "There are many other dining halls and Guest residences, you know."

Deena said, "That I know. I ran into one the other day. All kinds of people in there I didn't recognize."

"They would be Guests from human worlds other than Earth."

"I kinda figured that."

"They tend to keep to themselves. So do the nonhumans."

"As do we," Dalton said.

"Nerds of a feather," Gene mumbled.

"Speak of the nonhuman," Dalton said.

Everyone looked up as Snowclaw came striding into the room with his huge broadax, blade wickedly gleaming, balanced across his shoulder. Snowclaw was an immense ursine-humanlike creature completely covered in fur of the purest arctic white. Yellow-eyed and sinewy, mouth ferociously toothed, Snowclaw was something you would not care to be politely introduced to in a clean well-lighted place, much less meet in a dark alley.

"Hi, everybody!" He came over to the table and threw the broadax down, knocking over a tureen of crab bisque. "Oops, sorry."

"Think nothing of it," Thaxton said, mopping his lap with a serviette.

"Your spell wore off," Gene observed. "We'll have to stop by Sheila's world and get you fixed up."

"So, Gene," Dalton said, "you and Snowclaw are off to war and revolution. Who are you overthrowing? What sort of potentate? King, prince, sultan, pharaoh, what?"

"I'm embarrassed to say that we're aiding the royalists against an anarcho-syndicalist regime that came to power by revolution. The regime's been so monstrous and bloody that it makes a monarchy look utopian by comparison."

"I'm surprised there are any royalists left."

"There are almost none in the country itself. Most of them are émigrés in a neighboring state."

"Well, it sounds like a good cause."

"It does kind of recharge the old moral batteries," Gene acknowledged.

"How do you feel about it, Snowclaw?"

Snowclaw sat down. "Don't know about that stuff. I just like it when the fur flies and the guts go splattering all over the place."

"Energizing the ethical dry cells, as it were," Thaxton said.

Just then Linda Barclay walked in with Melanie in tow, Jeremy bringing up the rear. Introductions were made all around.

Deena asked, "How do you like it so far, Melanie?"

"Fine, so far."

"Wait till the creepy stuff starts happening."

"Uh . . . like what?"

Deena set her coffee cup down. "Well, let's see. A while back we had the Blue Meanies invadin'. Then the devils from Hell. But that's nothing compared to when the whole place goes crazy and the walls turn to rubber and things start shakin' and shiftin' around."

Dalton said, "The castle has been unstable at times. And there are permanent areas of instability. But you keep away from those parts."

"Oh."

"Soon you'll acquire a sixth sense about the place, and you'll be able to find your way around. And depending on what your magical talent is, you'll be able to use that to advantage as well."

"Magical talent?"

Linda explained, "Most people acquire the ability to do magic when they get to the castle."

"Most people," Gene said. "Then there are the retards, like Snowy and me."

"Don't listen to him. Gene's the best swordsman in the castle, and Snowy can teleport."

"Not very well," Snowclaw said. "Last time I tried it I slammed myself into a wall and got knocked out for an hour."

"You never mentioned it," Gene said. "That's strange."

"It hurt."

"Do you have to run to start teleporting?"

"No, I usually stay still and just think. Then I take like one or two steps, and I'm where I want to go."

"Then how did you wind up slamming into a wall?"

"You tell me."

Gene thought about it. "You must have materialized inside the wall."

Linda flinched. "Oh, my. That's a terrible thought. Don't do it again, Snowy."

"I won't. I never liked doing it."

Dalton looked at Melanie. "Most people's talents don't get them into trouble if they exercise a little discretion and watch what they're doing."

Melanie nodded. "I see. What will my talent be?"

"Oh, there's no telling. Anything from materialization to teleportation, to—"

"Dowsing," Gene said. "Necromancy, palm-reading."

"Not *that* stuff," Linda jeered.

"Channeling?"

"It'll be something useful, Melanie."

"Channeling is useful," Gene said.

"Right."

"I happen to channel a thirty-thousand-year-old high priest of Lemuria."

"You do?" Melanie said, a trifle awed.

"Sure. On the astral plane he's thought of as a very wise being."

Dalton asked, "So what's the name of this wise astral being?"

"Well, if you're just going to scoff," Gene said.

"Sorry. I'm asking nicely now. Who is he?"

"No, your skeptical vibes are queering my karma."

"Oh, come on," Dalton mock-pleaded.

"Only if you're sincere."

"I'm sincere. What's the name of the entity you channel?"

"Murray."

"Murray?"

"But he likes to be called Skip."

Melanie turned to Linda. "They're kidding, right?"

"They're *always* kidding. Pay no attention to them."

"It's going to be a while before I get used to all this," Melanie said.

"You will," Dalton assured her.

"After lunch," Linda said, "I'll give you the Cook's tour."

"Is it lunchtime?" Melanie asked.

"Well, it's after nine P.M. Eastern, so maybe you're not hungry."

ᴏᴏ"I didn't eat dinner because I didn't have any appetite, but I'm kind of hungry now."

"Try this cheese plate," Thaxton suggested. "The Camembert is the real thing. And these truffles are authentic, if I'm any judge."

"I like this curried lobster," Deena said. "You like curry?"

"Quiche?" Dalton said, proffering a dish past Gene's nose.

"Get that wimp food out of my face," Gene said.

"A thousand pardons."

"We dashing, non-quiche-eating types stick to meat and potatoes." Gene pointed to Snowclaw. "He, on the other hand, likes beeswax candles dipped in Thousand Island dressing. But, as they say, *de gustibus non disputandum est*, cha-cha-cha."

"I like paraffin candles sometimes," Snowclaw said. "It depends on my mood."

Gene noticed that Melanie's green eyes had gone apprehensive. "I'm sorry. Didn't we introduce Snowclaw?"

"No," Melanie said in a small voice.

"Melanie, I want you to meet Snowclaw, a friend of ours."

"Hi, Melanie," Snowclaw said.

"Hi."

"I'm not as scary as I look, Melanie."

"Very nice to meet you, Snowclaw."

"Same here. Reason I said that was that I noticed you weren't looking at me."

"I was a little scared. I'm sorry."

"It's okay."

"He's a pussycat," Gene assured her. "Really. Tell her about your hobbies, Snowy."

"My hobbies?"

"Yeah. Needlepoint, cloisonné, batiking—a real dweeb."

"What the heck is batiking?"

Melanie giggled nervously.

"And a rabid birder," Gene went on. "You can see him every morning out in the fen, field glass in hand, lusting for a glimpse of a chaffinch, or a chevroned waxwing, or even a partridge—a quail perhaps—nesting in the tall gorse."

Linda rolled her eyes. "Gene, really."

"Sometimes I don't understand a word he's saying," Snow-claw said, shaking his furry head.

"Gene is our resident Wit, capital W," Linda explained.

"I'd append the prefix *nit*," Dalton said.

"Resident twit," Thaxton suggested.

"Thank you, thank you," Gene said, rising. With a sweep-ing gesture he put on his plumed hat. "And I'd love to continue this pleasant badinage, but we have a revolution to run." Left hand on the hilt of his sword, he turned to Snowclaw. "*Garscon?*"

"Are you talking to me?" Snowclaw said.

" '*Allons, enfants de la patrie.*' "

"Wrong period for the costume," Dalton said.

M. DuQuesne sang, " '*Le jour de gloire est . . . ar-ri-vé!*' "

"Let's go, D'Artagnan," Gene said, slapping Snowclaw's shoulder in passing.

Snowclaw was still shaking his head. "I dunno." He got up and shouldered his ax. "Nice meeting you, Melanie. See you around."

"Bye."

The two adventurers left the hall.

"They're interesting," Melanie said.

"Oh, decidedly so," Thaxton agreed. "They're always up to something. I, on the other hand—"

"You're as boring as I am," Dalton said. "Let's go play some golf."

"Oh, God," Thaxton said, with a hopeless look ceilingward.

"Golf?" Melanie said. "There's a course outside?"

"There's a course *inside*," Dalton corrected. "There's not much outside but a four-hundred-foot drop to a desert."

Thaxton threw down his serviette. "Well, if I must, I must."

Linda said, "Mr. Thaxton, if you hate golf, why do you always give in and play?"

"For the simple reason that I have nothing else better to do."

"But the castle has no end of worlds."

He gave her a wan smile. "Yes, but you see, my dear, I'd be in them."

Linda nodded glumly. "I think I know what you mean."

Dalton thumped Thaxton on the back. "Buck up, old man."

"Oh, I don't want to give the impression that I'm unhappy in Castle Perilous. I think it's perfectly marvelous here."

"Then let's get out on the links."

"Right you are. Very nice to have met you, Melanie."

"Same here. Have a good game."

"Well, we shall certainly try."

All this time, Jeremy had been stuffing himself in silence. When the two golfers left, he leaned back and delivered a tremendous belch.

"Excuse me."

"That was really ignorant," Deena said.

"I said excuse me."

Linda looked down at Melanie's tattered jeans. "Do you want me to whip up an outfit for you, or do you want to keep wearing those clothes?"

Melanie tugged at her sweat shirt, from which the lettering NORTHEASTERN STATE had faded. "These? Everybody else is wearing fancy stuff. Maybe I should too."

"Do you want a dress, a gown, or pants?"

"Pants."

"I think you'd look good in shorts over tights. What color tights?"

"Uh, black?"

"You have green eyes. What if I go for a match?"

"Okay."

"Fine. Stand up."

Melanie stood. "What for?"

Linda waved her right hand. "How's that?"

Melanie looked down at herself. Gone were the sweat shirt, jeans, and white athletic shoes turned gray with grime. Instead, she was attired in forest-green tights, brown leather short pants, matching boots, and a thonged jerkin over a green puffed-sleeve blouse. Her old clothes and shoes lay in a pile at her feet.

"How did you do that?"

"Magic. What do you think?"

"I look like Robin Hood."

"Yeah, I—"

"What's the matter?"

With a sudden look of despair, Melanie slumped to her seat. "I was just thinking, I have a calculus test tomorrow."

"Well, we can always send you right back."

"You can?" Melanie thought about it. She shook her head emphatically. "I don't want to go back. But what will people say about my just vanishing? And my parents—?"

Linda said, "It used to be that there was no way back from the castle, and people wound up as missing persons or listed as possible murder victims. But Lord Incarnadine reestablished the Earth portal, and now we have almost complete control of it. What we can do now is set up some kind of cover story to explain your absence."

"What would I tell my parents?"

"That you're dropping out of school for a while and staying with friends, which would only be the truth. You could keep in touch with them by letter or phone."

"You can phone from the castle?"

"With the castle's mainframe, we can tap into any communication system in the world."

"You can even fax a letter," Jeremy said.

"Really?" Melanie let out a breath. "I guess I don't have any excuse not to stay."

"No, you don't. Why don't you have a bite, and then we'll introduce you to Lord Incarnadine. Jeremy, have you seen him lately?"

"Last time I saw him he said something about going to his sister's garden party."

"Princess Dorcas? Oh, that's right. Well, that's one party we can't crash. Maybe later. Go ahead and eat, Melanie."

Melanie pulled up the cheese plate and bit into a wedge of Camembert. She was hungry, and everything looked so appetizing. *Don't feel guilty about stuffing yourself*, she thought. *After all, you're eating for* . . .

She froze, a puzzled look on her small freckled face. By dint of some flashing insight, she was aware of what was inside of her, the small bud of flesh that had taken root in her uterus. She knew its structure and its potential, and she knew with a

certainty that could only come with seeing with her own eyes.
She did see it, somehow.

How? Was this sight of the unseen her talent?

A glowing smile spread slowly across her face.

You're eating for three *now*.

KEEP—WEST WING

"I'VE GOT IT."

Switching his golf bag from one shoulder to the other, Thaxton asked, "You've got what?" He kept walking down the gloomy corridor.

"A clerihew," Dalton said.

"Give."

"Okay, here goes.

> "Sergei Rachmaninoff
> Turned his lights on and off.
> An old Late Romantic,
> He was really quite frantic."

Dalton looked at his golf partner. "Well?"

Thaxton lifted one eyebrow. "Never cared much for Rachmaninoff."

"I'm asking for your opinion of my clerihew, sir."

"Adequate."

They continued down the hallway toward a pool of light. When they reached it they discovered that the illumination came from an archway that led out into the open, affording a pleasant prospect of stately trees, lawns, sunshine, and shrubbery. A formal garden of hedgerows and flower beds was set in the midst of all this, and a party was going on in the middle of everything. Canopies had been set up, tables underneath laid with food and drink. Several dozen people in widely varying costumes were enjoying the affair, many servants attending. Music came from a small orchestra. A game of croquet (or something to do with balls and mallets) was in progress on a greensward beyond.

"What's all this?" Thaxton said, stopping to watch.

"I do believe that's Princess Dorcas's family reunion."

"Oh?"

"A servant told me about it. Most of Incarnadine's family were invited. Cousins, uncles, Prince Trent, the whole crowd. The castle nobility."

"Really. You rarely see them."

"Most of them keep to their worlds. And they don't think much of Guests."

"Ah, yes," Thaxton said. "I suppose we're N.O.C.D. to them."

"'Not our Class, Dear'?"

"Right you are. Are they all related, do you think?"

"Most are, distantly," Dalton said, "from what I understand. They're the remnants of the aristocracy that once ruled the Western Pale and its adjacent kingdoms. Hundreds of years ago, thousands, maybe, when the territory wasn't the wasteland it is today. Over the years they took up residence in Perilous, and most of them live in one aspect or another."

Thaxton hefted his bag. "Well, we're not invited."

"Not hardly."

They walked on.

"Wait a minute," Thaxton said. "I feel one coming on."

"Eh?"

Thaxton cleared his throat, then versified as follows:

> "J. S. Bach
> Liked to run amach.
> His three-part invention
> Caused much dissension."

"Not bad, actually," Dalton said. "Have you discovered, like I have, that there's no good rhyme for Mozart?"

Thaxton considered the matter. "Goat's fart?"

"Not the most felicitous. Beethoven's hard too, if not impossible."

"We could change category. Or we could—what's the matter?"

Dalton had stopped to peer into a small alcove to the left. A pair of stockinged legs was sticking out from behind the arch.

"What have we here?" Thaxton said.

They entered the alcove and found a man lying face up. Dark-haired and bearded, he was dressed in a blue fur-lined gown and long-skirted orange doublet. The gown was finely embroidered with gold thread. Everything he wore was very well tailored and looked expensive. Gold and enormous jewels ringed almost every finger.

The man's lips were blue, the face ashen. The eyes looked off into nothingness in a lifeless final stare.

Thaxton knelt over the body and took the right wrist. "No pulse." He palpated the neck, then bent and put an ear to the chest. "No heartbeat. He's still warm, though. Must have died minutes ago."

Dalton went to one knee and looked at the face. "What of, do you think?"

"Could be anything. He looks about forty. You couldn't rule out heart attack."

"There's no telling age with these castle people. Some of them are centuries old."

"Quite right. And who knows if they're susceptible to the usual medical inevitabilities? With lifetimes on that order, I would tend to think not."

"But they're not immortal," Dalton said. "It's just a matter of time before nature catches up with them." He looked the body over. "No bruises. No blood. Look at that jewelry. A thief wouldn't leave those. I suppose we could rule out foul play."

Thaxton scratched his chin thoughtfully. Then he said, "Let's turn him over."

"Should we touch the body?"

"We can always put him back. Get his legs."

They shifted thc body to its side, then gently rolled it over. Thaxton's eyebrows rose. "Hello, hello, what's this?"

"Then again, foul play just might be the ticket."

A small rent in the fabric of the gown, a dark stain surrounding it, was located between the shoulder blades at a spot a little to the left of the middle of the back.

"Knife wound?" Dalton asked.

"Stiletto, I should think. Let's get this overgarment off and see the wound."

They struggled to undress the limp body. Finding a matching hole in the doublet, they wrestled with that until they had exposed a white cotton undergarment, against which the bright bloodstain stood out.

"There's the entry point," Thaxton said, fingering the cloth. "Not much blood. A thin dagger of some sort, that's certain. Deep thrust, right into the back of the heart. The attacker's aim was bad, though. Probably just nicked the aorta, causing a not-too-fast leak. Slow enough to let the victim walk out of the party and back into the castle. He got this far before internal bleeding did him in."

"The party? Is that where he came from?"

Thaxton nodded. "Have you evcr seen him before?"

Dalton shook his head. "But he could be a Guest."

"Perhaps. Has the look of nobility about him, though."

"True. But do you really think he was attacked at the party? Didn't look like there'd been any ruckus."

"No," Thaxton admitted. "If it was done there, it was a quiet job."

"Why would he have come back to the castle?"

"Who knows? To get help?"

"Wouldn't he have told someone first?"

"Doesn't make sense, does it?" Thaxton shook his head. "I dunno, just a hunch. Maybe he was attacked here or nearby. Maybe he isn't one of the gentry. We'll know soon enough."

"I'll go fetch Tyrene," Dalton said, getting to his feet. "You want to stay?"

"Golf's off for today, I should think."

"I'll be as quick as I can. Be careful. The culprit could still be around."

"I'll be on guard."

Dalton hurried off.

It was quiet in the alcove, too quiet. Thaxton had a rough time getting the body dressed again, but managed to return things more or less to the state they had been found in.

He got up and stepped back, viewing the body. He exhaled. Right.

He began to search the floor around the corpse, widening his field of operations until he was back out in the hall. He found nothing, not even a drop of blood.

He went back inside and stood over the body, thinking.

Footsteps sounded out in the hallway. Thaxton looked over his shoulder.

A man in quasi-Renaissance dress went walking by. As he did he glanced into the alcove. He did a double take and halted.

"You there," he said. "What's going on?"

Thaxton turned his head to look down at the body.

"I asked you a question," the man said as he came into the alcove. His gaze locked on the body. "Ye gods!"

Thaxton stepped aside.

After kneeling over the corpse for a moment, the man stood up and faced Thaxton. He was tall and black-bearded, like the dead man. He looked somewhat younger. His eyes were fiercely blue.

"What do you know of this?" he demanded.

"Not very much, I'm afraid."

"When did this happen?"

"My golf partner and I found him not five minutes ago," Thaxton said, "right where he is."

The man regarded Thaxton suspiciously for a moment, then turned around to view the body again, his chest rising and falling rapidly. "What happened?"

"I'm afraid I don't know that either. May I ask . . . ?"

The man gave Thaxton a sharp look. "Yes?"

"Might I ask who this gentleman is?"

"The viscount Oren, of course!"

Thaxton nodded.

The man turned his head again and said quietly, "My brother."

"You have my condolences," Thaxton said.

"Thank you," Oren's brother answered dryly. "Did anyone see him take ill?"

"I'm afraid I wasn't at the garden party."

"Weren't you serving?" The man looked Thaxton up and down. "Oh. You're one of *them*. I should have known by the ridiculous costume."

Thaxton glanced down at his knickerbockers and saddle shoes, then coolly scanned the man's attire—a rehash of the viscount's but heavier on the embroidery.

"I rather think that's a case of pots calling kettles, don't you?"

The content of the remark sailed over the man's head, but not the implication. "How dare you! I'll have none of your impertinence, do you hear? And you will address me as 'my lord.' "

Thaxton coughed quietly into his hand. "Don't you want to examine the body?"

"Eh?"

"There may be clues." Thaxton added, "My lord."

He understood. "Oh, yes. Yes. The body." He began a motion to stoop, but halted. "Run and fetch someone. Tyrene."

"He is being summoned, my lord."

"Ah. Good." He knelt, then looked up. "What is your name?"

"Thaxton, my lord. And whom do I have the honor of addressing?"

"Arl. Lord Arl."

Thaxton watched Arl fumble with the corpse's clothing. "Might I suggest we turn the body to one side?"

Thaxton helped him, lifting the body toward himself. When Arl's eyes found the hole in the gown, they went round and wild.

"Merciful gods!"

He shot to his feet. "He's been murdered. My brother's been murdered!"

"So it would seem, my lord," Thaxton said. "Frightfully sorry."

Arl looked helpless, confused. "It can't be. It simply can't be."

Running footsteps came from the hallway. Breathless, Tyrene—Captain of the Guard—burst into the alcove, followed by two Guardsmen. He immediately went to his knees and examined the wound.

"Gods," he said in a whisper.

Presently, Tyrene stood and faced Thaxton. "Did you see anybody in the hall just before you found the body?"

"Not a soul," Thaxton said.

Arl was still standing over the corpse, unmoving.

"My lord, did you see anybody?"

Arl wrenched his gaze from his brother's body. "No. I—no."

"Was the viscount at Her Highness's fête?"

"Yes," Arl said. "It can't be more than a quarter-hour since I saw him there."

"Did you see him leave, my lord?"

"No. No, I did not. I grew bored and left early. I was passing in the hall when I saw this man, here. And my brother . . . lying there. Dead."

"My sincerest commiseration is yours, my lord, in this your hour of grief."

Arl nodded absently.

Dalton puffed into the alcove, halted, bent over and put his hands on his knees for a moment and breathed deeply. Then he straightened and leaned toward Thaxton. "Just a little winded," he whispered.

"I'm sorry; I should have gone. Not thinking."

"You seemed to have had the situation well in hand."

"My lord," Tyrene was saying, "can you give me any information at all concerning your brother's actions during the fête that would shed light on the question of who may have attacked him?"

Lord Arl took a deep breath and let it out slowly. Then he said, "I can tell you little. As you may know, my brother and I were not on speaking terms. We did not speak at the fête, nor did we associate. I saw him playing hedge ball. Then later I saw him sup with Lady Rilma. That was not very long before I departed. I thought I'd left him at the fête."

"My lord, did you see him speak or associate with anyone else besides his wife?"

"He was playing hedge with Lord Belgard and Lady Rowena."

"Very good, my lord. My lord, if it be not too inconvenient, might we continue this line of questioning later? I must to the fête and inform Her Highness and the other guests."

"Yes. Yes, by all means, Tyrene."

"Thank you, my lord."

Two more people arrived: a young page, who carried a folded leather stretcher, and a gray-haired older man in a brown cloak. Although Thaxton had never availed himself of the man's services, he recognized Dr. Mirabilis, the castle physician. Thaxton wondered about the state of forensic medicine in the castle.

"Obviously a dagger or other sharp instrument," Dr. Mirabilis pronounced after examining the body. "I'll know more after I perform an autopsy, but I'd say there's a good chance that the viscount died as a result of the wound. There's been a great loss of blood, probably bleeding into the chest cavity. As I said, we'll know for certain later."

"When can the autopsy be performed, Doctor?" Tyrene asked.

"Immediately. If you can have the body brought to the infirmary."

The body was lifted onto the stretcher. The page produced a sheet to drape the body, then he and one Guardsman bore the stretcher away.

"I'll have my report messengered directly to you, Captain," the doctor said. Then he departed.

"His Majesty must be informed immediately," Tyrene said. "Was he at the fête, my lord?"

"He hadn't arrived by the time I left," Arl said. "But I'd heard he would be late." He looked away for a moment, then added, "I will inform Lady Rilma."

"I should be grateful to be relieved of that burden, my lord. Thank you."

Tyrene turned to Thaxton and Dalton. "I wonder if you two gentlemen would mind accompanying me to the Formal Garden? I imagine His Majesty would like to hear from your mouth any testimony you have to give."

"Certainly," Thaxton said. Dalton nodded.

Tyrene, Lord Arl, and the other Guardsman left.

Thaxton began to follow. Over his shoulder he said, "Let's go, old boy."

"What about the bags?" Dalton said, pointing to the dropped golf clubs.

"We'll send a servant. Come on, man. The game's afoot!"

CONSERVATORY

THE CONCERTO WAS DRAWING TO A CLOSE.

The pianist was animated, beads of sweat at his brow. With masterly skill and artistry, he threw off a sparkling glissando that swept from the one end of the Bösendorfer's keyboard to the other. The flurry of notes climbed high, coalescing into a cloud of rippling chords in five-beat rhythm, sounded first in the upper registers then repeated an octave lower.

Behind him, the "orchestra" rested for the cadenza.

There were no musicians.

There were, however, many instruments. All the traditional symphonic instruments of Western (Earth) music were represented—strings, woodwinds, brass, and percussion—but there was only one piece for each section: one violin, one viola, one horn, and so forth, except for percussion, which had the full complement. The instruments rested on chairs or tables or, like the contrabass and cello, were propped against the wall.

The cadenza finished on the highest G octave on the keyboard. Then, with a resounding chord in C major, piano and orchestra came in together, *fortissimo*, restating the main theme of the third movement, which had twice before been played voluptuously, rapturously. Now, for the final time, it unfolded with grandeur and majesty, yet was still charged with an uncontainable passion.

The piano alternated massive chords and syncopated accents to the orchestra's melodic line.

Among the strings, bows bowed, held by invisible hands. Stops and valves depressed in the woodwinds and brass. Although there was only one of each kind of instrument, the sound was of a full orchestra. The conservatory reverberated to the climax of the concerto.

The main theme done, the pianist launched into technical pyrotechnics while the orchestra played staccato cadences, sharply banging out the finale. Complex stacked chords cascaded down the keyboard at a furious rate. An impossible display of virtuosity. The whirlwind of sound rose again into the rarefied reaches of the upper octaves before resolving with a crash into four final notes hammered out at the bottom of the keyboard.

Rachmaninoff's Piano Concerto No. 2 in C minor, Opus 18, was over.

The pianist sat back, took a cloth from an inner pocket of his doublet, and wiped his forehead.

He looked around the chamber. "What, no standing ovation?"

He waved a hand and the room erupted in tumultuous applause. He rose and bowed to the invisible audience. Turning to the orchestra, he raised his arms. The instruments rose from chair and table, standing on end. They all tilted forward in a comic semblance of a bow.

The soloist waved his hand again, and the applause cut off abruptly. The instruments settled back down.

"Thanks, guys. You can sit this next one out."

He seated himself again, rubbed his hands, dried his palms on his purple gown.

Then he essayed the lugubrious opening bars of the Beethoven *Pathétique*.

A servant walked in.

"Sire . . ."

Incarnadine—liege lord of the Western Pale, and, by the grace of the gods, King of the Realms Perilous—was annoyed. He lifted his hands from the keyboard.

"What is it?"

"Sire, your pardon for interrupting, but something of extreme urgency has come up."

Incarnadine's fist pounded the keyboard. *"Merde!"*

"Sire?"

"Dorcas's party! I forgot!" He scowled at the young page. "Why didn't you remind me?"

"Sire, I was just about to when a messenger came from Captain Tyrene."

"Oh. It had better be damned important. Where's the message?"

"It was oral, Sire. I am to tell you that the viscount Oren was found dead inside the castle, a short distance from the Garden aspect. Murdered."

Incarnadine blinked. "Did you say murdered?"

"Sire, I most certainly did."

"I see." Incarnadine rose from the piano. "Was the viscount at the party?"

"That is all there was to the message, Sire."

"I'd better get down there right away." Incarnadine took a few steps and halted. "No, wait, I want to get changed first. Tell Tyrene to start his investigation immediately, on my personal authority. Tell him I have every confidence in him."

"Yes, Sire."

Incarnadine hurried to the door, passing displays of musical instruments from hundreds of worlds. At the threshold he stopped.

"Wait, another thing. Tell Tyrene that no one at the party is to leave the Garden aspect until I get there. That includes my sister."

"Yes, Sire."

"Have to keep them contained. They're a slippery bunch."

Out in the corridor, he made a right at the first intersection, walked a few paces to a stairwell and entered it.

He climbed six stories. On his way up to the seventh he was huffing and puffing.

"Gods, I'm out of shape," he mumbled.

He stopped.

Standing in the gloom of the stairwell, he thought the problem through while he caught his breath.

At length he said, "Seems like cheating, though."

He continued up the stairs and exited at the next landing. Out in the hall he stood in front of a blank wall and said, "I need an elevator."

In a moment, one materialized, a section of wall to his right transmuting into metal doors that parted to reveal the interior of a modern elevator. He entered, and the doors slid shut.

"Family residence," he said to no one who could be seen.

The elevator rose, rumbling and humming.

His study was lined with books and filled with endless curios. Quaint astronomical gear occupied one corner, alchemist's paraphernalia another. Maps and star charts covered areas of wall not taken up by books. There were several desktop computers in the room, and some of these were unusual. Instead of CRT screens, they had crystal balls.

He sat at the terminal of one of these morganatic marriages of the magical and the technological and tapped out a few commands.

The ball, mounted on a wooden base sitting on top of the computer, began to glow.

He peered into it, keyed in more commands, looked again. Shadows flickered dimly in the depths of the glass.

He kept at it until he saw something come to life. He watched intently.

After a good while he sat back and grunted. He hit a key and the light inside the ball faded.

"Well now, that's interesting," he said abstractedly. "Veddy, veddy interesting."

He sat for a time thinking, absently stroking his cleanshaven chin. His hair was long and light, and his eyes were brown this month. He had a habit of changing his appearance now and then. After three hundred years one could grow tired of one's looks. He refrained from transforming his face into something unrecognizable; that would confuse the servants and Guests.

But he was wont to alter his hair and eye color slightly with a simple spell. Underneath he remained the same: dark-haired, blue-eyed, strong of chin, thin blade of a nose. Generally a good face; perhaps even a handsome face, disregarding that the brow was a little low and the chin a shade too prominent.

Handsome or not, he was a lord. The peerage had devolved to him down through thousands of years. But he was also a king, and for that regal title he owed an ancestor who had got the notion that the lord of Perilous, master of thousands of worlds, should have his honorific upgraded to something more impressive. So Incarnadine was "King of the Realms Perilous," and actually did directly reign in several of the castle's domains. He had a hand in the politics of a hundred worlds, interests in thousands more. The piano-playing had been time stolen from a full schedule.

No time now.

He rose and began walking toward the door, but something rang off in a corner, and he turned and moved toward it. The device was an old-fashioned telephone, the upright kind with a conical mouthpiece and detachable earphone. Behind it, though, was a television screen, and beside that was a small device that looked like an automatic answering machine. Before he reached the desk on which all this lay, a somber recorded voice was already on the line:

You have reached Castle Perilous. We cannot answer your call at this time, but if—and let me emphasize the 'if'—you have some matter of great moment to impart, you may leave your name at the sound of the trump. On the other hand, if your call is being made on some contrived pretext, or, worse, is in the nature of an annoying solicitation, you run a grave risk.

He sat back down, propped a hand under his chin, and watched the screen. A form wavered on it, a face.

—we do not need storm windows, we do not need aluminum siding, we most certainly do not care to be the 'lucky winners' in some transparently fraudulent giveaway scheme. Let me now enumerate and quickly describe the variety of calamities that could befall you should any of the above conditions obtain. You could be incinerated on the spot—

The image on the screen clarified and sharpened: a thin-faced man with glasses.

—colonies of fire-lice could suddenly infest your spouse's—

He hit a switch on the answering machine and interrupted the recording, then unhooked the earpiece and put it to his ear.

"Howland, I'm here. Go ahead."

The man on the screen look relieved. "I gotta say, that is one intimidating answering-machine message."

"It screens out the bothersome calls."

"No kidding. I was half tempted to ring off myself."

"Glad you stuck it out. What's up?"

"Well, it's Tweel. He's made his move, I'm afraid. His dengs moved in on all our operations across the river—casinos, sporting houses, joy dens, wire parlors, everything."

"A hostile takeover, eh?"

"I should say. All the upper-level managers were let go, and Tweel's creatures installed."

"Did he even try to make it legal this time?"

"Oh, sure. The stock transactions are on record. He acquired controlling interest in all the subsidiaries through the usual junk bond issue. Then he sent out his demons to do the actual dirty work and make it stick."

"Any resistance on our part? We lose anybody?"

"Yes, two of our boys bought it. Curt and Tully. A little scuffle when they moved in on the Fifty-eighth Street sporting house. Curt was feeling a little protective of one of the girls when one of the dengs tried to take her upstairs."

Incarnadine shook his head. "They had standing orders not to offer any resistance."

"Curt was a hothead, but I can't say I blame him. The girl was screaming her head off. Not that I blame her, either. Anyway, it was pretty gruesome. Tully tried to help, and both of them . . . well, they had to practically shovel them into the morgue wagon."

"They should have known better, but that doesn't make me feel any less awful about it." Incarnadine drummed the desk top with his fingers. "So what does Tweel expect me to do, do you think?"

"Hit back with all you have."

"What do you advise, Howie?"

"Well, as your counselor I have to advise you that if you do retaliate, we'll have a major war on our hands."

Incarnadine nodded. "That's inevitable."

"We'll lose a lotta people. And you can't kill a demon."

"Who says?"

Howland shrugged. "Unless this boils down to a shoot-out between the two of you."

"Is that what you think he has in mind?"

"I think he's setting something up like that. He knows you don't want all-out gang warfare. He's got you."

"So you figure he's calling me out."

"That's about the size of it, boss. Word has it that he holed up out in his place with extra guards ringed around it. He says he's waiting for you to make your move. Oh, by the way, I saved the worst for last. He's got Helen out there."

"She's there willingly?"

"I don't know. Boss, you know he's got her spelled somehow. I really think he loves her. Always has. Funny. He could have almost any woman he wants. But he carries a torch for the only one who ever jilted him. I know she loves you. Maybe that's why."

"I wouldn't be surprised. Anyway, so he says he's waiting for me?"

"Yeah, and he's claiming that he's the more powerful magician now. Says you're all washed up in this town." Howland pursed his lips and shook his head. "Boss, we sure could use some dengs on our side."

"You inevitably lose when you traffic in the Dark Arts."

"Pardon me, boss, but it seems like we're the ones who're losing at the moment."

"It only seems like it. But what are you advising? Cutting some sort of deal? Give up Hellgate?"

"Cut our losses," Howland said. "Get out with all the cash we can grab. We have areas of the city in which we're a lot less vulnerable."

"For how long? Tweel doesn't want any competition anywhere in the city."

"That's true."

"So, how long do you think we can hold him off?"

Howland shrugged. "I grant you there's an inevitable time factor, but buying time isn't all that bad an idea for now. Besides, boss, I don't think we have any choice."

Incarnadine sat back. "Maybe not. Howie, you go ahead and open up negotiations with their counselor. Stall them. I'll be at the Pelican Club inside of an hour."

"What are you going to do, boss?"

"While you're negotiating, I'm going to pay Tweel a visit out at The Tweeleries."

"Are you talking *alone*?"

"That's what I'm talking. He wants a showdown, he's going to get one."

"You'll never get near the place, boss. He's got the boys out in force, extra dengs he's conjured up, trip spells, all kinds of devices. And that place of his is like a fortress."

"The dengs are his trump suit. The rest is just dressing. And I can deal with demons pretty well. I happen to live inside of one."

"You oughta know, boss. I'll be at the office if you need me."

"Good. Take care, Howie."

"Good luck, boss."

"Thanks."

Incarnadine hung up and the screen faded to black. He let out a breath and shook his head.

"Tyrene will have to handle it," he said. He got up and made for the door, but again was thwarted by the jangling telephone.

"Things come in threes," he murmured.

The man on the screen had his back to the camera (of which there was none anyway, but no matter).

Incarnadine picked up the earpiece.

"Yes?"

"Is this the castle?"

"Yes."

"I was told to report."

"I see. Where are you?"

"In the village. I don't understand why I was summoned, or what I'm supposed to do."

"Ah. Well, I'm sorry, there's no one here who can answer your questions at the moment."

The man sighed. "It's always like this."

"I'm so sorry."

"It matters little. Shall I call again?"

"It's up to you. By the way, who shall I say phoned?"

"Call me 'K.'"

"Uh, K., listen—again, my apologies, but we're really up to our butts in alligators here."

"I understand. I'll wait around here for a while, if you don't mind."

"As I said, it's up to you. Sorry to cut you off, but I have to run."

"Goodbye, then."

Shrugging, Incarnadine hung up.

"Trials and tribulations," he complained. "But that's to be expected."

He ran for the door.

LIBRARY

"THERE SURE ARE A LOT OF BOOKS HERE," Melanie said.

"You bet," Linda said.

The library was several stories high, spiral staircases communicating between levels. The second and third levels were galleries that looked out onto the main floor. The open stacks were on the ground floor, and they seemed endless. The place was as big as the biggest city or university library, if it wasn't a lot bigger. For all that, the place abounded with inglenooks and carrels and other cozy places to curl up with a good book. There were certainly enough books; most of them, however, were hardly what could be called light reading: ponderous tomes bound in ancient leather, formidable and daunting.

But not all.

Osmirik sat at a table with a stack of paperbacks in front of him. He was examining them one by one and making notations on index cards. A small-boned man with dark hair, he wore a simple brown cloak and soft black shoes with pointed toes.

Linda and Melanie came walking off the main floor and into the alcove where Osmirik was at work.

"Hi, Ozzie!" Linda said.

Osmirik looked up. "Ah. Lady Linda, how good of you to drop by."

"Just giving Melanie a tour of the library."

"Only too happy to have you." ⸗

"Melanie, meet Osmirik, the Librarian. Ozzie, this is Melanie."

Melanie smiled. "Nice to meet you, Osmirik."

Osmirik had stood, and now he bowed deeply. "The honor is mine, Mistress Melanie."

"What're you doing, Ozzie?" Linda asked.

"Cataloguing some new . . . acquisitions."

Linda looked. "Oh. More weird paperbacks, huh?"

"Yes. Not castle books, however. For that, we might be grateful."

"What have we got? Let's see. Boy, they all look interesting."

Osmirik said sardonically, "Interesting is an understatement. I was unfamiliar with this sort of literature until these books began showing up. They have greatly broadened my literary horizons."

Linda picked one up. *"Foundation's Robots*?"

"Deathless prose! Its use of allegory is on the order of pure genius."

She selected another and glanced at the cover. "What's 'cyberpunk'?" She tossed the book down. "Well, if you say so. Me, I never read this kind of stuff."

"I must confess that I, too, am at a loss as to what to make of them. But they have appeared here in the library. There must be some significance to that fact."

"Are you going to shelve them?"

"Oh, yes. I have already instituted a paperback shelf. They will be catalogued and become part of the General Collection."

"Can anyone use the library?" Melanie asked.

"All are welcome here," Osmirik said.

"If you can find anything good to read," Linda said. "Most of this stuff—pardon me, Ozzie, but most of it's pretty off-the-wall."

Osmirik nodded. "I must agree. But all of it is quite

interesting. And useful, as far as the Recondite Arts are concerned."

"He means magic," Linda explained.

"Oh."

"Yes, magic and other occult subjects are somewhat over-represented," Osmirik said. "Given the nature of the castle, this is hardly surprising."

"Lord Incarnadine does a lot of research, doesn't he?" Linda said.

"Oh, yes. And some of the castle nobility, as well."

"Really? I rarely see any of those people in here."

"Most send call-slips, and the books are delivered, though some do come personally to search the card catalogue. The Earl of Belgard is a not infrequent visitor. And . . . oh, yes, Lord Arl was here just this morning."

"Don't believe I know either of them," Linda said. "Well, we're going to mosey on down to the natatorium. Melanie, do you feel like a swim?"

"Well, kind of. Sure, that might be nice."

Linda rubbed her neck. "This morning I woke up with stiffness right along here. Maybe a soak in the hot tub will work the kinks out. You'll like the pool, it's Olympic-size."

Melanie gave her head an unbelieving shake. "Just how big is this place?"

"Uh, *real* big."

Osmirik asked, "How much have you seen of our castle, Melanie?"

"Oh, the lab, the dining hall, the bedrooms, the kitchens, the ballroom—"

"And a few of the permanent aspects," Linda added.

"Yeah, they're something," Melanie said. "Forests, mountains, deserts, every kind of place you could think of. Some of them are strange."

"There are a lot of strange aspects," Linda agreed, nodding. "And wild aspects."

"What're those?"

"Ones that pop up out of nowhere. But we're not in a wild area of the castle."

"Do people live in these worlds?"

"Sure, some of them. There are a few that are deserted. Ruins and stuff. But some of them have people."

"And you say Earth is one of these worlds."

"Yup."

"How come more people don't know about the castle?"

Osmirik said, "You have hit on an interesting point, Melanie. The fact is that not all may pass through these portals."

"Really?"

"That's what we've come to understand," Linda said. "The portal may be there, but not just anybody can come through to the castle. It may be that not everybody can sense the portal."

"You may consider yourself among the Elect," Osmirik said with a smile.

"I guess I should," Melanie said. "Sometimes I think I've died and gone to a weird kind of heaven."

"Nah, you're still alive. Come on, let's whip up a bathing suit for you. Or would you rather skinny-dip?"

"That sounds like fun."

Osmirik reddened slightly. "It was very nice of you to visit, ladies."

"Thanks, Ozzie. See you."

Osmirik watched them leave, then set back down. He picked up another gaudily covered paperback.

"*I Remember Rama*," he said, shaking his head. "Postmodernist, perhaps?"

The water in the pool was warm. Melanie floated on her back and looked up at the immense skylight, a ceiling of glass held up by ribbed columns of stone. Sunlight streamed through it, and the bright blue sky beyond it was clear and pure.

The irregularly shaped swimming pool, fed at its farther end by a waterfall, was surrounded by a lush botanical garden. The tops of tropical trees brushed the skylight. The water wasn't chlorinated, and lily pads floated at one end of the pool. No Olympic facility was ever like this.

Melanie swam to the edge of the pool and waded up a stone stairway. She and Linda were alone in using the natatorium, but Melanie had a feeling that no one would have given their nudity a second glance. Linda lay on her back on a chaise longue, eyes closed. Melanie dragged another chaise close and stretched out on it. Lacing her hands behind her head, she watched the waterfall and let the sunlight warm and dry her.

"I feel so good," Melanie said.

"I like it here, too. One of the few places in the castle where you can get some real sun. Besides the solarium. And one or two of the sitting rooms. Or six or seven."

"I never heard of a castle with a glass roof."

Linda opened her eyes. "You know, now that I think about it, that can't be the roof. We're in the castle keep, which is Lord knows how many stories high. But the natatorium is only six stories above the . . ." Linda frowned. "It doesn't make sense. There should be about forty stories above us."

They looked up.

"Doesn't look like it, huh?" Linda said.

"That's the sky."

"Yeah. Well, it only goes to show you. Forget about anything making spatial sense inside the castle. It isn't laid out in normal space—whatever that means. But Gene says so, and he's real smart."

"I'm not going to try to figure it out," Melanie said. "It's all too wonderful. It might disappear if I analyze it too much."

"It might. I mean it all could just disappear. In the past it almost has."

"Tell me about it."

"You'll hear the stories in the dining hall. Jeremy still brags about how he saved the castle from the Hosts of Hell."

"The Hosts of Hell," Melanie said with a shiver. "Whoever they are, they sound scary."

"They were. And the Blue Meanies. And the strange stuff that was going on when Gene and I first got here. I never did figure out what that was all about. A lot of it is fuzzy in my mind."

"Fuzzy?"

"Yeah," Linda said, rising to one elbow. "It all seems like a dream now. In fact, Incarnadine sometimes kids me that it was a dream. That it never really happened."

"What never really happened?"

"Oh, it's hard to explain."

"Can you try?"

Linda chewed her lip.

Melanie said, "If you don't want to, you know, it's okay."

Linda drew a breath and let it out. "No, I guess you should know just how crazy things can get around here. When I first got here, I was lost. Then I met Gene and Snowclaw, and we wandered for days. Then . . . something happened. But maybe it didn't happen at all."

"But what didn't happen?"

"The castle—disappearing. And this huge dragon . . ." Linda seemed to look far away. "More than a dragon. Some horribly evil thing, huge, monstrous. It killed. Men died, screaming. It was horrible. And the dragon took off into the sky. Me, I'm back home, back on Earth, and it's starting all over again, as if it never happened, and then the dragon comes back—" Linda's stare turned inward, pensive.

Melanie was watching her, puzzled and concerned.

Linda grew aware of Melanie's gaze. She smiled bleakly, then lay back down and sighed, shaking her head. "I'm not going to think about it. I've tried before and never got anywhere."

"Does it really bother you?"

"No, not really. The castle *is* a dream. Anything can happen, and does. You just have to live with that."

"I can live with it," Melanie said. "I can live with anything but facing the real world."

"Sometimes this world is all too real. Like I said, there's a dark side. A dangerous side. It ain't called Castle Perilous for nothing, honey."

"You don't seem scared by it."

"Well, I'm not, now. At first I was. Very scared. Then I got my magic powers, and that scared the stuffing out of me. But after that I learned to use the powers and got good at it. They've saved my life on more than one occasion."

Melanie looked up at the sky again. How could there be any doubt that this world was real?

But what about the "worlds" through the portals? During Linda's guided tour Melanie had been reminded of going through a museum of natural history, passing by one diorama after another. Linda hadn't conducted her through any aspects, and Melanie wasn't quite ready to accept one more strange reality, let alone 144,000 of them.

They lay soaking up the sunlight. The long afternoon wore on. Everything was quiet except for the splashing of the waterfall. Scents of tropical flowers hung in the humid air.

Melanie had almost dozed off when Linda shook her and dumped a towel in her lap.

"We have time to see the armory, the gaming room, and a few other places before dinner," Linda announced. "Or are you tired yet?"

"No, just nodding," Melanie told her. "There's more to see?"

"Much more, but I'm going to skip the rest of the tour bit. You'll have plenty of time to explore on your own when you get your sea legs. Besides, I've got duties. There are a few more Earthies I might want to recruit. You could help with that."

"Sure, anything I can do," Melanie said as she dried her long reddish-brown hair.

"Good, but at this point you can't do much but be there and reassure people that they're not going bonkers."

"You know, I never thought that, not for one minute."

"Well, just in case."

They both dressed and left the natatorium, which was adjacent to the gymnasium. The latter was a huge chamber with squash courts, dumbbells, Indian clubs, a duckpin bowling alley, and other strenuous opportunities.

Exiting the gym, they came out onto the landing of a great stairway that wound around a three-story-high court. They went down the stairs, talking and laughing. On reaching the second landing, they found a group of people standing there chatting, and one man turned and grinned amiably. Linda went to him, hugged him, and joined in the chatter. Melanie hung back and watched for a while, then went to the railing and looked out. Below was a fountain with a statue of a dragon spilling water from its mouth.

She left the rail and went down the hallway a short distance without finding anything of interest. On her way back she

found light pouring through a wide doorway that she was sure
had not been there before. There was no door, just an oblong
taken out of the wall. How could she have missed it? Maybe
the door had slid open.

She walked through and stepped out into a forest glade of
huge oaks and beech. Birds twittered in the treetops. Little
toadstools grew on a rotting stump to her right. Forest smells
were strong. A brook ran through a ravine below.

She realized before long that this was an aspect, and a very
pleasant one. The air was temperate, and bright sun played
atop the leafy canopy overhead, sending shafts of light through
to dapple the shade. She walked out farther from the aperture,
then turned around to view it. The portal looked like a huge
3-D photograph standing upright. It was flat, like a screen,
with nothing behind it. Yet within its depths the corridor was
still there, in three lifelike dimensions.

She marveled at the sight, then turned away to stroll down a
well-worn path.

She didn't get very far. Hearing Linda call her name, she
turned back. When she reached the portal, Linda was standing
on the other side, shouting down the hallway.

"Here I am." Melanie took a few steps toward the portal.

Linda whirled and looked dismayed. "Melanie, get out of
there! That's a—"

Then Linda disappeared, along with the corridor and the
castle.

Without warning, the upright oblong had vanished, closing
off the hole leading back to the world of Perilous, and leaving
Melanie utterly alone with birdsong and the soft rustling of
leaves in the wind.

FORMAL GARDEN

THE EARL OF BELGARD WAS INDIGNANT.

"You mean to say we're trapped here until His Majesty makes an appearance?"

Tyrene nodded and gave an apologetic shrug. "I'm afraid those were his explicit instructions, my lord."

The earl mumbled something which Tyrene tactfully ignored.

"Might I ask again, my lord—when was the last time you saw the viscount?"

"If it was not when we were playing hedge, I do not know when it was. And I must tell you I highly resent this line of questioning."

The earl was a tall man with a handlebar mustache, dressed in morning coat, striped trousers, and top hat. He carried a Malacca cane and wore a monocle.

"My lord, I have been charged by His Majesty himself with the task of investigating the murder of the viscount, and I am acting in his behalf. I beg your cooperation."

All over the garden, lords and ladies sat idly by, waiting. They looked bored, nervous, and put out, all at the same time.

The earl took his monocle out. He rubbed it on the sleeve of his coat and re-fit it over his right eye. The lens was, Thaxton guessed, a double affectation. The earl probably didn't need spectacles at all. The monocle was extraordinarily good, though, for projecting pique.

The earl said, "And I tell you I have nothing whatsoever of value to relate. My wife and I played hedge ball with the viscount, but as to the last time I saw him, I do not remember exactly where or when it was. I take little notice of trivialities."

Tyrene bowed slightly. "Thank you, my lord. My apologies."

The earl huffed again and turned away.

"Well, nothing so far," Tyrene said to Thaxton, who, along with Dalton, had been standing within earshot.

"You have a few people yet to interview," Thaxton noted.

"Quite a few, and if they're all as helpful as the earl, I'll get nowhere and Lord Incarnadine will have me thrown in the oubliette for incompetence."

"I doubt it. He realizes the problems involved. These upper-class types are a touchy lot."

Tyrene looked glum. "I was exaggerating about the oubliette, but I hope His Majesty will be understanding just the same. Nobody here seems to have seen anything."

"Perhaps there was nothing *to* see. But what do we have so far?"

"Naught, I'm sorry to say," Tyrene replied. "According to Princess Dorcas, the viscount arrived at precisely one o' the clock, castle time. He talked with almost everybody, seeming in good spirits. He played hedge ball with Belgard, Lady Rowena, and Count Damik. He ate—quite a bit, as he has a good appetite—then, quite suddenly, he left the party and walked back into the castle."

Dalton said, "Then it's pretty clear he was murdered in the castle."

"Which fact," Thaxton offered, "swells the suspect list to something near infinity."

"Aye," Tyrene agreed, with a pained expression. "All too true."

"And gives everyone here an ironclad alibi," Thaxton pointed out.

"I don't know whether to feel relieved at that or to wish for some clue gainsaying it," Tyrene said.

"A clue to the contrary would narrow things down a bit," Thaxton said. "But we don't have a murder weapon, or even a good suspect, yet."

"Has there ever been a murder in the castle?" Dalton asked.

"Not within recent memory," Tyrene told him. "Gods be thanked, Perilous doesn't seem to attract the murdering sort. A few thieves now and then, but no cutthroats."

"And since the viscount's jewels were left, we can rule out robbery as a motive," Dalton said.

"Might you two have frightened the thief away?" Tyrene asked.

"Possibly," Thaxton said. "But we would have seen him leave the alcove. Otherwise he heard us coming very far off. In that case, any self-respecting thief would have grabbed those rings."

"Quite right," Tyrene agreed. "Unless . . ."

"An aspect?"

"Yes, there is an intermittent aspect in that alcove. At least the castle registry lists one. The name eludes me at the moment, but the murderer could have escaped through there. If he knew the periodicity of the aspect."

"Know what's on the other side?"

"Not offhand, but it can be checked. In any event, it might be beside the point. The murderer could have dragged the body into the alcove simply to hide it from view."

"He didn't do a very good job," Thaxton remarked. "We were just passing by."

"I happened to glance in," Dalton said. "Otherwise we'd be playing golf now."

"But where was the viscount bound?" Tyrene wondered. "He was walking in a direction opposite from the one he'd have been going in had he been on his way home."

Thaxton looked over Tyrene's shoulder, and the captain turned, following his gaze, to find Princess Dorcas approaching.

"Your Royal Highness," Tyrene said, bowing.

The princess was dressed in something like a sari, but even more colorful. She wore large gold earrings shaped like butterflies, several gold bracelets, and a heap of gold chain necklaces. A single diamond was somehow affixed to the middle of her forehead. She was a pretty woman, if somewhat overweight and, by consequence, somewhat matronly. Her hair was an almost-black and her eyes were large and very blue. The eyes had a penetrating quality, belied by an ever-present smile, which, though still present, was now not quite so wide or all-embracing.

"Tyrene, any word from my brother?"

"No, madam. The messenger has not yet returned."

"He must not mean for us to stay here forever."

"I think not, madam, but I must await word."

"Of course. The king's word is law."

"I think it will not be long, madam. I sent word that, so far at least, there is no evidence to suggest that the murder was committed here in the garden."

"Can you be sure?"

"My investigation will continue, of course, but as of now there is no prima facie reason to hold everyone here."

"I'm sure my brother had his reasons for ordering that no one leave the garden."

"As am I, madam. But I think he will rescind that order."

The princess looked off toward the playing green. "Of course, if the murder was committed here, the murderer might escape easily if he is let back into the castle."

"If we had to track him through all 144,000 aspects, madam, I assure you, we would. He—"

"Or she," the princess interjected.

"Of course—he *or* she would not escape."

"But it would be a task, would it not? Tracking the culprit through Creation."

"Aye, it would, madam. But we're up to it."

"I'm sure you are, Captain Tyrene. Quite sure."

Thaxton had detached himself from the conversation and wandered over to one of the huge oak tables that must have taken six servants apiece to haul out from the castle. He surveyed the food. It was quite an ostentatious spread, even for the castle, all colorful garnishes and frills. A towering blanc-mange executed in scrolls and involutes stood in the middle, a single gouge taken out of it. For main dishes there was everything imaginable, from honeyed partridge to prime ribs au jus to whole suckling pigs mouthing apples.

He looked around casually before helping himself to a stuffed mushroom. Chewing briskly, he sauntered away from the buffet toward a long dining table on which lay plates that held the cold, half-eaten remains of an interrupted meal.

He almost bumped into Lord Arl, who was crossing from the right, looking at the ground.

"Pardon, my lord," Thaxton said.

Arl nodded and moved on. Thaxton watched him. A young man of about eighteen, dressed in a costume matching Arl's, came up to the lord and spoke. He looked like a younger version of Arl, without the beard, and when Arl put his arm around him, Thaxton assumed him to be the nobleman's son.

Thaxton took a few paces forward and stopped.

He saw something on the ground and bent over to look.

He swallowed the mushroom. "Hello."

There on the grass was a knife with plain wooden hilt and a narrow blade. A stiletto. The blade was encrusted with blood.

"Hello, hel-*lo*." He straightened and looked toward Tyrene, who was still talking with Dorcas. He waved and caught Tyrene's eye. He and Dalton came walking over.

"What is it?"

Thaxton pointed.

Tyrene stooped and examined it. "Ye gods and tiny pink salamanders."

"It's a wonder no one saw it before," Dalton said.

"And I wonder why," Thaxton mused.

Tyrene fished out a kerchief and picked the thing up by the blade.

"I think we have our murder weapon," Dalton said.

"Unless someone was paring their nails and slipped," Thaxton suggested.

"That proves it," Tyrene declared. "The murder was done here."

"No," Thaxton objected. "That only makes it likely that the murderer was here at some point to drop the weapon."

"But why would he drop it here?"

"Could have been inadvertent. But I'm just playing demon's advocate, don't you know. I'd say there was a good chance the murder was done in the garden, however unlikely it seems."

"It does seem unlikely," Dalton said. "If it was done anywhere here, it was a mighty stealthy job."

"I'll grant you that, but I still stand by my statement."

"What are you basing it on?"

"The murderer would hardly come back to the party with the murder weapon and drop it."

"Nobody left the party," Tyrene said, "except Lord Arl, and that was later."

"No one was *observed* to leave the party," Thaxton corrected. "But I don't think anyone did."

"Well, this thing gets sent to Dr. Mirabilis straightaway. We'll know soon enough if it was the murder weapon."

"I was wondering . . ." Thaxton said.

"Yes?"

"Just what have you got in the way of . . . well, modern police methods in the castle?"

"Do the terms nanotechnology or DNA pattern identification mean anything to you?"

"Good Lord! That modern?"

"Well, yes. Dr. Mirabilis keeps quite up-to-date."

"He keeps in close contact with Earth developments?"

"Earth? Oh, I doubt it. Earth is hardly the most advanced aspect in the field of forensic medicine. Or anything else, for that matter."

Chastised, Thaxton murmured, "I see."

"Not only can we positively identify the victim by the blood sample, but we can identify the murderer if he left any dead skin cells on the handle."

Dalton and Thaxton exchanged bemused looks.

Thaxton decided not to ask about fingerprints.

"Tell me, why not use magic to identify the murderer?"

"Castle law," Tyrene informed him. "No magic is to be

employed in the investigation of a major crime or introduced as evidence in a trial resulting from such an investigation."

"Really. That seems most enlightened."

"His Majesty is a most enlightened man."

"Oh, yes," Thaxton said. "Yes."

Tyrene summoned a Guardsman, gave him the knife wrapped in the kerchief, instructed him, and sent him off.

"Well, this is another hue of steed entirely," Tyrene announced. "I'll have to send word contradicting my last word. I shouldn't have spoken so soon. Damn their eyes."

Dalton said, "Whose?"

"My men. They were told to search this area thoroughly. And there it was, right under their drippy noses. There'll be many a black mark awarded, I'll warrant. And some promotions denied."

"It was under all our noses," Thaxton said. "I swear I walked past that spot, and I didn't see it."

"No one did," Dalton added. He insinuated one saddle shoe into the grass. "Grass is a little high. Maybe it got tramped down."

"Likely so," Tyrene said.

"Or it was dropped there just a short while ago."

Thaxton frowned. "Isn't that the chair where the viscount was sitting just before he left?"

Tyrene walked over to it. "And Lady Rilma sat next to him, here. And you found the knife in this spot, directly behind the viscount's chair."

"So," Thaxton asked, "would the murderer come back and deliberately or accidentally drop the murder weapon at the very spot where his victim had been sitting?"

Tyrene said, "Then you're saying the murder was committed here, where the viscount supped with Lady Rilma?"

"Yes, that's more or less what I'm saying. And the knife was dropped immediately."

"Why was it dropped?"

"Don't know that," Thaxton admitted.

Tyrene reached a finger up to scratch his shoulder underneath his leather cuirass. "Damn me. But Lady Rilma—?"

"Must have been looking the other way."

Dalton said, "But with all these people around?"

Thaxton sighed. "No, it doesn't make sense, does it? But murder often isn't well thought out."

"Oh?" Dalton said, with interest.

"Hardly ever. Ninety-nine percent of murders are done on the spur of the moment. Impulsive acts. Your locked-room mystery is a creation of fiction writers with overblown imaginations."

"Really."

"We'd better have a talk with Lady Rilma again," Tyrene decided. "As much pain as it causes."

Lady Rilma was sitting in a canvas chair beneath a stately weeping willow, which was appropriate, because she was still wetting a white embroidered handkerchief. Three ladies attended her.

Tyrene approached. "My lady, I realize—"

Lady Rilma burst into full cry again.

Tyrene regarded the sky for a moment. Then he said, "If I might have a further word with you, milady?"

Sniffling, she nodded.

"Is there something, anything, you can tell us about what happened shortly before your husband left?"

Lady Rilma was wore a red wimple and little makeup. Her nose was long and her teeth were small and somehow feral-looking. She looked to Thaxton like a nun in a colored habit.

"I told you," Rilma said. "We were dining, quite pleasantly—"

"Alone?"

"Yes, as I told you."

"Were you talking?"

"Yes. I can't remember exactly what about, but we were indeed talking, yes."

"Did he mention that he was afraid of something, that he feared something would happen?"

"No."

"Did he mention that he had had words with someone, some argument?"

"No."

"Did he . . . ?" Tyrene scratched his head. "My lady, did

he ever at any time express to you the fear that someone might make an attempt on his life?"

"No." Lady Rilma was offered a fresh hanky and took it. She blew her nose loudly into it.

"Now, what exactly happened just prior to the time your husband left?"

"Why, nothing, I told you. He just got up and left."

"Did he say something?"

"Yes. He said, 'I must leave.' "

"Were those his exact words?"

Lady Rilma shrugged. "I don't remember his *exact* words. He said, 'I'm going' or 'I must be going now,' or something to that effect."

"Could you tell me anything else that might be helpful. How did he look?"

"Look?"

"Did he look frightened or upset?"

"No." Lady Rilma honked into the hanky again, then thought. "He did look . . . well, I don't quite know how to describe it. He did look a little . . . strange."

"Strange? In what way, midlady?"

Lady Rilma inclined her head to one side, then the other. "In a *strange* way. How else can it be put? He had a strange look on his face."

"How strange? Slightly strange? Very strange?"

Lady Rilma glanced heavenward. "Gods! Yes, *slightly* strange, if you will."

"I beg your indulgence, my lady. He gave you this strange look, then he said that he had to leave?"

"Yes."

"At that point he got up and left?"

"Yes, he got up and left."

"He said nothing else?"

"Nothing."

Tyrene looked off for a moment, halting a motion to scratch himself again. "Yes, I see. I see. And nothing untoward happened up to that point."

"No, nothing."

"No one came up to your husband, no one approached?"

"Well, yes, someone did, but that was well before he left."

"Who talked with him?"

"Count Damik."

"And what did the count say?"

"I didn't listen. I was busy watching the hedge players."

"The count and your husband exchanged words. How long did they talk?"

"A very short time, as I recall."

"And you did not hear what was said."

"I *think* I said that."

"Sorry, midlady, simply repeating for the sake of emphasis. Did anyone else talk to the viscount while you dined?"

"No. I don't recall anyone else."

"Are you quite sure, my lady?"

"I think so. Wait a moment. Yes. Someone did approach before Count Damik. Lord Arl."

"He spoke with the viscount?"

"No. He simply passed by and touched my husband's back, as if he wanted to get his attention. I thought it strange, since the viscount and his brother weren't on speaking terms. Perhaps his touching him was simply accidental."

Tyrene slumped a little. "Well, I shall trouble you no more, my lady. Thank you very much for your kind cooperation in this very difficult moment."

Lady Rilma sniffed again. "Only too happy to oblige."

Tyrene bowed and began to walk away.

"There was one other thing."

Tyrene halted. "Yes, my lady?"

"He grunted. Just before he left."

"He . . . ?"

"Made a sound. I thought . . ." She gave a tiny giggle. "I thought he belched. But it was a funny sound."

"What . . . pardon, milady, but what *sort* of funny sound? You say it was a grunt?"

"Yes, he just made this funny grunting sound and sat up straight suddenly."

"Ah. Did you look at him when he made this sound?"

"No. As I said, I thought he belched. He does that. Did that.

I've often complained." She shook her head sadly. "No matter."

"And you didn't look at him."

"No, not immediately. I continued watching the players, then I turned to look at him and he was sitting up straight. He usually slouches when he eats. And he was sitting up. He put down his fork, and that was when he gave me the strange look."

"Then he told you he was leaving?"

"Yes. And he left. Got up and walked away. That was the last time I saw him."

"When you heard this grunt, Lady Rilma—" Tyrene said. "Please think carefully now. Could there have been someone near your husband at that time?"

"I was looking in the other direction."

"Yes, but did you hear someone?"

"No . . . wait."

Tyrene looked at Thaxton and Dalton with raised eyebrows.

"Yes," Lady Rilma went on. "I remember now. Someone was passing by at the moment. When I looked, he was walking between our table and the banquet table."

"How close would you say he was the moment you first saw him?"

"Oh, about as far away as these two gentlemen here," she said, pointing to the two beknickered golfers.

"And he was walking away from your husband?"

"Well, it's hard to say. I thought he was just passing by."

"Could he have been near your husband when you heard the viscount grunt?"

"Yes, I suppose he could have been."

Tyrene drew a long breath. "And who was this person?"

"The king's brother. Prince Trent."

THE PELICAN CLUB

IN AN OFFICE ON THE SECOND FLOOR of a big nightclub, a huge
vanadium steel vault door opened and a man stepped out. He
wore a black dinner jacket with black bow tie, boiled shirt with
onyx studs, cummerbund, striped trousers, and black patent
leather shoes. A white carnation boutonnière adorned the
jacket's left lapel. His dark hair was slicked back, highlights
glistening in the track lighting.

He looked sharp as a tack and twice as jaggy.

The office was lavishly furnished in blond wood and
chrome, the floor a meadow of plush white carpeting. He sat at
the expansive oval desk and reached for a silver box, from
which he withdrew a cigarette. Lighting it with a silver lighter,
he inhaled deeply. He shot smoke into the still air.

He lifted the receiver of a white desk phone and dialed three
numbers. After waiting a moment he said, "I'm here. What's
up?"

He listened.

"Where? At the bar? Uh-huh. Who is she?"

He nodded.

"Right. I'll be right down."

He got up and went to a bar that fronted a mirror. Selecting a bottle of whiskey, he poured himself two fingers, then hit the stuff with a shot or two of seltzer. He swished the mixture around, then drank it off.

He put the glass down and took a look at himself in the mirror, angling his head one way, then the other. Satisfied, he left the room, closing the door behind him.

The piano player was on between sets, doggedly plugging away at standard ballads. Nobody was listening. There was a big crowd, and they were noisy, awash with drink, giddy with laughter. Wreaths of smoke hung in the air. Smells of liquor and perfume and cigarette butts. Ice tinkled, silverware rattled. Busboys bused, and waiters waited.

He came down the curving staircase slowly, one hand in his pocket. He paused midway, took the cigarette from his mouth, and surveyed the floor.

A woman waved. He flashed a smile and raised the cigarette hand.

A man shot his arm up. "Johnnie!"

He waved back. There were several tablefuls of people he knew. He came down the stairs and wound his way over.

The woman who had waved met him halfway. She had short dark hair and a pale complexion.

"Dara, darling."

"You big lug. Where have you been sequestering yourself?"

"Don't ask personal sequestions."

"Ho-ho, you're fast tonight. Always the verbal quick-jabber, aren't you? I like the way you handle your litotes, kid. How'd you like to fight for me?"

"Would I have to take a dive?"

"One and a half gainer into a dry witticism."

"It seems to me I haven't seen you around here lately."

"Too fucking busy and vice versa," she said.

"Still writing for the magazine?"

"On and off. Book reviews, the occasional casual, or the casual occasional. Not much, really. Mostly I drink and stare out windows."

"How's that novel coming?"

"I did three whole pages two years ago. I'm a sprinter, John."

"Some of those shorts of yours are superb."

"I'm blushing. But what's this 'some' stuff?"

He laughed.

She pecked him on the cheek. "Everybody's here tonight," she said. "Too many friends in one room is boring. There's no one to talk about behind his back."

"I'm glad I'm here."

"You I say only good things about. I'm going to apply some powder to this hooter of mine. See you later."

"It will be my pleasure, Mrs. Porter."

"Don't go sappy on me."

He walked over to a group of tables, recognizing many faces: Gerald and Izzy Goldfarb, Oliver Lebanon, Rafe Larimer, Geoffrey S. Katzman, Monk Calahan, Rupert Bartleby, Walston Alcott, and Ephraim Skye Fitzhugh and his wife, Selma, among others.

"Hi, everybody!"

"John Carney, as I live and breathe," the rotund Walston Alcott said.

"Don't hold your breath," Katzman said with acerbity.

"No winter tan," Alcott said, scrutinizing Carney through small round spectacles. "You weren't in jail, so far as I know. Did you join a monastery?"

"No," Carney said. "But I hid out in a big castle."

"I've heard you're having problems."

"That's why I came back, not why I hid out. Everybody enjoying themselves tonight?"

Yeas all around.

"Except for that funeral music," Jerry Goldfarb said, scowling.

"You think you can do better?" Carney scoffed.

"Does a whale pee in the ocean?"

Carney waved to the piano player, then pointed at Goldfarb. The piano player nodded and stopped, got up. Goldfarb dashed to the baby grand, sat down, and launched into a medley from his new show, jazzing it up with brilliant improvisation. He sounded as if he had four hands.

"You've got Goldfarb music for the rest of the evening," Izzy said. "Free of charge. Enjoy."

"I like a Goldfarb tune," Rupert Bartleby said. "How about you?"

"I pay the Composers' Guild a bundle every year," Carney said. "Jerry'll get his nickel."

"But you're not getting the best part," Izzy said with a grin. "The words."

"Izzy, get up there and belt them out. They're your words."

"Me? I should have a bucket to carry Jerry's tunes."

"I'm going to write a show," Oliver Lebanon said, "and it will be vastly better than anything you two could scribble."

"Ollie, you've a wicked tongue," Izzy said.

"Well, I've tried to lead a wicked life to match."

Skye Fitzhugh got up and spoke into Carney's ear. "There's one of Tweel's dengs at the bar. With a woman."

"Yeah, I know. Going over there in just a bit."

"Your boys were afraid to tangle with it."

"No, they're under orders to take it easy, for now."

"Right. What kind of woman would take up with an incubus?"

Overhearing, Selma said, "Didn't you know that dengs are supposed to be extraordinarily well-equipped?"

"That's an old wives' tale," Fitzhugh retorted.

"I'm an old wife."

"You're a kid. You're not thinking of leaving me for a deng, are you?"

"I might, you never know. A woman likes to raise a little hell, too, now and then."

"Have another drink, Selma."

"I will."

Carney said, "Dengs tend to use up women fast. An affair with one is life-shortening."

"Short," Selma said, "but sweet. Unlike the present one, which is just nasty and brutish."

Fitzhugh said, "Selma's not as unhappy as she sounds."

"Speak for yourself."

Skye Fitzhugh shrugged helplessly, sat back down, and tossed off his drink.

"See you people later," Carney said. "Have some business."

"Don't sign anything in blood," Monk Calahan warned.

"At least not without your agent," Geof Katzman said.

Carney waved casually and left, threading his way across the floor. He saw Tony Montanaro coming toward him.

"Boss! Hey, you finally showed up. We got trouble."

"How's my nightclub doing, Manager?"

" 'S okay. Tweel can't move in on us here, though I bet he's gonna try."

Tony wore a white dinner jacket and a red bow tie. He had longish graying hair combed back with a part down the middle. For all the silver in his hair, he still looked young. His eyes were dark and his eyebrows almost met over his nose—but there was something delicate about his face, almost babylike.

"Howie told me about Tully and Curt."

"Yeah, that was nasty. But they shoulda known. When you mix it with dengs without magic backup, you might as well have your *candelòtto* in your hand." Tony made a motion. "You know what I'm sayin'?"

"I know whereof you speak. What else has been happening?"

"Things are happening all over town. Duke Holland got zotzed."

"Tweel?"

"Word's out on the street that that's who it was. He's movin' in on everybody, not just us. All over town, everybody's got trouble from Tweel."

"He's got the muscle. He feels he has to use it."

"He's got the dengs. Not too many bosses have a line to the real power."

"Duke Holland had some pretty good voodoo going for him," Carney said. "His protection spells were first-rate. Tweel must have moved up a notch on the infernal scale. Down, I should say."

"Tweel's dengs zotzed Holland's zombies. Holland wasn't exactly a great human being, but I feel sorry for the guy. He sells his soul, then he finds out too late he got rooked. Imagine setting up a protection circle, and then, there you are, looking like a big *chichrool*."

"Embarrassing. Well, I guess we have to deal with our visitor."

"Yeah, he's emptied out the bar, and he's running up a hell of a tab."

"I'll deal with him. How's the action in the back room tonight?"

"House has the odds, as usual. Business is good."

"Fine. By the way, is Father Sealey here tonight?"

"Yeah, I think I saw him." Tony looked. "Over there, by the bandstand. He's got a cute little number with him."

"Tony, do something for me, will you? Send to the bar for a seltzer bottle and have a boy bring it over to the father's table."

"Seltzer? Yeah, okay. But the father takes his hooch straight up."

"I know."

"Sure, boss, sure."

"And after that, get out of the monkey suit and into street clothes. I want you to drop me somewhere."

"Okay, boss. I'll get Andy to take over."

Carney crossed to the bandstand. Jerry Goldfarb was still banging away on the baby grand. A crowd had gathered around him, raptly attentive, some people singing along with the show-stopper he was currently into.

Father Sealey was entertaining a young lady. She was pretty—short brown hair, short gold lamé dress.

"John, long time no see," Father Sealey said, smiling, his bald pate shining in the pinspots. He rose and extended a chubby hand.

"How's it going, Father?"

"So-so. I'm still without a parish, temporarily. The bishop still equivocates about assigning me."

"He doesn't know what a good man he's toying with."

"Thanks, John. But His Excellency and I differ on where the souls are, the souls that need saving. They're here, not in the churches. Old ladies in babushkas have their tickets stamped already." He waved around. "Whereas these jokers don't know where the boat docks."

"They just might have a boarding pass to Charon's dinghy."

"That might be true. John, may I present my niece, Shauna Sealey. Shauna, Mr. John Carney, the owner of the Pelican Club."

"Hello," Shauna said with an engaging dimpled smile.

"Hi." Carney took her small hand. "City University?"

"How'd you know?"

"Let's see. Sorority. Omicron Upsilon Kappa?"

Shauna was mildly amazed. "O. U. Kid. You guessed it."

"Majoring in . . . mathematics."

"History. But I changed from math!"

"Your boyfriend's name is Chuck, and he's in engineering. He likes football, and he gave you a huge stuffed teddy bear for your birthday, along with that gold friendship ring."

Fingering the ring, Shauna shook her head. "You must be the magician they say you are."

Father Sealey laughed.

Carney said, "Your uncle talks a lot about you."

Shauna reddened slightly. "You're a bit of a tease." She turned to the priest. "But how did you know about the teddy bear? I never mentioned that."

Nonplussed, Father Sealey lifted his shoulders.

The boy arrived with the seltzer bottle.

Carney took it and set it down. "Father, I wonder if you'd do me a favor."

Over at the bar, Tony Montanaro was practically spitting into the deng's face:

"I said, you're shut off. You hear? No more!"

"What's it take to get a stinkin' drink in this joint?" The demon's voice boomed deeply. He added a few choice profanities.

He—or, if you prefer, it—was about six feet six inches tall, massive frame swathed in a black gabardine suit with wide lapels. Black shirt, white silk four-in-hand. The face was strangely distorted; lantern-jawed, bony-browed, it was not quite normal, and the skin was tinted faintly green. For all that, there was something forcefully masculine, not to say compelling, about its looks. The ears were pointed, the only straight-forwardly anomalous feature.

"For you, deng-breath, it's impossible. Now, move on out of here!"

"So that's how you treat your customers? How do ya like that, babe?"

The "babe" was a small brunette with heavily lined dark eyes and full red lips. Despite all the makeup, she was attractive. She had on a black cocktail dress and was smoking a cork-tipped cigarette. After blowing smoke at Tony she said, "I've gotten thrown out of better places."

"Who's throwing *you* out, honey?" Tony said. "You can stay. *He* goes."

"You're gonna haveta prove it, human."

"Prove it? Whaddya you talkin' about, prove it? Get the dung out of your pointy ears, deng. I said you're shut off. No more hooch! You can sit there all night for all I care."

The deng swore again, this time obscenely and at great length and elaboration.

"Watch that filthy hole you call a mouth, mister," Tony warned. "There are ladies around."

The babe laughed.

"You and what bunch of human pantywaists are gonna stop me?"

Tony took a bottle of bourbon by the neck and raised it threateningly.

"Tony."

Reluctantly, Montanaro put the bottle down and sidestepped away.

The incubus turned to the speaker.

"So! It's the boss, at last. I was wonderin' when you was gonna show up. You're a little late. We got half the city already, and we're gonna take the other half."

Carney took his station at the bar, about ten feet from the demon. He set the seltzer bottle on the bar.

The babe was between them. She turned to Carney, her dress hiked halfway up her thighs. A sly smile spread over her lips.

"Not if I get to your boss first," Carney said. "By the way, who's the young lady?"

"Velma," she said as she crossed her legs.

The deng laughed. "Actually, he's expectin' you. He wants to see you. I'll take you to him, if you wanna. I'm nice that way."

"Hi, Velma. Just to talk, I expect."

"Yeah, a nice little chat. Cozy like. Couple of drinks. You two fellas ought to be able to talk this out."

"Sounds lovely. I accept. But I'll get there on my own hook, thanks."

"Hey, anything I can do to help."

"You can help by leaving."

The deng was deeply offended. "I offer to do you a favor, and this is the kinda hospitality I get. That stinks." The demon lifted his glass and dumped ice into its mouth, where large white teeth crunched it up. "You stink."

"You're entitled to an opinion."

"Yeah, and if I say all humans are cesspool runoff, I'm entitled to that opinion, too."

"By all means. But how about taking your opinions and your business somewhere else?"

The deng chuckled. "Everybody keeps sayin' that, but I don't see no action." Onyx eyes took in the room. "I like it here. Real nice place. Great. I think I'm gonna stay." He reached into his jacket and brought out a hip flask. "And I brought my own."

"Leave now," Carney said, changing his intonation, "or you'll get hurt."

The demon guffawed. "You? Gonna hurt *me*? This I'd like to see."

"Then get the dame out of the way. Or are you going to hide behind her?"

"Huh?" The demon reached out. "Okay, babe, move it."

With one easy motion he yanked her off the bar stool. She wound up sprawled on the floor with her skirt up over her buttocks, which were not inordinately hidden by brief black silk panties. She got to her knees and crawled off a distance, then sat up and turned around. She appeared neither offended nor hurt.

The deng lifted the hip flask to its lips and drank. Lowering the flask, it smiled toothily. "Take your best shot, fart-face."

Flame shot toward the demon, originating from somewhere in Carney's vicinity. A ball of fire enveloped the deng's huge form.

It stood there burning, black smoke rising to the ceiling and pancaking out. The whole nightclub was silent except for the crackling. Burning scraps of fabric fell from the demon's body, and black ash like dirty snowflakes floated away.

The flames died. Most of its clothes burned clean off, the demon calmly took another swig from the flask.

Velma's eyes had gone wide at the sight of the demon's strange genitalia.

Tony Montanaro was on the other side of the bar with a .45 automatic in each fist. He leaned over the counter to look.

"Hey, boss. Kinda handy to have a spare, ain't it?"

"I don't think that's the exact function."

The demon threw the flask across the room, slid a forearm across its mouth. Naked and defiant, it laughed. "What gave you the idea that fire was gonna give me any trouble?"

"Didn't think it would," Carney said.

"Now it's my turn," the incubus said, advancing.

Tony opened up with the .45's. Slugs bounced off the muscular green-tinged carapace.

Carney said, "But I did sort of figure you wouldn't like this."

He picked up the seltzer bottle and gave the deng a spritz.

The water doused its chest and belly. With a suspiring hiss, steam rose instantly.

The demon stopped and howled, its darkened face contorted with surprise and pain.

"What *is* that?" it roared.

"Holy seltzer." Another stream of carbonated water arched out and splashed.

The deng screamed and backed off. Carney advanced, continuing to hose his adversary down.

"No! No!"

"Then get out."

"All right!"

The deng backstepped, then turned and hurried out of the barroom.

The Pelican Club gradually came back to life. The Goldfarb medley resumed, and low conversation filled the air. Glasses chinked. A woman laughed nervously.

"Nice work, boss," Tony said, sweeping brass casings from the bar top.

"Thanks." Carney went to Velma and helped her up. Her eyes looked a little glazed. He eased her onto a bar stool.

"What were you drinking?"

She looked at him and her vision seemed to focus. "Sloe gin fizz."

"A pink lady for the lady," Carney called to the bartender.

"Thanks."

"Was that a friend of yours?"

"Sort of."

"He treated you pretty rough."

"He's a guy. All guys are bastards. Either that or they're simps."

"Bastards or simps. Quite a dualism." He lit her cigarette.

"Thanks."

"You a friend of Clare Tweel?"

"Oh, yeah. Real close."

"You're being catty."

"He has a lot of friends. Lots of girls, too. Did you know he has a new one?"

"Really?"

"Yeah." Her drink came and she took a sip. "Her name is Helen. Helen Dardanian."

"For some reason I'm supposed to be affected by this revelation?"

She smiled. "I'm sorry. I don't want to make trouble for you. You're nice."

"Does that make me a simp?"

"You're no simp. You took care of my date quick enough."

"Then I'm a bastard."

She giggled. "A nice one."

"That's reassuring. Want a lift home?"

"Yeah. Thanks."

"Where?"

"The Tweeleries."

Carney lifted the glass of neat Scots whisky that the bartender had set in front of him. "That's where I'm going."

He took a healthy belt. It went down like the stock market on Black Whit-Monday.

THE JAUNDICED AYE

THERE WAS A CROWD THAT NIGHT. There was usually a crowd at the Jaundiced Aye, and it was always the same mixture of adventurers, poetasters, bohemians, ne'er-do-wells, and spottily employed cavaliers. Thrown into this pot was the odd hooligan, and one or two respectable burghers seeking a bit of slightly disrespectable diversion. For there was always good cheer and camaraderie to be had at the Aye, to say nothing of all the uproarious jokes and japes. And there was never a shortage of improvised sonnets or witty epigrams, available from any thin-faced scribbler for the price of a tankard of ale.

The young man with the blond beard made his entrance into this milieu, sniffed the air—stale tobacco smoke, smells of fried fish and spilled beer—and wished he were elsewhere. Nevertheless, he entered the tavern and shut the door. He was dressed in the manner of a young gentleman—lace collar and cuffs, short-waisted doublet, trousers, boots with lace tops, and a proper hat. But he did not wear the costume well. Perhaps the problem was his slender frame, his narrow shoulders, or his oddly flaring hips. At any rate, he drew skeptical stares and the peremptory sneer or two.

All attention seemed to gravitate toward a pair of cavalier sorts at the middle table. One of them was huge, an anomaly in boot-hose nearly twenty-five hands tall, his head topped by a cloud of snowy white hair. The other was a youngish man who wore no wig.

Gathered around these two, a crowd of admirers hung on every word of the smaller of the pair, who had been regaling everyone with a tale of derring-do. Apparently it had all happened earlier that night.

"Tell it again, Eugéne!"

Eugéne waved disdainfully. "It grows wearisome."

"Again, please! How many of the Legate's men vanquished?"

A modest shrug. "Twenty-eight . . . or nine. Thirty perhaps."

"Between the two of you!"

"Imagine!"

Eugéne raised his mug to drink. "It was nothing." He drank.

"Nothing, he says! Nothing since Shem prevailed against the Ashkelonians with the thighbone of a ram!"

The newcomer found himself an empty table toward the back. The barkeep eventually noticed and grudgingly came.

"Mulled cider with cloves and cinnamon, if you have it," the young man said.

The innkeeper curled his lip. "No spirits?"

"Oh, throw a shot of something in it, I don't care."

"Anything to eat?"

"Nothing, please. Um, tell me. Who are those two, er, gentlemen that everyone's gathered around?"

"Troublemakers, I call 'em," the barkeep said. "Ragueneau's thugs will have their hides soon enough. I just hope it happens out in the gutter and not in here, where I'll have to clean up the mess. Cider. That all you want?"

"Yes, thank you."

The barkeep left. The young man looked around. He didn't like the looks of some of the patrons. Some of these looked as though they didn't particularly care for him.

"It's not so much the heroic deed," one of the crowd of rowdies was saying, "as the manner in which the deed was done. While composing a ballade!"

"A trifle," Eugéne said. "Something to occupy the mind so as not to let fear take hold. A simple trick."

"Fear, bah! Hardly the babblings of a timorous versifier. Rather, the lays of a warrior-poet."

"Recite it again!"

"Yes, we'd like it again!"

"Especially that part about 'And as I end the envoi—lunge through!'"

"Yes, yes, that's the best part!"

"Gentlemen, please. I grow weary. The hour is late."

"Lord Snowden, you tell us, then."

The huge white-haired one shook his massive head. "Hey, don't look at me. I don't know any poetry."

"Tell us again how you killed three at one time. Forget the verse."

"Well, okay. I took two and cracked their heads together, see. One of 'em was kinda little, so I used him like a blackjack and brained another guy."

"Astounding!"

"Amazing!"

"Fantastic!"

"An astonishing story!"

Eugéne scoffed, "Fantasy and science fiction. He exaggerates."

"No, there were witnesses. We've heard all the stories. You can't deny it, Eugéne."

"Please, a little less enthusiasm, I beg you."

The blond-bearded young man's cider was delivered, and he drank of it. It was bland and weak, and tasted like dishwater. He made a face and looked toward the bar, trying to catch the barkeep's eye.

"Well, what have we here?"

The young man turned and found two cavaliers standing over him.

"Good evening," he said pleasantly.

One said to the other, "A Northern type, I warrant."

"Yes, it has the look."

"Pallild and phthisic."

"Yes, how pale his beard, his face."

"Tell me, young popinjay, what brings your sort here?"

"Uh, just out for a drink . . . gentlemen."

The other looked to the one. "It has a strangely lilting voice."

"High enough to chant descants."

"A coloratura, I'll wager."

"A protégé of the Legate, most likely. He's a patron of the arts, you know."

"Look, if you gentlemen will just leave me alone . . ."

The one on the right screwed up his face. "Might it be a citizen of the Cities of the Plain?"

"Thought I smelled salt and brimstone."

"Well, see here, young Zeboimite, if that you be, take care to guard your tongue in this place. If Eugéne and Snowden get wind of you, you might end up skewered in a way you had not bargained on, or stuffed into a firkin and set out as salt meat."

"Or both."

The young man nodded. "Yeah, I'll watch my step."

"It would be wise."

They left.

The young man's eyes smoldered. "Rotten macho creeps . . ."

"The poem again, Eugéne! Please!"

Eugéne downed the rest of his muscatel. "Oh, very well. But not the same poem. An improvisation from memory is your moron's oxymoron. No, I'll improv new lines, afresh. And on a new subject."

"Bravo!"

"Hear, hear!"

Lord Snowden sat back and regarded the rafters.

Eugéne mounted the table and drew his rapier. Putting one finger to his temple, he said, "One moment, while I choose my rhymes."

"Oh, brother," the young man murmured, rolling his eyes.

"I have them," Eugéne said presently. "Now to begin:

> " 'Twas brillig, and the slithy toves
>   Did gyre and gimble in the wabe;
>   All mimsy were the borogoves,
>   And the—' "

"Up yours!"

Silence. Everyone slowly turned to look at the source of the outburst.

Eugéne cast an imperious eye in that direction. Pointing, he said, "Who . . . is . . . that . . . *man*?"

"One of the Legate's catamites, we've surmised."

"Does this creature have a name?" Eugéne asked.

The young man shouted, "Baron Lyndon of the castle!"

"Baron Lyndon of the cas—?" The wind spilled out of Eugéne's sails. "Uh . . . oh. Well, fine."

"Eugéne! You'd let the impertinent puppy live?"

"Forget it. Has a right to his opinion."

Unbelieving looks were exchanged amongst the audience.

"The poem, then!"

"Yes, the new poem."

"Where was I? Uh, yeah.

 "'In Xanadu did Kubla Khan
  A stately pleasure dome decree:
  Where Alph, the sacred river, ran—'"

"Plagiarist! Throw the bum out!"

The crowd was outraged.

Lord Snowden stood. "Who *is* that?"

"It's a perilous night, Snowy!"

"Hey, I know who that is "

Someone shouted, "Make mincemeat of him, Eugéne!"

"Everyone out!" Eugéne shouted.

"But, Eugéne!"

"Leave him to us! Go on, get out. Come back later."

"But Ragueneau's men—"

"We'll meet you back here in an hour. Come on, guys, take a hike, okay?"

Grumbling, the troop of cavaliers left. Soon the tavern was empty but for the barkeep.

The two men advanced on the blond.

"Linda!" Gene whispered. "What are you doing here in that ridiculous get-up?"

"They don't let women in bars here. Think *I wanted* to come in drag?"

"You know, men's beards are almost never blond."

"Yeah, so I found out. Jeez, it was almost impossible to get close to you guys. I chased you all over town, from one dive to the other."

"Well, we're on the Legate's poop roster, so we have to keep on the move. What's up? What the matter?"

"It's Melanie. She—"

"Melanie? Who's that?"

"Melanie McDaniel, the new Guest—at lunch? Remember?"

"Oh, yeah. Yeah. Sorry, go ahead."

"She wandered into a wild portal and it closed up on her."

"Damn. That's tough."

"It was my fault. I let her out of my sight."

"What were you doing in a wild area?"

"We weren't! The portal popped up in one of the safest parts of the castle."

Gene clucked ruefully. "Well, it's been known to happen. Even the stable areas aren't one hundred percent."

"And it had to happen to Melanie. Gene, we've got to do something. That's why I took the chance of coming here. I had to talk to you. I feel so awful. What are we going to tell that poor girl's parents?"

"Would they believe us? Nah, best to say nothing."

"But we have to do *something*."

"Like what? You know how the castle works, Linda. Wild portals can lead anywhere, any universe, and not necessarily one listed in the books. No telling where she wound up. That portal might never open again."

"Gene, we have to take the *Sidewise Voyager* out and search for her."

Gene sat back and let air into his lace collar. "Linda, that's going to be a problem, seeing as how the thing's wrecked."

"But Dolbert and Luster say they can fix it."

Gene laughed mirthlessly. "Those two. They've been fiddling with it for months."

"It's not an easy job."

"I'll say. The thing needs parts. Where're they going to get 'em? That thing was built in a universe that I'm not sure even exists in the ordinary sense."

"Dolbert has been building some parts from scratch in the castle smithy."

"I dunno," Gene said doubtfully.

"Jeremy says Dolbert's a mechanical genius."

"Yeah, well, idiot savant he may be, but he's still an idiot. Besides, I wouldn't stake my life on Jeremy's judgment. He's somewhat of a cretin himself."

"That's not fair. Jeremy's—"

"Forget it. That's not the point. The point is travel in the *Voyager* is risky, even at best. What does Incarnadine say?"

Linda looked downcast. "He's disappeared again."

"He'd probably say the same thing."

"Gene, please. I'll never forgive myself. Never. That poor girl is alone in a strange universe. She might be in danger right now. She might die, Gene."

Gene let out a long sigh. "Oh, well. Trouble is my business."

"But if you're afraid—"

"My dear, you're talking to a man who has laughed in the face of death, sneered at doom, and chuckled at catastrophe. I'm petrified. But let's get back to the castle and see what we can do." Gene started to rise. "Which, I'm afraid—" He sat back down.

"Trouble?"

"Well, it so happens the portal is in the Legate's part of town. The city is divided up between the king's regent, who's kind of weak in the power department, and the Legate Ragueneau. Local politics, it's complicated."

"What about the revolution you were talking about?"

"They had it without us. The peasants revolted and over-threw the Directorate. Got fed up with starving. But it turned out that Ragueneau was backing the regime because he was buying grain from them at bargain prices and selling it on the . . . but forget about that. It's real complicated, and anyway it's beside the point. The point is, we're on the

Legate's hit list, and his goons are out in force tonight looking for us."

"Great. How are we going to get back?"

"I dunno. How's your magic in this world?"

"Iffy. I cast a little number to keep my voice low, but apparently it wasn't very effective. How's your swordsmanship?"

"Great, but I'm not Superman."

"Oh? What was all the bragging about?"

"Hey," Gene said with some embarrassment, "we were just having some fun, okay?"

"Just a bunch of the guys out for a good time."

"This isn't the twentieth century here. In fact it's the—"

"We'd better go. We have to make a run for it."

Gene grunted. "Right. You game, Snowy?"

"For a fight? You bet."

"Guys, please! This isn't a game. We just have to make it back to the portal. The thing is to *avoid* trouble."

"It's late, and there'll be patrols."

"We'll have to duck in and out of alleys."

"Yeah, do the stealth bit. Right. Okay, let's go."

Linda looked Snowclaw up and down. "Sheila did a good job on you."

"I hope I can last until we get back to the castle," Snowclaw said. "I've been feeling kind of shaky. It's rough being human."

Gene said, "No kidding, Philip Marlowe."

MILL

SHE HAD WANDERED ALL AFTERNOON without seeing signs of intelligent life, and when she found the dilapidated mill house she was overjoyed. She had begun to think that this world was uninhabited. The old mill, floorboards half-rotted, beams sagging, proved that it at least had been inhabited at one time.

It was dusk when she finished gathering enough tall grass to make some sort of mattress to lay over the plank flooring up in the loft. As bedding, she made do with two old gunnysacks. They were scratchy and mildewed, but when the chill of night came on, she was grateful for them.

Nocturnal chirping and twittering came out of the forest. The moon was out, outlining the small window above her and throwing an oblong of blue light on the floor. The wind played in the trees.

An owl hooted. She thought it was an owl.

She wondered about nonhuman worlds. Was this one? The mill looked human enough, but how could she know for sure?

She turned over and tried to fall asleep, unsuccessfully. A cricket trilled very near, then stopped. The old mill creaked and groaned.

She heard something, far off. She listened intently. The sound grew. It was a thumping . . . a stamping . . . the sound of hooves. They came nearer, nearer. They were right below the window. She froze, her heart bouncing against her breastbone.

The hoofbeats stopped.

Below, footsteps. Someone had come into the mill and was looking around. Something crashed. A male voice uttered an unintelligible curse. More crashing. Whoever it was went outside again, then came back.

She listened as more activity went on below. Gradually it subsided. Then everything was quiet again.

Someone sighed. Coughed. Cleared his throat. Then let out a long breath.

In a little while, she heard snoring.

Whoever it was, he sounded human enough. But she was still afraid. Highwayman? Rapist? Murderer? All of those, maybe.

She was afraid to relax her body, afraid to move a muscle. Her back ached, and her stomach churned.

She was worlds away from the existence she had known just hours ago. It seemed like years. The short time she had spent in the castle seemed like another life, and this, still another.

Was this all a dream? Yes. She'd be waking up soon in her room in Haberman Hall. There was a calculus test to cram for. She'd have a few hours to do it if she got up early enough. What time was it?

She felt her wrist. Her Phasar Quartz was still on her wrist. It had a night light. Slowly, she ducked her head under the sack and pressed the tab on the side of the watch.

The tiny digital readout seemed to light up the night.

7:39 A.M.

Okay, the sun should be up by now. So how come it isn't?

No, she was not on Earth. She was somewhere else entirely. Where? The trees and flowers and plants had looked earthlike enough, but they were also different somehow. She'd seen no maples, but something that looked like an oak. That was it as far as her tree-knowledge went. The sun had looked like the sun, and she wasn't about to get up to look at the moon.

The crickets sounded like crickets. Some help there. Maybe this was Earth, but the past. No, Linda had said nothing about traveling in time.

She wondered if she would ever see her world again.

Through the window, the sky was gray. It was morning. She marveled that she had actually fallen asleep. How long had she slept? What about . . . ?

She rolled over. A tall man was standing over her. She threw the sacks off and jumped to her feet.

The man sized her up. Apprehensively, she did the same to him.

He was young, about twenty-five, with a light beard and hazel eyes. He had on a hooded doublet and cape and wore high boots. A cross-hilted sword in an ornate scabbard hung at his left side.

He said something, and for some reason she understood him, though he hadn't spoken English. He had said, "So you *are* a woman. You dress like a boy."

He eyed her up and down. "Not a bad woman at that. Young. Run away from your parents?"

"No," she said. Then: "I'm lost. Can you help me?"

The man frowned. He didn't understand. She couldn't understand why the comprehension was one-way.

"A foreigner, eh?" He took a step toward her, and she edged back against the wall.

He stopped, smiling. "You've got nothing to fear from me," he said. He had something in his hand. It looked like a brownie or a piece of sheet cake. He was offering it to her.

She took it. It smelled okay, and she took a bite. It was chewy and tasted like an oatmeal cookie with ginger and cinnamon. It was good. She smiled at him.

"Yes, break your fast, because you've got to be on your way. My kindly half-brother's paladins are close on my heels, and they leave no unprotected woman unravished."

He laughed, more or less to himself. "Why am I telling you this? You don't understand, and their having at you might be all the diversion I need to get clean away. I know they won't pass one like you by. You even have all your teeth."

She understood all of it. The language sounded like Scots, burred and broad-voweled, but with a hint of something like French in it. Anglo-Saxon? No, she remembered what that had sounded like; the prof for EARLY ENG LIT, as her class schedule printout had put it, was given to dramatic readings of *Beowulf* and other incunabula. This was different. Medieval French? Maybe, but she doubted it.

"Come along, then." He went down the rickety ladder to the ground floor. She followed.

Outside, she watched him saddle his horse. The tack was of a type totally unfamiliar to her; it looked unwieldy and not at all comfortable. The horse was a chestnut mare and had a long flowing mane.

He mounted. "Well, then, girl, it's farewell. I'd advise you to be on your way. You're a pretty wench, and I'd like you for myself, but I don't intend to be caught with my breeches down. God go with you."

"Wait!"

He halted. "What is it?"

"Take me with you."

His brow lowered, but he appeared to understand. "I think not. Much as I'd like to have my bedding warmed, you'd be a millstone round my neck."

"I'm lost. Please help me. I have no one else to turn to."

He scowled. "What a *strange* tongue you speak. Sounds like a mallard in heat. Whereabouts do you—"

He suddenly looked off, his expression tightening.

"Damn them. They usually lie slugabed."

He turned back to her. He extended a hand.

"Come on, girl. Hurry."

She clambered up and took a precarious seat on the animal's rump, circling her arms around the man's waist.

The horse headed down the trail and away from the stream, first at a trot, then a walk, then breaking into a canter. She found the canter easier on her backside than the trotting. The horse's hard bony spine knifed between her buttocks. It hurt. She wondered how long she could ride like this.

Hoofbeats behind. The man gave a quick look back, then heeled the horse into a full run.

They plunged headlong through the woods. Melanie held on desperately, but there was little riding experience in her background. She had no idea of how to maintain a seat on a mount, much less how to hang on riding tandem. She bounced and slid, shifted and recovered, not daring a look behind.

But she could hear the pursuit, their hoofbeats sounding on the beaten dirt of the trail, closer, closer still.

They rode up a hill, ran along the crest, then down into dense trees, branches whipping at them from both sides. Splashing through a brook, they mounted a shallow bank and came back onto the beaten path.

It happened when they tried to take the next steep incline. The horse hesitated at the bottom, then leaped. Melanie lost her grip and slid off, hitting hard, her head slamming against the ground. The rider kept going, not looking back.

She was stunned momentarily. When she lifted her head she saw three men on horses standing around her. She sat up.

"Well, look what we have here," said the one with the dark beard and small eyes.

All three were in chain mail, their heads bare in the warm weather.

The three dismounted. "He's getting away."

"He can wait. Besides, we can always say we killed him."

"He's right. Who will gainsay it?"

"Who's first, then?"

"I am," said the black beard, unstrapping his scabbard.

Two grabbed her. She didn't fight; she was still woozy.

Soon they had her stripped and spread-eagled on the ground.

The black beard was down to his knit tights, but something he saw made him stop.

"What's this?" Looking back up the hill, he guffawed. The two other paladins released Melanie and got to their feet.

Melanie sat up and looked. The rider had reappeared on foot at the top of the hill, sword drawn, and was now slowly descending, his face set resolutely, as if confronted with an unpleasant but necessary task.

Laughing, the two casually drew their swords, waiting. The black-bearded one hurried to dress.

Without thinking about it, almost as though her body were

obeying an inexorable law of its own, she crawled, naked, to the dropped scabbard. She slid the huge sword out, its two-edged blade oiled and gleaming. She stood. She approached the black-bearded one from behind, slowing raising the sword.

When she was directly behind him, she brought the heavy weapon down as hard as she could.

She was surprised by how deeply the blade cleaved the skull. Two geysers of blood erupted to either side of the wound. She let go of the sword as the man fell.

One of the other paladins turned his head and registered momentary shock. Then he advanced toward her menacingly. At the same time the rider began to charge down the hill.

The one coming at Melanie looked back. She turned and ran, but didn't get far. The paladin soon caught up, grabbed her by the hair, and whipped her to the ground. He raised the sword high to do the job.

Her penultimate thought, before the blade came down, was that she didn't have to worry about the calculus test.

Her last thought was for her two sons who would never be.

GARDEN

PRINCE TRENT WAS A STRIKING MAN, hair the color of country butter, the blue of his eyes matching patches of sky among the puffy clouds overhead. He was dressed in a white tennis shirt with red piping, tan slacks, and gray suede shoes. He looked a young forty. His smile radiated charm.

"I expected to see Sheila here," Dalton said.

Trent chuckled. "My relatives are a little snooty. Sheila's a commoner, and, worse, a castle Guest. That puts her a notch or two below a scullery maid."

Trent was seated on the edge of a table, arms crossed, one leg casually dangling. He seemed totally indifferent to the fact that a murder had taken place.

"I see. Too bad."

"Oh, she didn't want to come. But I couldn't very well turn down my sister."

Tyrene said, "I'm reluctant to bring it up, sir, but did you not have a slight altercation with the viscount over this very matter?"

Trent's smile faded a little. "Actually, yes." The charm

came back again. "Are you *sir*-ing me, Tyrene? When I was in the Guard it was 'Y. R. H.,' old fellow.'"

Tyrene smiled. "That was many a year ago."

"Yeah, too many. But I like to be called Trent, now. No 'Your Highness' or even 'sir.' 'Y.R.H.' only if you must."

"As you wish, Trent."

Tyrene waited.

Trent chuckled again. "I'm being evasive. You wanted to know about the run-in with Oren. Yes, I brought Sheila to a soirée shortly after our marriage. Oren was among those who made it known that she was not welcome. Then the son of a bitch made a pass at her. Not a short screen, either. I mean a long bomb into the end zone. He practically tore her bodice off."

"And you struck the viscount."

"Yup. I let him have it."

"And you challenged him to a duel."

"No. Actually, it was he who challenged me."

"I see."

"It was later, and he was drunk. He told me that no man could strike him and live."

"Is it not true that you answered with words to the effect that sexual assault was a crime punishable by death in any civilized world?"

Trent eyed Tyrene at the level. "Yeah, I said it."

Thaxton was sitting at the table eating a slice of blancmange.

"That any good?" Trent asked, turning his head.

"If you like blancmange," Thaxton said. "Pity to let all this food go to waste."

"It is getting close to supper time," Dalton said.

Trent asked Tyrene, "My brother's still out?"

"Yes, last word I had. He didn't tell anyone where he was going, which means he doesn't want to be reached."

"He must have had pressing business. Or maybe he didn't care for Oren either, though I don't think the two ever associated much."

"In any event," Tyrene said, "his declining to make an appearance is putting me in a spot. I have explicit orders to bar anyone from going back to his home aspect until the king commands otherwise."

"What are you going to do?" Trent asked. "Pitch tents?"

"Oh, they'd never stand for it. No, Peele Castle is where we'll spend the night."

Dalton said, "Peele Castle?"

Trent said, "It's an old fortress about, oh, five miles from here, down by the shore. Sits on a cliff over the sea. Very picturesque. My brothers and I used to play there when we were kids. Talk about a long time ago."

Tyrene said, "It'll be a hardship, but we'll make do. I've already given orders to get horses up here, as some of the ladies are not up to walking."

"Is the place habitable?" Thaxton asked.

"Oh, yes," Tyrene replied. "It's been refurbished over the years. It's still sometimes used as a weekend resort. Completely furnished. But we'll have to haul supplies."

"And the ladies' toiletries and night-things will have to be fetched," Trent said.

"Gods, yes. I have fifty servants fanning out to gather all the necessary stuff."

Thaxton wiped his mouth with a satin napkin and stood. He drank off a glass of champagne. "That should hold me till dinner."

"You're presuming," Dalton said. "Tyrene, there's no need for the two of us to come along, is there?"

Tyrene said, "I wish you would. Mr. Thaxton, here, has a sharp eye. Besides, His Majesty's orders cover anyone connected with this affair."

Thaxton said, "After all, we could have killed him."

Trent laughed. "Two homicidal maniac golfers, in knicker-bockers yet."

"Oh, yes, you can bash a head in good with a niblick."

"Sure, and I suppose you stabbed him with a tee."

"Y.R.H., if I might reintroduce a note of sobriety," Tyrene broke in.

"Sorry. Yes, by all means."

"You say you have no specific memory of passing by the

viscount and Lady Rilma at the moment, or shortly before the moment, that the viscount got up and left?"

"Well, no, not really. I mean, I must have walked by that spot once or twice, but I didn't see the viscount leave. Wasn't aware of him at all, really. And I certainly—"

Trent looked off for a moment. "Wait a minute. Now I remember. I did walk by there, and the reason that I recall it is that something flew by my head."

"Flew by your head?"

"Yes. Something swished past. Don't know what it was. I thought it was a bird buzzing me. Didn't see anything."

"What sort of sound did it make?"

"Not very identifiable. Just a fluttering. Or maybe it wasn't that, just a hiss or a swish. Maybe it was an insect. There're usually dragonflies around the pond over there. It wasn't very obtrusive at all, and I really didn't take any notice of it."

"Very interesting indeed," Tyrene said. "Where were you exactly when this occurred?"

Trent got up and walked a few paces out from the table, looked around, then sidestepped out a few paces more.

"About here," he said.

Tyrene walked to him and looked back toward the table. "So you were almost directly behind the viscount at the moment that this thing came past."

"Almost. A little past him. Yeah, it seems so. I could be off a couple of paces, but this is more or less where I was at that exact moment. I'm pretty sure that the thing whizzed by the back of my head."

"And you have no idea what the thing was."

"Well, now. Since I've recalled this, several possibilities have come to mind."

"Such as?"

"The obvious."

Tyrene nodded. "A thrown knife, perhaps?"

"Yes. Even though a stiletto isn't a good throwing knife, the thought did occur to me, yes."

"A stiletto is not a good throwing knife at all. But I suppose we must consider the possibility that it was thrown. Did you see anyone in a position to throw it?"

Trent looked to his right. "That hedge is man-high. Someone could have stepped out from behind there and done it."

Tyrene looked. "Yes. Possibly."

"Well, there you are. That's what happened."

Tyrene looked doubtful. "Why would the murderer take such a risk?"

"Unless he were an exceptional knife thrower."

"Ah. And do you have such a person in mind?"

"Tyrene, I'm rather hesitant about casting suspicions on anyone. Besides, I think you know who I'm thinking of."

"My apologies, Y R H. I just wanted to hear someone else vocalize it. Yes, I have someone in mind. But I have a problem. Why would the murderer choose to throw while you were in the way?"

"I may have been the target," Trent said.

"I suppose we cannot rule that out."

"Or he simply might not have seen me. I may have walked into his blind spot."

"Also possible. But if it was this certain person I have in mind, only the second reason would apply, since the man is an old friend of yours."

"Damik," Trent said. "Yes, he and I go way back. Damn it, Tyrene, I said I didn't want to compromise anyone."

"I have no reason at the moment for believing that the count was the culprit. His being an excellent bladesman does not instantly bring him under suspicion. There are many such among the inhabitants of Perilous and its environs."

"I'm glad you realize that, because Damik's no murderer."

"There is no reason in all the universes to imagine that he is. In fact, I believe he was a friend to the viscount as well."

"No accounting for taste."

Tyrene looked at the trampled grass. "Yes. Well. I'm very grateful to you for this interview, sir."

"Only too glad to help."

Tyrene looked back toward the portal. "Here be the horses." He heaved a sigh. "And now, it devolves to me to inform these gentle lords and ladies, every Jack and Jane of them my better, that they're all going to spend the night in the lockup. Gods have mercy."

Tyrene moped off.

"Where is this castle?" Thaxton asked.

"Just follow the sun down to the sea," Trent said. "There's a bridle path that runs by on the other side of the pond. Takes you right there."

"What say, Dalton, old boy? Ready to walk it? It's only five miles."

"Oh, I suppose I'm up to it. I'm not much of a horseback rider."

"I'd join you gentlemen," Trent said, "but I'm waiting for my wife. I sent word to her, and she sent back that she was coming, hell or high water notwithstanding."

"Are you going to take Sheila to Peele?" Dalton asked.

"If she wants to come. I don't give a damn what anyone thinks."

"Well, I suppose we'll see you both there," Dalton said. "Later."

"Wouldn't miss the fun."

The two erstwhile golfers circled the pond, in which grew a profusion of pretty water plants. On the other side they found the bridle path winding through hedges and thickets of forsythia. Here and there were lilac trees, all blooming in endless shades of lavender.

"How do you suppose they get horses up into the castle?" Dalton asked.

"Freight lift?"

"Have you ever seen a freight lift in the castle?"

"Can't say as I ever did, but that, as you well know, means nothing."

"Right. More important," Dalton said, "do you think Trent is still as hotheaded as he was reputed to be in his youth?"

"Which was about two hundred years ago," Thaxton pointed out. "Who knows? Don't know Trent very well. He and Sheila don't come out of their island paradise much."

"Myself, I've never found him to be anything but the soul of civility. But castle legend has it that he once challenged Incarnadine for the throne."

"I've heard that. But that's all patched up, isn't it? Besides, what's it got to do with Trent's being a likely candidate for the viscount's killer? That is what you're insinuating, isn't it?"

"Yup," Dalton said. "He could have thrown the dagger, or simply slipped it in as he passed."

"Odd way to do someone in, that," Thaxton ruminated. "*En passant*, at a picnic, with people around."

Dalton said, "And all because the guy made a pass at his wife."

"Unless . . ."

"Hm?"

"Unless," Thaxton said, "there's something more to it. Something more to the pass, that is."

"You mean Sheila . . . and the viscount were—?"

"Well, that sounds unlikely. We both know Sheila. But we don't know the circumstances of the alleged incident. 'Long bomb into the end zone.' If I know my American rugby that's serious business. Suppose it were more or less a rape?"

"Okay, I see what you're driving at, but we don't know what happened, and I don't see how we could find out. Trent is certainly not going to elaborate."

"Yes. But 'sexual assault' is a tad bit more serious than a pass, isn't it?"

"I would have to agree," Dalton said, smelling the lilac.

NECROPOLIS

IT WAS DARK IN THE ALLEY behind the Pelican Club, a single bare bulb glowing above the back door of the oriental restaurant next door. Kitchen fans blew food smells to blend with the reek of garbage. A rat skittered across the broken concrete of the pavement, stopped to sniff at an oily puddle, moved on.

Carney and Velma waited in the shadows, her hand on his arm. He was in topcoat and hat, she hatless in a dark seal coat. It was chilly, but there was no wind.

A car made the turn into the alley and approached. It was a long cream-colored sedan with flaring fenders, a continental kit on the driver's side, white tires, and a big front grille of gleaming chrome. The radiator cap was topped with a winged Nike.

The car pulled up behind the nightclub. Montanaro was at the wheel. Carney ushered Velma into the front seat and got in, closed the door.

"So, boss," Tony said, "Where to?"

"Velma's place. Tell him where you live, Velma."

"The Tweeleries."

Tony grinned. "Boss, you either have some powerful

mumbo jumbo workin' for you tonight, or you've gone nuts."

"Neither. But I figure the straightforward approach is best."

"You're just going to call him out, or what?"

"Actually, just going to call *on* him. Tweel likes to talk."

"He likes to do the talking. Boss, I don't think it's a good idea."

"No, but it's inevitable. Something's up, and I've got to find out what—what his game is. What's eating him, maybe. Do you know, Velma?"

"Clare doesn't have anything eating him," she said. "He's an eater. He feeds."

"It's a rough universe."

"Yeah, yeah," she said, pulling out a cigarette. "Can I smoke?"

"Sure," Tony said, as he slid the ashtray out of the dashboard. "This baby has everything." He took the cigarette lighter out of the dash, flicked it. Flame danced, limning her rouged cheeks, her glistening red lips. She puffed. He put the lighter back and closed the door to its tiny receptacle.

She inhaled deeply, then let it out. Smoke billowed against the windshield. "Yeah, it's rough. There are the eaters, and those that get eaten. Clare's an eater." She looked at Carney. "You are, too."

"How about me, babe?" Tony wanted to know.

"You're dumb, but cute."

"Let's see if I have this straight now," Carney said. "There are bastards and simps, and the consumers and the consumed. Have I got it all now?"

"You got it."

"Where do you fit in?"

"I just swim along with the current. Just swim along."

"Okay, now you have a marine metaphor going. Big fish, little fish."

"Big fish with big teeth, little fish with suckers. That's pretty much it."

They pulled out onto Whiteway Boulevard, merging with the stream of late-night traffic. Crowds were just getting out of the darkening theaters, couples arm-in-arm on the sidewalks, still laughing at the gag lines, humming the tunes, occasionally pausing to window-shop. Drunks threaded in and out of the milling throngs. Beyond the canyon walls the many-footed city murmured in the neon night-mist, a monster stirring in its sleep.

"They gotta be tailin' us," Tony said.

Carney gave a look back. "Don't see anything yet."

"Wait till we turn off. Boss, this is gonna be suicide. One, they're gonna try to zotz us before we cross the river; two, if we do get into Hellgate, we get wasted before we drive a block; three, say you do get to the Tweeleries. They either let you have it at the check station, or they take you in and do it, maybe for Tweel to watch."

"Drive to Manny's Garage first," Carney said.

Tony nodded slowly, then smiled. "I gotcha. Change cars, huh?" The smile faded. "But they'll just wait for us to come out."

"You drive in, drop me off. You take the new car and drive out with Velma. They won't follow you. I'll slip through the celebrity duck-out hole into Lucky's basement. I'll go up into the restaurant and out the front door. You pick me up there."

"That's great, boss."

"Nobody but Lucky and his celeb customers know about the hole. And Manny. And me, since I own half the joint. And Manny's employees." Carney chuckled. "Now that I think of it, it's not such a big secret. Still, it should work."

"It's a little risky, but I like it," Tony said. He shrugged. "Hey, you gotta take a shot, you know what I'm sayin'?"

"You pays your money and you falls on your face."

Tony laughed. "Yeah, that's exactly what we're gonna do if they tail me, maybe thinkin' you're hidin' in the trunk or some stunt like that."

"If they do split up to tail you, what you do is—"

"Hey, boss, whaddya think, I'm some kinda *mamaluke*? If they tail me, I drive around until they get sick of it. I lose 'em and then I come back for you."

"Hey, you gotta some brains."

Tony cackled, then checked the rearview window. "Hell, I see 'em already. That's Seamus Riordan's Durant Roadmaster. I can tell by the grille."

"Seamus got first crack," Carney said. "But he won't have time."

Tony turned right onto 43rd Street and went half a block before turning into a steep ramp under a sign that read MIDTOWN PARKING.

Down in the garage, Carney got out near the glassed-in office.

"Park it. Get the new car and get over there as fast as you can. If you're delayed, when you pull up in front of Lucky's, blink your lights. The doorman will let me know, so I don't have to stand out there waiting and maybe get spotted. Got it?"

"Got it, boss."

"Manny will take care of you, or whoever's on tonight."

"Check."

He closed the door and went into the office. The night manager was Billy Pinsk. Carney ordered a nondescript rental car.

"Got just what you need, Mr. Carney. A Leland sedan, gray, no flashy stuff."

"Tony Montanaro's out there. You fix him up. Right now I need you to let me through to Lucky's."

"Door's unlocked, Mr. Carney. Always. You know where it is?"

"That door back there and to the right?"

"That's it, Mr. Carney. Straight to the end of the corridor, you can't miss it."

"Okay, thanks."

"Dark back there, Mr. Carney. Watch your step."

"Right."

He walked to the back of the garage, opened the steel door, and stepped through. It was quiet on the other side. He turned right and proceeded through gloom until he came to another door. It was ajar. He went through and followed a short corridor, came out among boilers and pipes, weaved through and around, then mounted a wooden staircase.

He pushed open the door at the top and let himself into Lucky's kitchen. It was big, full of men in white aprons and hats working furiously at counter and stove. Steam mushroomed to the ceiling. The odor of chopped onions stood out among myriad others.

Nobody gave him a look as he walked through. He thumped through swinging doors and passed the men's room. He gave a fleeting thought to relieving his bladder *pro forma,* not really needing to, giving Tony a little time. But he was anxious and in a hurry.

He went to the front door by way of the smaller of the restaurant's two rooms, not seeing anybody he knew.

Outside, he looked up and down the street. No Tony. The doorman asked if he needed a cab, and he shook his head. He stepped back under the sidewalk canopy and gave it three minutes, looking for signs of Tony's Leland or Riordan's Durant.

Neither showed. He beckoned to the doorman, spoke his instructions, and handed the man a fiver.

"Sure thing, Mr. Carney."

"Just let Alphonse know. I'll be at my table."

"Yes, sir."

Inside, after he had checked his hat and coat, Alphonse greeted him with a smile.

"Your table, Mr. Carney?"

"Yes. I probably won't be staying long. Just enough for a drink."

"Anything you say, Mr. Carney."

A waiter showed him across the main floor. On the way he saw a table occupied by the Bakunin triplets—Grumpo, Cisco, and Heppo—and two chorines, all in for a late bite after another performance of their long-running hit musical comedy, *Have I Gotta Deal For You!* He detoured over.

Cisco took his nose out of a racing form to say, "Johnnie, sweetheart." It was always a little disconcerting to hear his normal voice, untainted by the put-on Latin accent of his stage and screen character. "Hey, what do you say?"

Grumpo smiled his lizard smile. "Killed anybody recently?"

"Nobody. Haven't zotzed a soul since, oh, it'll be a year come Michaelmas."

"Well, that's disappointing. Next thing you know you'll be taking stray kittens home."

Heppo's childlike grin was as wide as the bald strip that ran from his forehead almost to the back of his neck. Without his wig and makeup he looked like a garment maven or a bookkeeper, anything but the brilliant comedian he was. "Hi, John," he said. "Haven't seen you in for lunch at the Penobscot lately."

"Crossing foils with that Penobscot Forum crowd is tiring. I can't stay up late writing ad libs."

"How do you think I feel sometimes," Heppo said, "mixing with the literati? Me with an eighth-grade education."

"They like you, Heppo."

"Dara Porter says I'm a rhinestone in the rough."

"She knows her gems."

"Rhinestones are a girl's best friend," Grumpo said.

"Me, I'll take the money," Cisco said. "What do you think, John? I got a tip on a twenty-to-one long shot, a two-year-old filly in the fifth at Via Appia tomorrow. She has a terrible track record, but I got the word in training-runs she clocks like the wind. Crazy? or should I bet my wad?"

Carney thought about it. "Yeah, it's only a matter of time before she overcomes her skittishness. Put it all down to win, Cisco."

"Hey, I will. Thanks."

Carney said, "Grumpo, how's the new show coming?"

"Lousy."

"What, with book by Geoff Katzman and music by Ira Bremen?"

"It's going to cost a fortune to stage, which means they're not going to offer us any more money than we're getting now. And I just bought a house. I need a raise."

"Didn't you just film *Have I Gotta Deal*?"

"Yeah, but I already spent that money on the down payment."

"Must be a terrific house."

"It was a steal. They stole my money."

"John, have a seat," Heppo said.

"Actually, I'm just waiting for my driver. He must have gotten a flat or something. He's late."

"Well, you got time for a drink, then. Sit down."

Carney dismissed the waiter and pulled up a chair. The two chorines smiled at him and he grinned back amiably.

"Hear you've been having trouble recently," Grumpo said.

"Nah, just a little misunderstanding," Carney said.

"*The Daily Times* is billing it as the biggest gang war Necropolis has ever seen. Pictures and everything. It wasn't pretty."

"I don't imagine. Still, they're blowing it all out of proportion, as usual."

"Yeah, they have the box office to think of, too," Grumpo said, phlegmatically munching the end of his cigar.

"Strange things are happening," Cisco said. "I got a friend in the mayor's office says they haven't seen him for two days."

"Who?" Carney said. "The mayor?"

"Yeah. Nobody knows where His Honor is. They got no message from him, nothing. The papers are sitting on the story."

"Interesting. But he's probably down in Palm Coast again with the phone off the hook."

"A reporter I know says he's at the Tweeleries. On ice."

"He and Clare are buddies. Or were."

"Yeah, but I don't think this is friendly."

Food arrived, stacks of sandwiches and piles of cole slaw. Carney ordered a drink, and it came with lightning speed.

"You want half my sandwich?" Heppo offered. "I can never finish these."

"No, thanks, Hep." Carney looked at his watch. "I can't imagine where my driver got to."

"You need a lift?" Cisco asked.

"You have your car?"

"No." Cisco chuckled. "Hey, I just asked you if you needed a lift."

"You ought to work on that material. It shows promise."

"Promises were made to be broken," Grumpo said. "I have a car, John, and you're welcome to it, if you can get it back from the finance company."

Cisco snorted. "He's always kvetching about how hard up he is. Bullshit—he's rich."

"Bullshit, I'm rich."

"Go on, you're rolling in it. I'm the one with the sob story. I lost fifty grand at the track last year."

"And that was after taxes," Grumpo said. "You know, Morris—"

The brothers (fraternal triplets) always called each other by their proper names.

"—just the other day someone said you were dumb."

"Yeah? What did you say?"

"I said, 'He's *shit*.'"

"Well, thanks, I appreciate it," Cisco said.

"If you can't stick up for your brother, who can you stick up for?"

"Stick it up your ass."

"Don't knock it if you haven't—" Grumpo turned to one of the chorines, who was convulsed. "You can choke to death that way, honey. Spit that corned beef out."

She swallowed and gagged. Grumpo slapped her bare back.

Carney checked his watch again, then gave a glance back to the maitre d's station.

"You seem a little nervous, John," Heppo remarked.

"Maybe I am."

"Well, take it easy. You're among friends."

"With friends like us," Grumpo said, "he needs all the enemies he can get."

"Don't listen to this guy. Momma always said his mouth would take him to the top, and then right back down again."

"Momma didn't raise any mute children, except you."

"I know my limitations. I can't talk for sour beans. Shoot a Moogie—"

Heppo made a grotesquely comical face.

"—that I can do. There was this guy below our place when we were kids, ran a fix-it shop. When he worked he screwed up his face like this." Heppo did it again. "His name was Mort, but they called him Moogie, for some reason. Anyway, I been cashing in on him ever since."

"An artist uses the material of everyday life," Carney said.

"And a comedian buys his gags from a good gag writer," Grumpo said.

"Grumpo," Carney said, "your best gags are your own. In fact, you're eponymous for the quick retort. Grumpoisms."

Grumpo looked rueful. "I wish I was a surgeon. Or a dishwasher. Anything but a professional wiseguy." He seemed to mean it.

The meal went on, the talk gravitating to show business. Carney decided to stay put for now, as he was reluctant to take a cab alone. Not because he feared an ambush—if one came it could be a litmus test by which to judge the possible outcome of the evening—but because the cabby might get hurt.

At some point, Cisco threw down his half-eaten sandwich. "Let's get out of here. It's late and I'm tired."

"Spoken like a trouper," Grumpo said. "Let's vamoose. John, you're welcome to share a cab with us."

"Thanks, I will."

Grumpo picked up the check and looked it over. "This is outrageous. John, if I were you—"

Carney's fifty was already in the tray, and the sight of it spoiled Grumpo's punch line. All he could do was grin awkwardly and say, "That's decent of you." Grumpo was not known as the world's fastest check-grabber.

Outside, Cisco herded the girls into a cab and waved goodbye to them.

"I'm bushed," he said. "Besides, I think they're both virgins. They're from out in the Midwest somewhere."

"Yeah, Virginia." Grumpo said.

"No, from some farm state."

"Aren't they all? Virgins are a cash crop out there. They ship 'em all east to the Boulevard."

"How about Studio City?" Cisco asked.

"Studio City? Virgins? Are you kidding?" Grumpo appealed to Heppo. "He's gotta be kidding."

A cab pulled up. Carney had been vainly searching up and down the street.

"Coming, John?" Heppo said.

"Yeah." Carney got in.

The cab pulled away, and Carney settled back, unsure of what to do.

"Where are you going, John?" Grumpo asked.

"Hellgate."

"Driver," Grumpo yelled. "East Seventieth and Bennington, then over the river for this gentleman here." He turned around on the little flip-down seat. "We'll pay the fare since you were stupid enough to pick up the check."

"Forget it. Hellgate's a long way."

"Well, if you insist," Grumpo said affably. "I like arguing with this guy. You always lose to your benefit."

Cisco turned the conversation back to virginity and related matters, and was in the middle of a story about a sporting house up in Eindhoven with an employee whose specialty was something akin to fruit arrangement, when Carney spotted a gray Leland parked on the street.

"She takes these pineapple slices, see . . ." Cisco was saying.

"Stop here, driver!" Carney called.

"Sounds so good I'd probably eat it myself," Grumpo said. "Are you getting off, John?"

"Good night, boys."

"Well, don't take any wooden Indians. Whatever that means."

"Take care, John," Heppo said.

Carney got out and watched the cab move off. The street was quiet. He walked back to the parked sedan.

Tony and Velma were intricately entangled, his hand lost in her dress.

He tapped on the glass.

Tony jumped. He rolled down the window. "Boss! Hey, we got tailed. They wouldn't quit, so I pulled over to wait 'em out."

Carney gave the street the up-and-down. "Looks like they were convinced. You can stop the verisimilitude now."

When Carney got in, Velma was reapplying lipstick and Tony was wiping it off his face.

"Sorry about that, boss," Tony said.

"You could have phoned the restaurant."

"I didn't want to leave Velma."

"Forget it. But I'm docking you a hundred out of your pay."

Tony was silent for a moment. He put away his handkerchief. "Gee, boss, I'm sorry as hell. I feel like such a *finòcchio*. I really shoulda figured some way to phone."

"I said, forget it. We lost them. Now let's get moving."

Tony started the car.

Velma gave Carney an enigmatic smile conveying a suggestion that she had meant to do some mischief and was delighted to have succeeded. But it was only a suggestion.

"Go up to Dutchtown," Carney said.

"Dutchtown? I thought we was going to cross the river."

"Later. I need to get in the spirit."

"Check."

The car moved off into the night.

VILLE-DES-MORTS

THE STREET WAS DARK AND DESERTED, decent people being in bed, sleeping or otherwise, at this time of night. There was, however, a fingernail-clipping of a moon that served to limn the cobblestones in a faint bluish light.

Linda, Gene, and Snowclaw kept to the shadows. They passed through alley after alley, sending gray ghosts of cats scurrying. Every so often they encountered a lighted window—someone sick, perhaps, or a literate citizen (in these neighborhoods quite rare) up with an absorbing book.

They did run across the odd person up and about, and twice, a group of rowdies. The rowdies they hid from, but in neither case did they suspect the passers-by of being members of Ragueneau's private police force.

They moved on through the old city.

"We could go through the sewers," Gene suggested.

"Yuck," Linda said. "Do you know your way around down there?"

"Nope. But I thought it would lend the right note of romance. Orson Welles in *The Third Man*. Zither music, you know?"

"Right."

"Wait." Gene stopped Linda with an outstretched arm. Snowclaw halted.

Voices up ahead. Gene motioned toward the mouth of an alley. With a light tread, they ran.

The other end of the alley gave onto a winding street. They turned left and proceeded until they heard more voices, these off to the left. They hurried.

They came running around a bend and into full view of three men talking in the middle of the square. They skidded to a stop.

One of the three walked toward them. "You there! Let's see your papers." He wore, as did his mates, the telltale purple brassard of Ragueneau's auxiliaries.

"Papers?" Gene said innocently.

The man kept coming. "Idiot! Your identification papers."

"No need to get personal."

"Eh? What's your name?" The man's right hand went to his sword hilt.

"Jose Ferrer. And we don't got to show you no stinkin' papers." Gene drew his rapier.

The man drew his weapon almost simultaneously, but backstepped until the other two arrived. Gene and Snowclaw went to meet them. Gene engaged the first man while Snowclaw, sans weapon, faced down the pair.

They didn't know what to make of him. Snowclaw kept advancing purposefully, and, momentarily intimidated by his size and his inexplicable behavior, the two men failed to stand their ground. Then one of them lunged for Snowclaw's massive chest. The point made contact; the thin sword bowed into an arch, and the astonished attacker withdrew.

"Ouch," Snowclaw said, stopping. He opened his shirt and examined his right pectoral. "That broke the skin, darn it." He sprang toward the culprit. "Now you're going to get it."

Both men dashed away.

Gene and his opponent were mixing it up rather well. Snowclaw stood by and watched imperturbably, but Linda gnawed a knuckle, giving a little shriek when Gene had to retreat from a killing lunge.

When the man realized he was alone, the fight went out of him. He backed off, looked over his shoulder, gave a weak, embarrassed smile, then turned and ran.

"You guys *are* good," Linda marveled.

"Get hurt, Snowy?" Gene asked.

"Nah. There's only one or two spots on me that those pointy things can jab into, but they haven't found 'em yet."

"Amazing," Linda said.

Gene poked him. "Snowy must have some kind of layer of cartilage under his skin. At least that's how I—"

Running footsteps came from beyond the bend, approaching.

The threesome took off down the street. They made a left at the next crossing and followed a narrow street lined with buildings fronting on the pavement. The sounds of pursuit remained at their heels. They ducked into an alley, ran along it. Snowclaw collided with a pile of debris and made a racket. Linda stubbed her toe, suppressed a curse, and went limping along. Gene was first into the street on the other side, and looked to the right. Five of Ragueneau's henchmen came spilling out of a courtyard. Gene jumped back into the alley, snagged Snowclaw before he blundered out, and turned Linda around. She grabbed onto him.

"Go back! Can you walk?"

"I think I broke my toe."

They worked their way slowly back up the alley. For all Snowclaw's caution, however, he stumbled over the same pile of junk, raising as much racket as before.

"I thought you could see in the dark," Gene growled.

"Who ever said that?" Something breakable shattered. "Darn it, anyway."

"Snowy, quit that!"

"I'm not doing it deliberately! I can't see a thing."

In fact, Snowclaw's eyes were designed to temper the harsh arctic glare of sun on ice and snow. The lenses of his eyes were like polarized sunglasses, and thus made for poor night vision.

A shadow appeared at the end of the alley.

"You there! Stop where you are!"

They turned and tried to run, but Linda could do little better than limp along. When they reached the other end of the alley, Ragueneau's goons were waiting to meet them.

Gene waded in, sword long since drawn, and engaged no less than three of the five. One grabbed Linda, but Snowclaw snapped his neck straightaway. The fourth goon tried to run Snowclaw through, but got his rapier broken in two and himself thrown through a window.

More of the Legate's henchmen came rushing out of the alley like hornets out of a disturbed nest, in numbers more than even Snowclaw could effectively deal with.

By that time Gene had skewered one opponent and punctured another's sword shoulder. Those two incapacitated, Gene took on two more, ran one through immediately and nicked the other's forearm. He fought furiously, his blade whipping back and forth from one opponent to the next. Steel clashed and rang.

But it was no use. Eventually Gene was surrounded and the fight was over.

Gene lowered his sword. "Snowy!"

Snowclaw was busy with an experiment: Could a man's leg be stuffed into his own ear? Not easily, as it turned out. Seven other goons were desperately trying to restrain him.

"What?"

"Give it up, Snowy. They got us."

"Aw, heck." Snowclaw dropped his slightly rearranged victim.

One of the captors, presumably the leader, swaggered up to Gene and took the rapier.

"Eugéne de Périlleux, I presume?"

"*C'est moi* all over."

"His Eminence, the Legate, craves the honor of your company," the man said with an ironic sneer. "But on the morrow. For tonight, deluxe accommodations await you at the Tower of Tears."

Gene muttered, "Yeah, I hear the Triple-A gave it five stars."

"Take them away."

Gene heard gasps and turned in Snowclaw's direction.

No longer did Snowclaw look human. In fact, he looked not

unlike an upright-walking polar bear dressed in seventeenth-century costume. But of course he looked more fierce than any bumbling bear; no bear ever had such elaborate dentition or yellow eyes that glowed in the dark.

He growled. The goons backpedaled away.

"Pay no attention to my friend, here," Gene said. "His therapist says he's getting better."

"Sorcerers!" one of them said, quailing.

Snowclaw tore off his clothing and threw the rags aside. "Boy, that feels better." He was a mountain of white fur.

"A devil!"

"Not really," Snowclaw said. He held up one pawlike hand. Gingerly, he touched the middle of the palm with one finger. In an instant bone-white claws, two inches long and wickedly sharp, sprang from the ends of his fingerlike digits. "But I like kicking a few butts now and then."

They ran.

Gene picked up his sword and sheathed it. "You had to go and spoil the fun."

"Sorry," Snowclaw said.

Linda let out a windy breath. "Oh, was I *scared*."

"We would have figured out something," Gene said. "Come on, let's get to the portal. How's your toe?"

"It's all right. Just stubbed. Gene, what's the Tower of Tears?"

"Oh, a prison, with a very good apprentice-torturer program."

"Get out."

"No, it's a sort of teaching hospital in reverse. Clients get personalized service."

"I'm not going to think about it."

"I really am sorry," Snowclaw said, tagging after them.

The portal was in the crypt of a collapsed cathedral that had never been rebuilt. The stairs descended into darkness. Gene went to a nearby niche, slid out a stone, and took a candle and matches out of the cavity. He lit the candle, handed it to Linda, then slid the stone back into place. The threesome went down the winding stairwell single file.

"I'd stash a flashlight, but I worry about it being discovered," Gene said. "Besides, batteries corrode. Never rely on a higher technology when a lower one will suffice."

They walked along a corridor with doorways opening off to burial crypts at either hand. Gene led the way into the third chamber on the right.

The far wall was pierced with a pointed archway, through which light spilled. They passed through it and entered Castle Perilous, stepping from one world to another as if it were nothing. And it wasn't much at all, as far as they were concerned.

Linda did an orchestra conductor's flourish. Her seventeenth-century outfit vanished, replaced with her usual castle duds. Gone also was the blond beard.

"Sheesh! Am I glad to get out of those. I wouldn't make a very good guy."

"I wouldn't touch that line with a fork. Do you think Dolbert and Luster are up in the graving dock now?"

"They sleep up there. We should go up and see what gives."

"It's only three floors. Let's take the escalator."

The escalators were a new feature, tricked up by Linda, Sheila, and a few other adept castle magicians. They seemed to be fairly permanent so far, subject only to minor fluctuations and uncertainties. The devices hummed and clanked satisfactorily, and they actually worked.

"Even if Dolbert manages to get the *Voyager* running again," Gene said as they ascended, "we still have the problem of locating Melanie."

"We need the locater spell. Osmirik has it in one of his dusty books."

"It works on Earth. No telling how effective it is elsewhere. Besides, she could be in any one of a million universes. It could take years to find her."

"Then we have to come up with a spell that will locate her quicker. That's all."

Gene had no answer.

They found their way through the immense castle with the ease possible only to veteran castle Guests. Still, it was a long walk to the lab.

On the way they heard something ringing ahead. They turned a corner to find a pay telephone on the wall.

"Have you ever seen a phone in the castle before?" Linda asked, amazed.

"Can't say that I have," Gene said. "Going to answer it?"

Linda picked up the receiver. "Hello? . . . Yes, it is . . ." She listened for a moment, then said, "Just a minute, please." She put her hand over the mouthpiece. "Do you know anything about a Land Surveyor?"

"Land Surveyor? Nope."

"Guy says he's the Land Surveyor and that he was sent to the castle."

Gene shrugged.

"Uh, sir? I'm sorry, but there's no one here who can help you at the moment . . . Yes . . . Uh-huh. You're welcome." She hung up. "I wonder what that was all about?"

"Who knows," Gene said.

When they arrived at the lab, Jeremy was at his work station as usual, typing away at the mainframe terminal.

Gene asked, "Are Dolbert and Luster back in the graving dock?"

"They never come out," Jeremy said. "I never see 'em."

Gene, Linda, and Snowclaw walked to the back of the lab and went through a large oaken door.

The chamber on the other side was immense, but not as big as the lab. The ceiling was the same arabesque of stone arches.

In the middle of the floor sat a strange bell-shaped object, a craft of some sort, up on jacks. There was an oval window in the hull; otherwise the silver-colored machine was smooth and featureless.

Two pairs of legs stuck out from underneath the craft, one pair a lot longer than the other.

Gene stooped. "Hey, Luster?"

"Yo!"

"Uh, you got a minute?"

"Wull, ah reckon ah do."

Luster slid out and stood up. He was tall, wheyfaced, and

thin. He wore filthy brown corduroy pants and work boots, and was shirtless except for the top section of his long underwear, which had originally been white, probably sometime early in the last decade. He wore a tattered, sweat-stained baseball cap of the style not seen since the last time Ty Cobb led the American League in batting. His irises were so pale they were almost indistinguishable from the white of the eye.

"Hullo," Luster said, smiling. "Ma'am," a nod to Linda.

"Hi, Luster," Linda said.

"Whut kin ah do for y'all?"

Gene said, "Gee, Luster, we hate to bother you, but we kinda wanted some idea of when you guys think you can get the *Voyager* back on-line."

"Say *whut*?"

"Uh, get it working again. Have any idea when?"

"Dolbert? You hear that?"

A high-pitched cackling came from underneath the craft. It sounded at once derisory, ironic, and regretful.

"Dolbert says he heard you."

"Uh-huh. Well?"

"Dolbert? Gene wants to know when."

Chittering, with a hint of sarcastic skepticism.

"Dolbert says it beats the livin' bejesus outta him," Luster reported.

Linda sighed. "We'll have to do it by magic."

"How?" Gene asked.

"Conjuring. I'll just conjure her."

"Can you do that?"

"Never tried it. When Incarnadine was stranded last time, I was tempted. But this time I think I'm going to try it."

"Well, that brings up a lot of philosophical questions," Gene said.

Linda suddenly lost enthusiasm. "Yeah, I know. For instance, will it be the 'real' Melanie, or just some fake? Like most of the stuff I whip up."

"Most of your stuff is pretty permanent," Gene said.

"Yeah. Good thing, too. Imagine suddenly losing your clothes. Embarrassing. But that doesn't mean they're real.

Even if it worked, if I could conjure Melanie, I could never really be sure that the real one wasn't still off in a wild aspect somewhere, lost and alone."

Linda slumped to a wooden crate. "Damn it."

"Somebody in trouble?" Luster asked.

Gene explained.

"Wull, that shore is a pity. Hear that, Dolbert?"

Sympathetic chirring.

"Yeah, I know it. Dolbert says he's shore sorry, but he don't know whut all he kin do beyond whut he's doin' right now."

"That's okay, Luster," Linda said. "I'm sure you guys are trying your best."

Dolbert slid out from underneath the *Voyager* and stood. He didn't look much like his brother. He was short and his eyes were darker. He wore no shirt under his bib overalls. His baseball cap was, if possible, even more rat-chewed and moth-eaten than his brother's. Grime covered him. His smile was wide and perpetual.

He guffawed and pointed to the crate Linda was sitting on.

Gene turned to Luster. "What did he say?"

"He says maybe that new particulator we ordered'll do the trick."

"Particulator?" Linda said, getting up.

"Yup. We done ordered it in one of them whatchucall yore *aspects*. Lord Incarnadine told us it might be had there. And shore enough, it were."

"What's it do?" Gene asked.

"Danged if we know. Jus' know that one that's in the *Voyager*'s cracked."

"Oh. And you think that might be the problem?"

"Could be. We replaced a couple parts so far. Dolbert even built one or two. They didn't do the trick. But this one jes might." Luster took off his cap, exposing a thicket of yellow hair. He scratched his head. "Then agin, maybe not."

Gene asked, "When do you figure you can install this gadget?"

"Dolbert?"

Dolbert laughed and shrugged his narrow shoulders.

Luster said, "Dolbert says there ain't nothin' standin' in the way o' doin' it right now."

Gene dragged up another crate, this one empty. He sat. "Mind if we watch you doctors operate?"

Dolbert giggled.

SEACOAST

PEELE CASTLE SAT WITH ITS BACK TO THE SEA atop a high chalk cliff. It looked like something out of a fairy tale, a fantasy of high towers and crenelated battlements. The sun declined behind it, throwing a sheen of reddish light over the water. Gulls wheeled in the evening sky, white against the darkening blue. Far out to sea, the dark stripe of a squall line edged the horizon.

Thaxton and Dalton sat on a knoll overlooking the scene.

"Looks like bad weather coming in," Thaxton said.

"Yup. God, isn't it picturesque?"

"It is that."

" 'It was many and many a year ago, in a kingdom by the sea,' " Dalton recited. " 'That a maiden there lived, whom you may know, by the name of Annabel Lee.' "

"Keats?"

"Poe."

"Oh, yes. American."

"Here's the princess."

They both stood as Dorcas approached barefoot, sandals in hand.

"Good evening, gentlemen. It was a nice walk, wasn't it? It seems we're the first to arrive."

"Couldn't pick a more charming spot to spend the night," Dalton commented.

"I've spent many a night in Peele," she said. "When I was young we came here often. I spent whole summers here."

"Are there any local inhabitants?" Thaxton asked.

"No. This land is deserted. The population disappeared long ago. Plague was the cause, it's thought, though it happened so far back, no one is sure."

"Pity. It's beautiful country. Reminds me of England a bit."

"This world is a variant of Earth, and this land was very similar to England."

Dorcas looked landward across the grassy plateau. "Here comes everybody."

A line of horse-and-riders was approaching, servants and others walking behind.

"Your Highness," Thaxton said, "may I ask about the jewel you wear on your forehead?"

"Yes, of course. It symbolizes the Interior Eye, the Eye of Yahura the Seer. It has to do with the religion of my adopted country, my husband's native land."

"How interesting. I'd like to hear more about it."

"Certainly. Later, if you wish."

"May I ask, ma'am, whether you knew the viscount well?"

"I knew him, his wife. I saw them at various affairs over the years. I couldn't say we were friendly. Still, it's a terrible thing that's happened."

"Oh, quite. Did the viscount have many enemies?"

Dalton seemed uncomfortable. "I'm sure Her Highness doesn't—"

"I can understand your interest," the princess said, "having discovered the body. It must have been a shock."

"It was. I hope you don't find my questions too impertinent, ma'am, but, as you said, our curiosity is naturally very high. And our concern, of course."

"As is everyone else's. The murderer must be brought to justice. He cannot be permitted to go free." The princess seemed to retreat into herself, her gaze deflecting momentarily.

Then she looked at Thaxton. "Yes. To answer your question, the viscount was not liked by many people. Whether he had enemies, I don't know."

"Thank you, ma'am."

She looked toward the sea. "I think I'll sit by the cliff and watch the sunset before I go in. I must meditate."

They watched her go down the knoll and walk toward the cliff's edge.

"Odd."

"What?" Dalton asked.

"When she said '*He* must not be permitted to go free' I got the distinct impression that she had someone specific in mind."

"I sort of did, too, now that you mention it."

Their room was small but had a spectacular view of the ocean through casements of leaded glass. The servant, an elderly man with a shiny bald head, swung the panes out to let in tangy salt air.

"Servant's quarters, I suspect," Thaxton said, looking around.

Dalton said, "It'll do. Hard to get used to an *ordinary* castle with limited space."

"One bed," Thaxton noted, dubiously eyeing the not-quite-double bed.

"I can fetch a cot, sir," the servant offered.

"Oh, don't bother on my account," Thaxton said. "One regrettable aspect of the current openness about things is that there's now something slightly questionable about two men occupying the same bed. Used to be no one gave it a second thought."

"I remember," Dalton said. "But I like to stretch out, and besides, I thrash in my sleep sometimes, or so my late wife used to tell me."

"I'll tell one of the boys to fetch it right up, sir."

"Thank you . . . ?"

"Ruford, sir."

"Thank you, Ruford."

Thaxton remarked, "You were at the fête, weren't you?"

"Yes, sir."

"I suppose you saw nothing suspicious, either?"

"Ah . . . no, sir. I did not."

"You didn't see the viscount get up and leave?"

"No, sir."

"See anything happen right before that?"

"Ah . . . specifically what, sir?"

"Oh, anything that went on, for instance, between the viscount and his lady."

Ruford looked away. "I did serve the viscount and Lady Rilma, yes, sir."

"Did they talk?"

Ruford seemed reluctant to speak.

Thaxton nodded. "I realize I'm asking you to talk about your employer—"

"Sir, I am not employed by the viscount. I am head of staff here at Peele."

"I understand your reluctance. But this is important. Did Tyrene interview you yet?"

"No, sir."

Dalton said, "Thaxton, maybe we'd better wait. After all, it's not our—"

"Hold off just a moment, old man. Ruford, Mr. Dalton and I are acting in an advisory capacity to the investigation. We will keep anything you say in strictest confidence."

Dalton gave his golf partner a strange look.

Ruford sighed. "Very well, sir. Yes, I heard them speaking."

"And?"

"They were arguing, sir."

"About what?"

"I didn't hear all of it, sir, but the lady said something to the effect that he ought not to have done it right in front of her."

"Done what?"

"Oh, dear." Ruford's face reddened.

"He was making improper advances?"

Ruford raised his thin eyebrows. "Yes, sir."

Thaxton's aside to Dalton was: "Just a wild guess." Of Ruford he asked, "To whom? Lady Rowena?"

"Yes."

"That's Lord Belgard's wife?"

"Yes, sir."

"While they were playing at hedge ball?"

"Yes, sir. I myself saw it."

"And Lord Belgard, too, I presume."

"Yes, sir, I suppose the lord did see it. He was right there."

"Interesting. Under her husband's nose. And the viscount and Lady Rilma argued over this. She berated him?"

"She did, sir."

"And what was his reaction?"

"He told her to be quiet. Then . . . he threw something at her."

"He did?"

"Yes, sir. A wing of capon."

"It struck her?"

"Yes, sir. In the face."

"And what did she do or say?"

"Nothing, sir. She just got the palest look on her."

"Pale? Was she afraid, do you think?"

"No, sir. It was anger, sir. The kind that drains the blood from the face and makes the lips waxen. That kind of anger, sir. Cold anger. She looked as though . . ."

"She looked as though what?"

"As though she were going to strike him back, sir. Only harder."

"Did she make any attempt?"

"No, sir. None. She just sat there."

"Did you hear or see anything else?"

"I'm afraid not, sir. That is all I have to tell."

"You didn't see Trent—?"

"Oh, please, sir. I saw nothing." Ruford cast his eyes to the floor. "It is not my place to talk about the brother of the king."

"In a court of law, you'd be obliged to," Thaxton reminded him.

"Yes, sir. I would. But not until then, and not until his lordship the judge puts the question, and I am bound by law and principle to answer."

"I see. Well, thank you, Ruford. That's all for now."

"You're quite welcome, sir. I'll see to the cot straightaway."

When the door closed, Dalton said, "That was hard for him."

"Well, servants, you know."

"I do know that there's more than one mystery to all this."

"Eh? What's that?"

"You."

"Me? Whatever do you mean?"

Dalton sat on a hard-backed wooden chair. "I've never seen you like this. I can't fathom this amazing transformation that's come over you."

"Just what amazing transformation is that, old man?"

"This is the first time I've ever seen you . . . *interested* in something. You're animated, you're involved. And you have the makings of becoming a damn fine amateur sleuth. Where on earth did you learn all that forensic medicine?"

Thaxton chuckled. "I'm faking it, old man. I don't know all that much about forensic medicine or, for that matter, anything else. What I do know was learned out of murder mysteries."

"You're kidding."

"Not at all. Used to read three a week sometimes when I was married. Not much else to do. Sayers, Christie, Chesterton, Bentley, the lot. And I was raised on Conan Doyle. Most fiction leaves me cold, but I love a good mystery. Gets the blood racing."

"Absolutely amazing."

"Detection? Hardly. All it takes is having no qualms about asking indelicate questions."

"No powers of deduction? No keen eye?"

"Overrated. I certainly can't tell from a spot of clay on a man's boots that he's recently been in Lyme Regis or that his dog has beriberi or any of that Holmesian nonsense. But it doesn't take much to deduce that someone killed the viscount and that it was probably somebody at the party, who either threw a knife or stabbed him in the back and dropped the knife."

Dalton nodded. "And now we know it could have been Lady Rilma."

"Yes, she now tops the list. And it makes much more sense

than the knife-throwing business. If the knife was thrown and it stuck deeply in the viscount's back, who pulled it out?"

Dalton tried reaching to the middle of his back. "I suppose he could have, though I can't imagine anything harder or more painful than pulling a knife out of one's own back. And . . . now, what I know about these matters you can't stuff a flea's backside with, and I've read Sayers and everybody else—but don't people *die* when they get stabbed in the back? I mean, immediately? I was always under the impression it was a pretty quick thing. All of which is leading up to saying that it just might be that he was stabbed in the castle."

"About murder, I only know what I see in films and read in novels," Thaxton said. "But one thing I do know. Somebody stabbed the viscount as he sat eating, and then either deliberately or accidentally dropped the knife."

"All right, but why drop the knife right there? Why not throw it in the bushes or in the pond? Why no attempt to dispose of something that could be traced?"

"Maybe it can't be traced."

"Fingerprints?"

Thaxton stared out the window. "Something tells me that there won't be any fingerprints on that thing."

"Why not, if Lady Rilma stabbed him, as you seem to be suggesting?"

"No reason at the moment. Just have a feeling it'll be clean as a choir loft."

"So you don't suspect Lady Rilma."

"She could have wiped the knife before dropping it."

"After stabbing him in a sudden rage? Maybe, but it doesn't sound convincing. Damn it." Dalton stood. "Nothing about this business makes sense, and the biggest thing that doesn't make sense is that nobody *saw* anything. A brutal stabbing, right out in the open, in broad daylight, and no one saw a damn thing."

Thaxton was silent.

Dalton heaved an uneasy breath. "I'm hungry. They said dinner would be in an hour or so. No lunch. I should have grabbed something at the picnic. But—"

"Magic," Thaxton said.

"Huh?"

Thaxton turned. "Magic's involved somehow. I don't know how."

"Well, that's interesting, because I was talking with Tyrene while you were off somewhere, about how this aspect doesn't have much magic in it. Or difficult magic, if any."

"Nevertheless, I still think magic's the key."

"Anything behind that bit of brilliant deduction? And please don't say it's elementary."

"I wasn't going to. Well, old boy, let's take a walk, shall we? Look around the place."

"Fine."

"We'll deal with alimentary matters later."

"Shameful."

Peele Castle was interesting in a quaint way. The furnishings were in various styles, ranging from the very old to the merely antiquated. The place was a museum. Unicorn tapestries draped the walls, suits of armor stood in corners. It was in many ways much more homey than Perilous. Proportions were on a human scale. Rooms were not overpoweringly large, and there were enough comfy chairs, ottomans, carpets, settees, lamps, and trivet tables to make anyone feel at home.

The lords and ladies were being served drinks in the drawing room. At the sight of so many disgruntled and resentful aristocrats, Thaxton and Dalton demurred and sought refuge in the library.

Dalton browsed the shelves while Thaxton sipped sherry.

"If only I could question them on my own," Thaxton mused. He clucked and shook his head. "Not bloody likely."

"Interesting books," Dalton said. "They look more readable than Osmirik's stuff, though there're a lot of foreign—wait a minute, here's some English. Good God."

Thaxton broke out of his reverie. "What?"

"Here's a book that's got to be mighty strange."

"Eh? What's that?"

"*The Moswell Plan*, by Dorcas Bagby."

"Aside from the unlikelihood of running into the name *Dorcas* twice in one day, what's strange about it?"

"It shouldn't exist. I was a literary agent, but I'm a bibliophile, too. I actually like books, especially obscure and interesting ones. This novel's somewhat of a legend in the obscurity department. Matter of fact, I once tried hunting it down, and my assessment of the whole matter was that it was a hoax concocted by a young fantasy aficionado out in the Midwest. But here it be. I guess I'll be up tonight reading this."

Thaxton got up and looked over the selection. Most of the books looked old, and some were falling apart. He inclined his head and read the lettering on the spines.

"Ever seen magic spelled M-A-G-I-E-K?"

Dalton looked. "Mageek?"

Thaxton pulled the volume out. It was old but in good shape, its sturdy boards covered in fine leather. He opened it to the title page. In spidery print it read:

YE BUK OV MAGIEKAL DIVERSHYNS
beeng divers discorses on Ye
emploiment ov wichrrye forr Ye
delectashyn & eddifycashyn
ov gentil fohkk
Ye athor beeng wone
Baldor o' Ye Cayrn

"Weird spelling but it's English all right," Dalton said. "I like 'wichrrye' especially. Those capital Y's have a *th* sound. So it's just the word *the*. I make the author out to be Baldor of the Cairn, or something like that. A cairn is a pile of Celtic rocks."

Thaxton thumbed through it. He found something of interest.

"Not what you call page-turning action, but you can make it out," Dalton said, looking over Thaxton's shoulder. "What's it on? Parlor tricks?"

"Interesting," Thaxton said. "Interesting. I think I'll be up reading, too."

A servant appeared at the door.

"Gentlemen, dinner is served."

DUTCHTOWN

"*SLOWLY, SLOWLY RUN, O HORSES OF THE NIGHT.*"

Tony Montanaro glanced at the passing carriage and chuckled. They were almost out of the park and into the uptown district on the west side of the city.

"Boss, I don't get it. What do they got up in Dutchtown that you need?"

"The seltzer trick is only going to work once. The old stuff gets stale eventually. I need something different, something new."

"And you're going to get it off some *melanzana*?"

"Maybe. We'll see."

They rolled out of the park and into uptown. The streets were still busy, a steady stream of patrons flowing in and out of the speakeasies. Expensive cars cruised the streets, pulling over now and then to engage tightly dressed women in conversation.

The majority of faces on the street were dark, but there was a substantial white representation. Some of the best clubs were in this part of town, and some of the very best music.

"You know where the Djinn Mill is, Tony?"

"Yeah, I been there once or twice."

Tony wheeled left and slowed to let a group of laughing bar-hoppers cross. "The place is always jumpin'," he said.

Tony made a right, then a left. He drove straight for six blocks, then went left again.

"I like Dutchtown," Velma said. "I need a drink. Are we going to stop awhile?"

"Yeah," Carney said. "Right here."

The Djinn Mill's front was not imposing. There was no sign, just a green-painted door with a light over it. Tony pulled up to the curb.

Carney opened the door. "C'mon, Velma. I'll buy you a drink."

"Sure." She smiled prettily at him.

"Tony, no disappearing act."

"Don't worry, boss, I'll be close by. Take your time."

The peephole opened in the green door and a black face appeared.

"Carney, John Carney. Is Biff Millington here tonight?"

"Evenin', Mr. Carney. Yessuh, I do believe he's here."

The door opened. Jazz came through, hot jazz, but served with a dollop of cool urban sophistication, a baked-Alaska of sound. They entered. A broad-shouldered, nattily dressed bouncer looked them up and down, smiled, and took a long drag on a rolled cigarette. Carney recognized him, and winked. The man nodded.

The maitre d' said into Carney's ear, "He's in the back."

Smoke was a swirling fog in the main room. Fake palm leaves hung from the pillars, "jungle" vegetation abounded everywhere. The dance floor was large but crowded. The stage held a ten-piece band and King Elmont at the piano, doing a fast, syncopated rendition of "Shake That Thing." The dance was a fast two-step. There were a lot of pale customers; the club catered to a largely white clientele, but there were some brown faces: celebs mostly, entertainers, along with prosperous Dutchtowners, the odd hood, and a politician or two.

They crossed the sea of tables. Friends and acquaintances shouted greetings along the way, their invitations to sit and drink reluctantly turned down.

He did stop to ask of one city councilman, "Where's Mayor Speranza?"

The councilman shrugged. "You haven't heard the latest. Three councilmen are missing. We're all worried."

"Tweel, do you think?"

"That's what's on the grapevine. There were dengs all over City Hall today, hanging around, looking like they owned the place."

"Maybe they think they do, now."

"We gotta do something to clean up this town," the man said, lifting his bathtub-gin martini. He took a drink. He smiled. "Present company excepted, John. If some ganglord has to run things, I'd rather it be you."

"Thanks for that vote of confidence, Stanley."

Delivering a reassuring pat on the shoulder, he moved on.

They crossed in front of the stage to get to the other side of the room. King Elmont took his left hand from the keyboard briefly, to wave. Then the hand dropped to sound an augmented ninth chord.

"Is there anyone in Necropolis you don't know?" Velma said.

"Long ago I learned how to win friends and influence people. Read a book on it."

"It must have been a good book."

The back room was busy, the craps table surrounded three-deep, the roulette even deeper. Blackjack dealers slapped cards down in front of the apprehensive players. Private poker games were over in one corner.

Stately, plump Biff Millington was seated at a green-felt table holding a pat hand, Caribbean cigar clamped securely between his teeth, one eye shut against smoke drifting back. His skin was a little darker than *café au lait*. His suit was custom-tailored and his nails were manicured, the white carnation on his lapel so fresh it could have been cut moments before and rushed from the hothouse with sirens wailing. Slowly, one end of his lip curled up, then down. His was not the best of poker faces. But he made up in luck what he lacked in skill.

One dark eye found Carney.

"Be with you in a minute," he said around the cigar.

"I call," said the player beside him.

"Straight, ten high," Millington said, showing him.

"Damn!"

"I should have stayed in," said another player. "I was working on a flush. But despair's my greatest sin."

"*Ego te absolvo*," Millington said. "*Nil desperandum.*"

"No capeesh. I flunked that subject, along with others."

Millington rose and picked up his cash. "Gentlemen, deal me out."

Carney and Velma had taken seats at the bar. The bartender was setting a gin-and-tonic in front of Velma when Millington arrived.

"John, nice of you to drop by."

They shook hands. "Biff, meet Velma."

Velma flashed her small even teeth.

"Hello, Velma. That's on the house."

"He's paying."

Millington blew more smoke into the smoky air. "Have a drink, John. On me. Then get the hell out."

Carney grinned. "Still sore about that brewery in Melville."

"I liked that little operation, and I didn't like having it salamandered."

"Your insurance paid off. Business, Biff, just business. Nothing personal. The profit margin didn't allow our dropping prices to match the competition. It was either fold up our tents or carry out a preemptive strike."

"Oh, I understand." Millington grinned back. "I simply didn't like it."

"I'll get, but first you might think about doing the unthinkable and helping me."

Millington laughed. "Oh, you lead a *rich* fantasy life, my friend."

"Don't rule it out just yet. Tweel's dengs are muscling in on everyone in town. Somebody has to put a stop to it."

"You, I suppose. Alone?"

"It's best. The other way would just kill off eighty percent of my boys. I'd win that way, too, but it'd be messy."

"You're mighty confident."

"I can't be anything else. Half the battle is the approach, the frame of mind."

Millington nodded. "True. Psychological considerations are paramount, especially in some sort of showdown. But I think you're overstretching yourself. You're a hell of a sorcerer, but maybe not enough to go up against Hell itself."

Carney munched some peanuts. "Funny the way you put that."

"Am I hinting that Tweel's dengs might be running him instead of vice versa? Yes, I'm hinting. They seem to have an agenda all their own." Millington puffed thoughtfully on the long green cigar. "In which case, it's inevitable that they'll be calling the shots in this town. Because if Tweel can't control them, neither can you."

"Maybe so," Carney said. "But I think I'll take a shot anyway. I have some experience."

Millington was dubious. "Where? When?"

"Another time, another place."

"Uh-huh. Well, there is this longstanding rumor about you, a bit of latter-day folklore, which says you're from another world. Just what other world is vague. Are you telling me it's true?"

"I'm not telling you it isn't. But forget that. You really think it's inevitable that they'll take over?"

Millington frowned. "I don't know. I hope not. But . . . not everyone can be big wheels. Some of us must be cogs. I know my limitations. I figure I'm a little wheel at best. But tell you what, I will think about your proposition."

"The dengs might shift gears and leave you spinning. If they run Necropolis, they won't need humans at the middle-management level. Or even lackeys. They have all the personnel they need. They are legion."

Millington regarded the ceiling, contemplating its painted stars and crescent moons.

"You have a point, much as I hate to admit it." He let out a sigh. "What do you want, John?"

"What spells are you using?"

Millington chuckled. "What fo' you wanna mess wit' colored, boss?"

"A fresh approach. An unusual angle. Unexpected."

"Yeah." Millington chuckled again. "Unexpected. Well, I'm not going to let you tap into my connection, that's for sure. You learn my charms and it's not just breweries on Great Isle that I'll be losing. But there are other consultants open for business around here. I can give you a name and an address."

"I'd appreciate it."

Millington took out a pen. Carney gave him a business card to write on. Millington thought first, then wrote.

"I think that's the number. Anyway it's on One Hundred Thirty-fourth Street next to a greasy spoon called Darby's Cafe."

"Much obliged," Carney said, taking the card.

"You're quite welcome, sir. I have a game to get back to. Be well, and if I don't see you in here again, it will be too damned soon."

The big man wheeled around and walked off a few steps before stopping and turning his head to say, "Oh, and good luck." He blended back into the crowd.

"Thanks."

"Nice music in there," Velma said.

"Yes. Want to dance?"

"Love to. You have the time?"

"One spin around the dance floor on our way out. Finish your drink."

She downed most of it and gave him a serious look. "You can't win against dengs. Who do you think you are? God?"

"There are those who cast out dengs in His name."

"Stow the sermons, parson."

"Not until I pass the plate. Drink up and let's get the hell out of here."

GRAVING DOCK

"How's it coming, Luster?"

Gene was on his knees, peering under the bell-shaped craft.

"It's comin'," Luster answered. On his back underneath the *Voyager*, spanner in hand, he was wrestling with a stubborn lug-nut. Dolbert was helping, manning a crescent wrench.

Gene got up. He had changed from the garb of Cyrano to something befitting a NASA astronaut: a sky-blue jumpsuit with velcro-sealed pockets.

Jeremy said, "At least the communications repairs are done. We'll be able to keep in touch by modem."

"Can't you rig voice communications some way?"

"Sorry, but there's only one channel."

"What about using magic?"

Jeremy scowled. "Hey, sending data via modem without a phone line or a radio relay *is* magic. And getting the signal from one universe to another is big-time magic. Whaddya want, miracles?"

"Sorry."

"Don't worry, we'll be in constant communication. That's an improvement over the way we've done things in the past."

Linda was eating a sandwich at a table laden with luncheon food. She had switched outfits too, dressed now in a futuristic silver-lamé two-piece utility suit with matching boots. The costume evoked 1930's-40's movie serials.

Snowclaw was sitting beside her, dipping citronella candles in ranch dressing. He had decided to try something new.

"Aren't you guys hungry?" Linda called. "Come and get it before it turns into pumpkins."

Gene came over with Jeremy. "I guess I should eat," Gene said, sitting down. "No telling when we'll get the chance next."

Linda said, "Jeremy, what about the locater spell?"

"Osmirik sent one down, and I fed it into the *Voyager*'s computer. Whether or not it's gonna work, I don't know. But it's like radar. You punch up the display on the screen, and when you see an echo, you know you're getting close to the target."

"The target being Melanie."

"Right. But of course, the problem is, what's the spell supposed to look for exactly? How is it supposed to identify the target?"

"Her old clothes aren't enough?"

"I don't know what I'm supposed to do with 'em. If this were just plain magic, I guess you'd just throw an old sock into the brew, or something—like for a love potion or something corny like that. But we're using a little bit of magic and a lot of technology. That makes it tricky."

"We need a bloodhound," Gene said. "You'd just let it get a whiff of the stuff and off it'd go, sniffing away."

They all sat thinking. Then their gazes intersected.

"Why not get a bloodhound?" said Gene.

"Yeah," Jeremy said. "Could you whip one up, Linda?"

"A dog? Well, I can conjure almost anything. I've cloned Gene and Snowclaw, but that was working with a known model. I don't even know what a bloodhound looks like."

"That's never stopped you before," Gene said. "You can conjure stuff you've never laid eyes on."

"Okay, but wait a minute. Say I do produce a bloodhound.

How's that going to help? We don't know what universe she's in."

"It'd have to be a bloodhound with very unusual talents," Gene said. "He'd have to be able to sniff out whole universes."

Linda shook her head. "That's a tall order. I don't know how I'd program an ability like that into anything I conjure. The best I could do would be a standard bloodhound—whatever that is."

Gene ruminated. "I seem to remember something about the castle having a hunt aspect."

"A hunt aspect?"

"Yeah. Riding to hounds. Fox-hunting, for the gentry. If so, there has to be a kennel. Royal hounds. Now, they'd be your basic hunting hounds—there are number of breeds—but they could certainly follow a human scent."

"But they'd still be just ordinary dogs," Linda said.

"Yeah, I guess." Gene took a bite of the sandwich he'd made. "But there's a kernel of an idea here somewhere. We need a natural-born tracker. A hunter."

Jeremy said, "How about Snowy?"

"Yeah, I can do that," Snowy said. "But I don't even really know what the heck a universe is."

"Yeah, that's no good," Gene said.

"Besides, I have a cold."

Gene said, "You get colds?"

"Sure. My nose gets all stuffed up and I can't smell a thing."

"No kidding." Gene set down his prosciutto-and-green-pepper sandwich. "What we really need is a psychic critter."

"Why not just a psychic?"

"A human one? What, are we going to look for Elvis? You want the scoop on the next stage of Jackie O's love life?"

"It was only a suggestion."

"There are castle people who have psychic powers," Linda said. "What do you call what I do?"

"Real magic."

"What's the difference?"

"There's a lot of difference. Besides, you said you can't conjure a human being."

"But there might be someone in the castle who could help."

"We need real tracking talent, not some self-styled 'psychic' who makes a hundred wild guesses, of which one might luckily pan out."

"Incarnadine could locate Melanie," Linda said.

"Probably, but he's not around. Want to wait for him to come back?"

"No, Melanie's in trouble. I can feel it."

"Talk about psychic vibes."

"No, I can't find her. My talent's not that way."

"Well, is there something you can remember about that wild aspect? What it looked like, anything to identify it?"

"It was just a dense forest, big trees. Looked like ordinary trees. It could have been Earth for all I know." Linda paused and thought. "There is one thing. The way Melanie moved when I saw her. She seemed to be in an old silent movie. Jerky, fast."

"Ah, a time-flow differential," Gene said.

"Time-flow?" Jeremy said.

"Yeah. Might be that the rate that time flows in that universe is faster than the one here. That's not so good. More time for her to get in trouble."

"Great," Linda said, sounding discouraged.

"But the differential doesn't appear to be too big," Gene said, wishing he hadn't brought it up. "Shouldn't be a problem."

"Anyway," Jeremy said, "the *Voyager*'s a time machine."

"I guess it is," Gene said. "It travels through all the dimensions, of which time is one. We might be able to adjust for any temporal displacement." Gene himself wasn't sure exactly what he meant or what such a remedy would entail.

Linda stared at the table. "Boy, this is going to be fun."

"Linda, I think our best approach," Gene said, "is for you to conjure a psychic dog."

"You don't believe in human psychics, but—"

"Hell, dogs *are* psychic. Everybody knows that. Besides, dogs I trust. Human con-artists, no."

Linda shrugged. "Okay. This is getting even crazier than what usually goes on in this place, but what the heck. Let's give it a shot."

Linda stood and walked out from the table a few feet and stopped. "Psychic dog. Right." She folded her arms and closed her eyes.

She stood motionless, her feet wide apart. The two men and Snowclaw watched. This went on for a longish minute. Nothing happened.

Linda relaxed and opened her eyes. "This is going to be harder than I thought." She shifted her feet, then resumed her stance. Folding her arms again, she shut her eyes.

"Dang it, anyway!" Luster griped from across the room, frustrated by some recalcitrant grommet.

Linda rocked slightly back and forth. Gene, Jeremy, and Snowclaw didn't move. Nothing happened for about thirty seconds.

Then, with no fanfare, a huge dog materialized on the floor in front of Linda. It was lying down. Startled, it lifted its head, looked around, and sprang to its feet.

The animal looked to have a lot of sheepdog in its ancestry, but something had gone wrong. Its fur was a dirty white, splotched with great patches of black and rust-red in a crazy-quilt pattern. Its head was enormous and the ears were long and floppy. The right eye was brown and the other looked different; it was a little larger, and had green in it. A black ring circled the smaller eye. All in all, it was a clumsy, confused mélange of a dog, oversized and shaggy. It was male.

Its ears went down, and it hunkered and growled. Then it barked.

"Easy, boy," Linda said.

"That's a psychic dog? That's the goofiest-looking mutt I've ever laid eyes on," Gene complained.

"Aw, it's cute. Sort of."

The dog's ears went up and its shaggy tail started wagging.

"See? It's friendly!" Linda knelt and petted it. "Good boy."

Gene shook his head. "That thing doesn't look like it could find its water dish."

"Don't listen to him, boy. You know what you got. You're super-psychic, right?"

"*R-r-rowf!*"

"Right!" Linda laughed, rubbing its head. "See, Gene? It's smart."

Gene came over and patted its back. "A complete selection of fine carpet remnants. Well, it looks healthy. How's that sniffer of yours, boy? Huh? How's the old hooter?"

"*Whorf!*"

"Hmm. It's either a nautical dog or a 'Star Trek' fan. How's the world been treating you, boy?"

"*R-r-ruff!*"

They both laughed. "I guess it is pretty bright at that," Gene conceded. "But possessed of powers far beyond those of mortal canines? Hardly."

"Let's give him a chance," Linda said.

"*Whoof!*"

"What do you think, Jeremy?" Linda asked.

"That's the dumbest-looking dog I've ever seen. But you never know. I'll go get Melanie's stuff."

"Snowy?"

Snowclaw got up and came over. The dog sniffed curiously at his legs, but kept wagging his tail.

Gene said, "He thinks you're human, Snowy."

"He *is* dumb."

"He's giving you the benefit of the doubt."

"What should we name him?" Linda said.

"After his species," Gene said.

"What's his species?"

"*Canis goofus.*"

"Goofus!" Linda said, laughing. "It fits."

"*Whoorf!*" Goofus's long pink tongue lolled out as he panted happily.

Jeremy returned bearing Melanie's old clothes and shoes. He threw them down in front of Goofus. The dog sniffed the pile with interest. He barked, sniffed some more.

"Looks like it's on to something," Linda said. "Find her, boy. Find her!"

Goofus looked at Linda and barked again. He snorted and snuffled with more animation, tail wagging furiously, following a trail away from the pile. He walked a few paces toward the *Voyager*, stopped, looked at the craft, and barked.

Gene scratched his chin. "That's weird. Now, how could he know that?"

"Psychic dog," Linda said. "Following a psychic scent."

"Yeah. I take it all back, fella. You are obviously one special puppy."

"*Whar-r-r-rooff!*"

"Well, who's going on this expedition?" Gene asked. "We can't all fit in that compartment."

"I'm going," Linda said.

"You, me, Goofus, and Snowy?"

"I guess."

Gene said, "Jeremy, you really should go. You have more experience piloting the thing."

"I did it only twice. Anyway, the craft will be under the mainframe's control at all times. It'll be much better than flying by the seat of your pants. At least I think it will work."

"Good, because that crash course in piloting qualifies me to turn the thing on and off, and not much else."

Luster pushed out from under the craft and stood.

"Wull, she's in."

"Is it working?"

"Don't know. Ain't turned her on yet."

Dolbert crawled out. He snickered as he wiped his hands on a grease-stained rag.

"What do you think, Dolbert?" Gene asked.

Dolbert laughed, then nattered unintelligibly.

Luster said, "He says he shore wouldn't like to be the one to take 'er out."

"Oh, now, that's encouraging. Ask him what he thinks our chances really are."

"He kin hear you, Gene."

"Sorry. Well, Dolbert?"

Dolbert shrugged and chortled at some length.

Luster took his cap off and dabbed his brow with a checkered handkerchief that had seen better days—circa 1923. "Dolbert says you got four chances. Slim, a Chinaman's, a snowball's in the devil's own wood stove, and Katie-bar-the-door."

Gene turned to Linda. "You still want to go through with this?"

Linda nodded emphatically. "Yes, sir."

"Uh-huh." Gene arched his eyebrows. "Yeah."

"Okay," Jeremy said. "I'm going to test all the systems, and then we'll be ready to try a trial run out into the interuniversal medium." Jeremy scratched his head. "But first we have to figure how we're going to use Goofus here. I'll have to think about that. Anyway, let me go do the tests."

Jeremy left.

"What supplies do we need for the trip?" Linda asked.

"Food, water, a first-aid kit, maybe. We can't take much. It's a tight squeeze in there. In fact, I don't see how we'll fit with Snowy and Goofus together."

"I'd hate to stay behind," Snowclaw said.

"I'd hate it, too," Gene said. "We could use you. Damn it, we're all just going to have to exhale and sardine ourselves in."

"Food, water, medicine," Linda said. "Anything else?"

"Weapons."

"You think?"

"You never know what you're going to run into when you go traipsing around in strange universes. 'Peace through superior firepower' is a good creed to follow."

"Okay," Linda said. She blinked. "On the table."

What was on the table was an assortment of small arms: revolvers, automatic pistols, carbines, lightweight machine guns. There were also exotic specimens. Gene handled a strange-looking pistol with a flaring bell-end.

"Laser?" he asked Linda. "Phaser?"

"I dunno. Try it out."

Gene looked at the thing. "Hey, there're settings here. STUN, DISRUPT, BURN, and VAPORIZE. You gotta be kidding."

"On second thought, don't try it. It sounds dangerous."

"Have to test it. It's on DISRUPT so I'll leave it there."

Gene took a jar of pickles and cleared a space around it on the table. He stepped back ten paces and aimed. Linda and Snowclaw moved back a safe distance.

Nothing happened. Gene examined the weapon.

"Oh, it's on safety." He flicked a small tab and aimed again.

The pickle jar exploded into green mist. There was no debris to rain down; the smell of brine was the only thing left.

"Hell, that ought to stop a rampaging bull elephant. One that's driving a tank even."

"I can't imagine what 'vaporize' does," Linda said.

"Let's hope we don't have to find out. Now all I need's a holster and I'm in business. Go ahead, alien creepoid, make my millennium." Gene made sinister faces.

Linda shook her head wearily. "Gene, stuff a sock in it."

"Sorry."

PEELE CASTLE

THE DINING HALL WAS UNCOMFORTABLY QUIET. A mood of apprehension hovered, the clink of silverware louder than the tones of hushed conversation. No one joked, no one laughed. A half-hogshead of wine was consumed.

The food was plentiful, mostly fish and fowl. The selection of wildfowl was especially cosmopolitan, including bittern, shoveler, pewit, godwit, quail, dotterl, heronsew, crane, snipe, plover, redshank, pheasant, grouse, and curlew. The catch of the day was turbot, baked with capers and lemon, but flounder, cod, pike, snapper, haddock, shad, and swordfish were available—broiled or baked with various garnishes—along with sturgeon, lobster, crayfish, oysters, herring, and shrimp. The only meat was wild boar with mint jelly. The soup choice was chicken consommé or julienne with asparagus tips. For dessert: fruit in abundance and variety, nuts, several kinds of fruit tart, cheeses, and an assortment of cakes, from hazelnut torte to raspberry-rum shortcake. Cognac and liqueur were served with chicory-laced coffee and herb tea.

The cooks tendered their apologies for the limited bill of fare, pleading short notice and Peele's primitive kitchen.

The lady Sheila Jankowski had arrived at Peele with her husband, the prince. Trent, Sheila, Dalton, and Thaxton dined together at a side table.

Sheila was red-haired and beautiful with a creamy complexion and bright green eyes. Her mouth was a trifle large but sensuous. She seemed in good spirits, but there was something anxious in her eyes. She was worried for her husband. She was also outspoken; at least she tended to be so in the company of Dalton and Thaxton, whom she considered friends.

"It may sound terrible," she said, "but if there was ever an s.o.b. who deserved it more, I don't know who it could have been, short of Hitler."

"Or Stalin," Trent added. "Everybody leaves out Stalin."

"I guess that sounds awful, huh?"

Sheila was looking at Thaxton. "We've been getting a progressively darker picture of Oren," he said.

"You don't know the half of it. Trent told me you know about the run-in we had with him."

"We know he assaulted you," Dalton said.

"Well, he nearly raped me. Two seconds more and it would have been rape, but Trent walked in. The creep cornered me in the conservatory and it was like dealing with an octopus. I mean, first he was charming and everything, but then he got grabby, and then . . . well, it was just amazing. I couldn't believe he was doing it with all those people around. The guy was nuts. I knew he made a play for just about every woman he met, but I didn't think he was a maniac. I guess he thought Trent had married this hooker or something, because he just seemed to assume that I put out for anybody who asked. He was actually surprised when I resisted. What a *creep*."

Trent was staring into his soup.

"I'm sorry, darling," she said with a hand on his arm. "Does it upset you when I talk about it?"

"No, not at all, dear. It's just that you wouldn't make a very good defense lawyer." He smiled. "Forget it. Eat your fish."

"I'm not hungry." Sheila let go of her fork. "I suppose I should shut my big mouth. I'm just setting you up with a good motive."

"Tyrene already has me at the head of his suspect list."

"Well, he's crazy. You're no murderer. What about it, guys? You don't think Trent did it, do you?"

"Never crossed our mind," Dalton said.

Trent chuckled. "I'll bet. Okay, I'll come out and say it. I wanted to kill Oren, and I would have if Sheila hadn't put her foot down."

"I told him I wouldn't stand for the dueling bit," Sheila said. "I sure wasn't going to sit at home sweating, wondering whether my husband was going to come home in a pine box. No way."

"She persuaded me to call it off," Trent said. "Chicken out. And I was about to send word to Oren that I wouldn't be showing up for our little affair of honor, when we got a note from his second saying that Oren wanted a postponement, pleading illness. Well, there the matter rested. He never broached the subject again, and neither did I. For all I know *he* chickened out, but he was a pretty able duelist, so the excuse might have been genuine. However, he was aware that I was the better swordsman. In my opinion, I would have killed him."

"If anyone wanted to kill him, it would be Lord Belgard," Sheila said. "Oren and Lady Rowena had been having an affair for years. I'm sorry, my big mouth again."

"Tyrene has known it for years, along with everybody else," Trent said. "But Belgard wasn't anywhere near Oren when the murder happened. If it happened when I walked past."

"We've heard that Oren made no secret of his liaison with Lady Rowena," Thaxton said.

"You're referring to his habit of playing grab-ass under Belgard's nose?" Trent said. "Rowena and Oren did that all the time. She despises her husband and enjoys the hell out of showing him up a cuckold. Belgard never spoke up because he knew that in order to stop it he'd have to challenge Oren, and he knew damn well that Oren would kill him. Belgard can't fence his way out of a paper sack. And he's a worse shot, so there's no help there either."

"I suppose that makes Belgard a poor candidate for knife-throwing," Thaxton commented.

"I don't know about his knife-wielding abilities," Trent

said. "Seems unlikely that he could have done it, but you never know."

"Seems unlikely that anyone could have done it, or would have done it in all that company," Dalton put in, "except that you heard the thing whiz past. That must have been the knife, and that means someone threw it."

Thaxton said, "Trent, the way you described it, I got the impression it made quite a racket."

"It was loud. And it didn't sound like a thrown knife. It didn't swish so much as it *shooshed*. By that I mean that it didn't sound as though it was rotating as it flew. This is just hindsight, mind you. I didn't give it any thought at the time. I just assumed it was a large bird or a bat or something. Or an insect, as I said."

"Must have been traveling at a terrific clip," Thaxton said.

"That's occurred to me," Trent said. "But who could have thrown it with such force?"

"I suppose there's no such thing as a knife catapult," Thaxton said. "Something on the order of a crossbow, only propelling a knife or dagger?"

"Never heard of such an animal," Trent said. "But there are any number of universes with stranger things in them."

"But the culprit would have had to conceal the thing on his person," Dalton said. "Or get rid of it quick. Stash it somewhere."

"Tyrene's lads would have found it," Thaxton said.

"They missed the murder weapon," Dalton said.

"We all missed the murder weapon." Thaxton took a sip of wine. "Still thinking about that."

"It is a puzzling aspect of this case," Trent said, "among others."

"There are a lot of problems," Dalton said. "Like, for instance, if the knife was thrown, who pulled it out and dropped it?"

"Maybe he was stabbed somewhere else," Sheila said. "I'm just going on what Trent told me on the way here. Couldn't someone have stabbed him in the castle and gone back into the garden and dropped the knife?"

"No one saw anybody leave the garden and come back in," Dalton said.

"Maybe someone in the castle?"

"But no one strange was seen to come into the garden. If the murder happened in the castle, you have to explain how the murder weapon wound up in the garden."

"What about a servant?" Sheila asked.

"Tyrene's questioned most of the servants," Thaxton told her. "At the time Oren left the garden, all the servants who were serving at the party were in the garden. They were all busy as the devil. No one was seen leaving and returning."

Trent said, "Suppose that sound I heard was a bird. Suppose there was no thrown knife. Let's say Oren gets a sudden urge to leave the party and gets up and walks off. Someone near the portal stabs him just as he walks through. Oren continues into the castle and dies a short way down the corridor. The culprit accidentally drops the knife near where the viscount was sitting. Just coincidence. How's that for a scenario?"

"Fine," Thaxton said, "except that no one saw anyone near the portal."

"No one happened to be looking. It was luck," Trent said. "Good for the murderer, bad for us."

"Possible," Thaxton said. "Possible. But the coincidence of the knife dropping at that spot strains credulity a bit."

"Lady Rilma's testimony about hearing her husband grunt makes me think that something happened at that moment," Dalton said. "In fact, I'm almost convinced of it."

Sheila snorted. "She's another one."

"How so, Sheila?" Thaxton asked.

"Another suspect. Trent, didn't you tell me that she once stabbed Oren?"

Trent nodded. "It was a good while ago. Rilma's unstable, always has been. She's been in and out of institutions. And, yes, she did actually stab Oren once. In the arm, with a pair of scissors. Superficial wound. But she did it, all right. She was hospitalized for a time after that. She hasn't done anything like that since, though."

"Nevertheless that's very interesting," Dalton said. "So she could have heard him grunt in pain all right, but maybe she's just repressing the fact that she was the cause of it. Maybe it was a case of temporary insanity. That would explain the dropped knife and her not caring or maybe even not knowing about it."

"Possible," Thaxton said. "You're thinking, old boy."

"So," Trent said, sitting back in his chair. "I'm walking by, and this bird buzzes me. I don't see it, and I don't see Lady Rilma draw a stiletto and stab her husband, and nobody else sees anything either. Oren doesn't say a word to anyone, just gets up and leaves, dying with each step."

All four of them were silent for a moment. Trent sat up and resumed eating his soup, which had gone quite cold. He took one slurp, put the spoon down, and pushed the bowl away. He sat back again.

"No," Thaxton said, "it didn't happen that way. No."

"But how did it happen?" Sheila said.

"No one knows. That's what makes a good mystery. Which, in a book, makes for enjoyable reading. In reality, here and now, it's frightful."

"And frightening," Sheila said. "To think the murderer is in this room. He or she is here right now, eating with us. And here we sit calmly."

"My palms are sweaty," Dalton said.

"You get that, too?" Sheila asked. "I've always had a problem with sweaty palms. I get so nervous sometimes."

"Here comes Tyrene," Thaxton said.

The Captain of the Guard came directly to the foursome's table and greeted each in turn.

"May I join you?"

"By all means," Trent said, pulling out a chair.

Tyrene sat. "I've got Mirabilis' report. It was a knife wound all right. The blade chipped a rib, penetrated the left lung, and just missed severing the pulmonary artery, making a medium-sized slit in it. Of course there was immediate hemorrhaging. But the rate of blood loss was slow enough to give the victim some time. There were signs of healing around the slit."

"Healing?" Dalton said. "How can that be?"

"Magic," Tyrene said.

"Magic?"

"Yes, healing magic, presumably cast by Oren himself. Here is what seems to have happened: When Oren realized that he'd been stabbed, he did the sensible thing. Forthwith, he left the garden aspect, where his magic wouldn't work, and went back into the castle, where it would. Now, as far as I know, Oren was no magician's magician, but as a castle resident he knew some potent enchantments, as do we all. Healing and general health-preserving spells are common, and he doubtless knew a few. He must have magicked like mad as soon as he got into Perilous, summoning all his powers. And they were nearly sufficient. He almost succeeded. However, he knew magic alone couldn't save him. Immediate surgery was required. He must have known that his heart had sustained a mortal wound. So he took a gamble. He could have returned home and gone to a hospital there, but his aspect is a ten-minute walk from the garden aspect. Dr. Mirabilis' office is just as far, and in any event the doctor is not equipped for major trauma surgery. There was a hospital close by, though, through the aspect in the alcove where you found him. He gambled in that he did not know whether that periodic aspect was open or closed at the time. He lost."

"What aspect was it?" Thaxton wanted to know.

"It's called Klingsor," Tyrene said, "and though it's not technologically developed in most respects, it does boast excellent surgeons who do wonders with relatively primitive equipment. And the hospital near the aspect specializes in trauma surgery. Oren might have survived had he made it to that hospital. But his magic wasn't strong enough. The wound was too severe, and he lost too much blood too quickly. He lost consciousness, the healing process stopped, and he bled to death."

"That explains why he left the party in a big hurry," Trent said, "why he went back into the castle, and what he was doing in that alcove."

"Yes, it does. And it puts to rest any notion that he was attacked inside the castle."

"Any report on the murder weapon yet?" Thaxton asked.

"There were no fingerprints. The instrument was completely clean."

Thaxton nodded, smiling half in regret, half in satisfaction.

"It's a common artifact," Tyrene continued, "manufactured in the Helvian aspect, and its like must be sold in a thousand street markets in that world. Cheap steel, plain boxwood haft, brass hilt. The blade barely holds an edge, but it will do the job as long as no fancy cutting is involved. Perfect knife for stabbing."

"If not for throwing," Thaxton said.

"No, it's not intended as a throwing knife, but it is balanced quite well, the only thing well-made about it. It's not entirely a stiletto, yet not quite a poniard."

"So it could have been thrown?" Dalton asked.

"I suppose," Tyrene said. "Though as of now I don't think it was. Someone stabbed the viscount at close range. That, I think, is certain."

No one asked the obvious.

"But my investigation is far from over," Tyrene went on. "I must interview anyone who could have seen what happened. And that means almost everyone at the fête. By the way, the blood on the knife matches Oren's blood type. There's no doubt it was the murder weapon."

Tyrene rose. "I have a number of people to interview. If you will excuse me . . . Lady Sheila, Your Royal Highness." Tyrene bowed stiffly.

"See you later, Tyrene," Trent said.

"Gentlemen," Tyrene said, then left.

"He just about came out and said he thinks I did it," Trent observed.

"I think he suspects Lady Rilma more than you," Thaxton said.

"Maybe I'm just paranoiac." Trent turned to his wife. "Are you through, darling?"

"I can't touch a thing. I'm so upset by all this."

"You really should eat something. No late-night snacks here."

She took a bite of snapper, chewed perfunctorily. "It's gone cold, and I'm tired, for some reason. Can't we—?"

"Good evening, Your Highness—Lady Sheila."

Trent looked up. "Damik. Hello."

Thaxton and Dalton stood.

Trent remained seated. "May I present Messieurs Dalton and Thaxton? Gentlemen, His Excellency, Count Damik of Ultima Thule."

The count clicked his heels and bowed his head. "Gentlemen."

The two hapless golfers bowed.

"Please," the count said, "be seated. I do not mean to disturb your meal, but there is something I must tell you, Trent."

"Sit down, Damik."

"Thank you so much."

"Some wine?"

"None, thank you. I've dined."

"What's up?"

"It's about all this business, of course. Tyrene suspects me."

"Whatever reason would he have?"

"Because of the succession squabble in Thule. Despite my pleas, Oren chose to throw his support to the House of Dou and against my allies and relatives, the Zoltans. He has—had—heavy investments in provinces controlled by the Dou clan. He chose to follow the dictates of his pocketbook rather than honor a friendship. On that basis alone, I am suspect. The fact that I also have an admittedly fetishistic love for knives and bladed weapons of every sort seems to be enough to condemn me out of hand."

"Rest easy, my friend," Trent said. "Tyrene doesn't really believe you did it."

"He doesn't? I wish he would be so kind as to point this out to me!"

"The investigation's far from over. He's not even at the hypothesis stage yet in choosing his suspects. Sure, you're on the list. So am I. Hell, lots of people hated Oren's guts."

"I didn't! That's the irony of it. I didn't hold his political decisions against him. He was a friend, though I will be the first to admit that he had many faults. But he was . . . he knew how to have a good time. He was a jolly fellow, sometimes."

Trent gave a half-shrug. "I wouldn't know. We never socialized."

"Yes, well, of course I understand completely why he was in bad odor with you. However, there is another disturbing fact that I wish to relate to you. I need advice."

"Shoot."

The count looked one way, then another. Leaning forward, he said quietly, "I know who the knife belongs to."

"You do?" Thaxton said, his eyebrows arching.

"I saw this person purchase the weapon when last I was in Helvius. It was at an open-air market in the village of Fliebas. I shall not name this person. At least not yet."

"You don't know that the weapon you saw being bought was the murder weapon," Trent pointed out. "Those knives are pretty common. I had one like it once, long time ago."

"Yes, but this was recently. True, my observation does not categorically establish the person's guilt, but this fact should be brought to light. I feel obligated to report it to Tyrene, compelled, if not by friendship for Oren, then by a sense of duty."

"Then by all means tell Tyrene about it."

"But . . . of course there is the inevitable odium attached to the act of informing."

"I understand," Trent said. "But you shouldn't let that deter you."

"Yes, I suppose you are right. I must give some thought to this matter." The count rose, drawing Dalton and Thaxton to their feet.

"Thank you very much for the advice," the count said to Trent.

"I'm sure you'll make the right decision," the prince replied.

"I think I shall retire early this evening. Gentlemen, the pleasure was all mine. Good evening, Your Highness . . . my lady."

"Good night, Damik," Sheila said. "Take care."

The count bowed deeply and left.

"I'd hate to be in his shoes," Sheila remarked. "Especially if it was a friend I suspected."

"I wish he'd told us who it was," Thaxton said. "But I suppose he couldn't go around making accusations, no matter how well-founded."

"That knife is a very common make," Trent commented. "No doubt the murderer chose it for that very reason."

"No doubt," Thaxton said.

Trent suddenly got up. "I forgot to mention something to Damik. I'll be right back." He walked out of the dining hall.

Conversation shifted to lighter topics while Dalton demolished a roast sage hen. He claimed that the sea air had sharpened his appetite. Thaxton was in the middle of telling a story about grouse-shooting in Dorset when a scream came from the anteroom of the dining hall.

Everyone rushed outside.

There, in the middle of the foyer, stood Princess Dorcas. At her feet lay Damik, eyes closed. Trent was standing close by, along with Lord Belgard and Lady Rilma. All seemed stunned.

Thaxton and Dalton got to him first. He was lying face up, a red stain marring his white blouse.

"Dead?" Dalton asked.

Thaxton took his hand from the count's neck. "Quite. The knife went right through the heart."

Tyrene elbowed his way through the crowd. Thaxton stood up and stepped aside while the captain examined the corpse.

"Dalton, old boy?"

Dalton came to Thaxton's side.

"What is it?"

"I just kicked something."

"You just kicked something?"

"As I stepped back, I felt my shoe hit something, and I heard something clatter. I don't see a thing, do you?"

Dalton looked around. "Nothing for it to hide under. Are you sure?"

"Quite sure. What do you make of it?"

"Thaxton, old fellow, I don't have a clue."

Thaxton stared at the count's body.

"I think I do," he said.

DARBY'S CAFE

THE GREASY SPOON WAS CLOSED. A door at the side of the building gave onto stairs mounting to a landing, where three doors led to separate apartments. The stairs were dark, the bare light bulb over the landing burnt out.

"No numbers," Carney said. "Which one, Velma?"

"You got me."

The building was quiet except for the far-off sound of a radio playing. Soft dance music.

Carney picked the first door on his left and knocked.

Nothing happened for quite a while. Then came sounds of latches being thrown. The door opened a crack, the chain still hooked.

Dim light inside; a woman's voice: "Yes?"

"Does a Mr. Lemarr Hamilton live here?"

"Who're you?"

"I'd like to engage his services, if he's not too busy."

"He in bed."

"I realize it's late, but I'm in a great deal of trouble. Mr. Hamilton can help me. Can you please wake him?"

"He don't do that stuff no more anyway."

"I can pay well. As I said, the situation is very urgent. In fact, it's a matter of life and death."

The eye on the other side of the crack was unblinking. The door closed momentarily. Then it opened wide. Carney and Velma went in.

A tall woman in her forties closed the door. She was tall and slim in a green flower-print housedress and worn slippers. She gave her visitors a distrustful frown. "Go on through there, into the parlor," she said.

It was a railroad flat. They passed through the kitchen, then through another room where a blanketed form lay sleeping on a cot in the corner. There was a larger bed and several other pieces of furniture. Ragged holes marred the ceiling plaster, and water stains billowed across it. The place smelled of frying grease and mildew. Otherwise the apartment was well-kept.

They passed through a short corridor with a door. The back room had comfortable, if threadbare, furniture. Carney and Velma sat on the antimacassar-draped couch. They waited, looking at family pictures on the wall.

Presently an old man came into the room. He walked stooped, his gray head inclined, his eyes up and aware. He was thin, almost emaciated, dressed in baggy pants and undershirt, black wool socks with a hole in one toe.

He looked at his two visitors, unsmiling, then sat in the chair opposite.

"You want somethin' with me?" His voice was strong, clear, belying his appearance.

"Yes," Carney said. "I wish to engage your services as a consultant in supernatural matters."

The old man studied him with penetrating black eyes. "Yes, suh." He smiled. "Yes, suh. I believe I know who you are. Can't say as I know the name, though."

"John Carney. I run a couple of businesses in this town. Some people say I'm pretty influential."

"I believe they right." The old man leaned forward, elbows on his knees. "What can I do for you?"

"I need the power."

They sat in silence for a while. The radio, far off, had switched to lively Latin rhythms.

"Everybody need the power," the old man said. "You got to have the power to live."

"I need more. I'm fighting something pretty big. I think you might know what it is. They've been in this town for a long time, and they're growing."

"Yessuh. I know it."

"I want to fight them. I am fighting them, though not very effectively up till now. But give me an edge, the slightest edge."

"Edge?" The old man grunted. "It ain't nothin' you can edge up on."

"Perhaps the metaphor . . . I need what power you can summon. What you can generate and transmit. Whatever this power is, or whatever its nature, I might be able to work with it."

The old man straightened up slowly, then sat back. He let a long contemplative quiet intervene before answering: "I can't transmit nothin'. I can't generate nothin'. It don't come like that."

"Can you describe how it does come?"

The old man shook his gray head. "Ain't no describin' There's feelin'. You got to feel it."

"What is it?"

The old man studied him for a moment. "You not the man for it."

"No?"

"No, suh. You not the man."

"Is it the color of my skin?"

Silence again. The old man looked off to his left, out a window that offered a view of darkness obscuring nothing worth viewing.

At length he leaned forward and spoke calmly but with underlying controlled emotion. "Ain't a matter of color. Matter of . . . experience. You born with a color, but every man, he live different. Do things different, different things happen to a man. He get to be different. He look at things his own way. No one can tell him, 'cause he know. It get into his blood and then he can't go back, he is what he is. It get to be part of him like it was his color, like he was born with it. A man's life ain't like any other man's life. It's his own. Can't do nothin' but live it his own way. He got his *pain,* y'understand. Livin' is *pain.* Don't matter nohow if he happy or he sad. Livin' is pain. Each man got his own pain. You got to take that . . . work with it. Shape it up. Use it. Then you got somethin'. But each man got his own. Ain't no use tryin' one man give it to another. Can't be give out. You got to keep it. You got to work with it."

The old man settled back in the easy chair again. His voice was soft as he said, "I don't rightly know if you the man *for* it."

"I'm willing to learn," Carney said. "I can pay very well."

The Latin rhythms went on—tinny conga drums, maracas like rattling gravel. Suddenly, the music stopped. Quiet. A horn sounded outside.

Carney cocked his ear. He heard nothing.

Velma had been sitting quietly. "You mind if I smoke, Mr . . . ?"

"No, I don't mind, miss. You go right ahead."

Velma lit a cigarette, looked around for an ashtray. She found one on the end table.

"You ain't had enough pain," the old man said.

"Maybe not," Carney said. "I can't say I regret that, but there it is. There are other considerations, though."

"Yes, suh. They other things. Maybe you got 'em."

"I think I do. As you said, each man is unique. The singular circumstances of his existence mold the clay of his character, the stuff of his inner substance, and the curves and contours are all his own, like his signature or the cracks in the palms of his hands." Carney's grin was lopsided. "That's a fancy way of saying exactly what you said."

"Mighty fancy."

"There is a kind of pain that comes from seeing too much. Of living too much. Too long."

The old man nodded. "I know. I know that for a fact."

"There's the pain that comes at the end of chasing down the wild possibilities until there's nothing left to surprise you. Of ringing the changes over and over until there are no more permutations, all the treble bob majors rung. A melody played once too often. There's a sickly feeling that goes with that, maybe a tiny hint of regret. Anxiety, too. You're facing the big Nothingness. Because what does it all matter at the end, when the end comes? It doesn't really matter what went on up to that point. I don't think it matters one whit. When you're faced with that yawning abyss . . . no, that's too dramatic. Think of finding your last cigarette crumpled, a crack in it. Think of walking through a fun house and coming out into a junkyard. Think of . . . but I think you know what I mean. You see? Pain is universal. There is only one kind. Because, as you said, living is pain. It's a struggle, from day to day, minute to minute. The heart works, pumping unceasingly, night and day, a complex machine beyond our comprehension. It sweats and strains and throbs, and if it muffs a rhythm, if it lets up for a second, we feel the life draining away from us. We're that close to it, one heartthrob away from oblivion. We eat and work and play, skating on the thin ice of contingency. One moment we're gliding along as usual, the next, into the chill depths, from which there is no returning. Do you get what I'm saying? The rub of it is that power, fame, or fortune won't ease up the pain one iota. Not even love will, which is another kind of pain. We're all inevitably alone with ourselves and with the awful realization that all of it means . . . *nothing*. Nothing at all. No matter what construction you wish to put on it, atheist or monotheist, nihilist or romanticist—"

Carney took a breath. He settled back into the worn velvet of the sofa and fanned himself with his hat, smiling. "Warm in here, isn't it?"

"Yes, suh." The old man smiled back. "Yes, *suh*." He laughed, a low, dyspeptic cackle.

Then slowly, he rose and shuffled out of the room.

Velma crushed out her cigarette. She took out a small mirror from her purse and checked her lipstick, put the mirror back. She looked at Carney.

"What's he have that you want, anyway?"

"Maybe nothing. Maybe nothing at all."

"I need a drink." She began the motions to light another cigarette.

"Maybe our host will oblige."

He took the matches she was fumbling with and lit her

cigarette. The flame danced in her eyes. She stared at him as she puffed. He reached across her to put the match in the ashtray.

"You have a lot of character in your face," she said.

"I paid for every line of it."

"No, you do. You have a very interesting face. Did anyone ever tell you that?"

"Not in so many words."

"I can tell about a person just by their face. It's all there. You can tell a lot."

"What does my face tell you?"

"It's strange. Interesting. You've done a lot, seen a lot." She took a long drag, blew smoke into the greasy air. "Nobody really knows you. You keep it all inside."

He nodded. "Ever work the carnival circuit? You have a good line of patter."

"I mean it. You think I'm kidding. I know you. I can see inside of you."

"Maybe you can." He inclined his head toward the doorway. "How does the old man's face read?"

She looked off and shrugged. "Old. Tired."

Carney tossed his hat onto the table beside the sofa. "It is kind of warm in here. Either that or I'm having hot flashes."

The old man returned bearing a bottle and a cloth sack. He set the bottle down on the table. He raised the bag, fiddling with the drawstring until he had it open. He reached inside, felt around, and took out a darkly gnarled object and handed it to Carney.

Carney looked at it. It was some sort of root or twig, almost black, of a hardness not usual for wood or plant material.

"High John's root?"

"Uh-uh. No, suh. That be Black Benjamin. You can't hardly find that."

"Really."

"I spent a week in the woods, just sneakin' up on it. You gots to sneak up on Black Benjamin. You turn around, you think you know where it is, and it gone, man. *Gone*. After I dug it up and brung it home, it just sit there and stew. It was madder'n hell I dug it out. It don't wanta be out. It don't want no one t'see it."

"It's sentient, then. It thinks."

"Yessuh. It knows. Got a mind of its own, Black Ben."

The old man rooted in the bag again and brought out a lump of a grayish substance. Carney took it. It was iron-heavy, and looked the part.

"Just a guess. Meteorite?"

"Yessuh. That's what they calls it. Sky iron. I found that forty . . . no, forty-five years ago. Just layin' on the ground. Sittin' there lookin' up at me."

"Nickel-iron," Carney said. "Partially melted."

The old man rummaged again. He brought forth a succession of odd stones, various roots, sprigs of henbane and liverwort, a bit of bone—other talismans.

Carney examined each item and pocketed it. When there was no more, he said, "Thank you."

"But that all don't mean a *damn* you not in the spirit. You gots t'get in the spirit."

Carney picked up the bottle. The glass was old and dark. There was no label. He popped the cork and sniffed it.

"I get you a glass."

"No, don't bother." Carney sniffed, then took a long pull on the bottle. He swallowed and started coughing.

The old man smiled with satisfaction.

"Jesus!" Carney gasped.

The old man cackled.

Carney caught his breath. "That went down hard." He looked at the bottle. It was about three-quarters full. "Applejack?" he asked.

"Ain't applejack."

"Tastes like it, a little. Stronger. Apple brandy with hydrochloric acid, maybe. Damn."

"You gots to drink it. A lot of it. The spirit's what does it."

"Yeah." Carney drank again. This time the stuff coursed down easier, like lava down the slope of a volcanic cone. He drank again; then one more time. His eyes were watering.

"I think I'm going to be in the spirit very soon."

"It do you good."

Carney offered the bottle. "Join me?"

The old man shook his head. "I ain't the one for it, either. Too old. Too used up. I threw it all away. I didn't use it to no good at all. Can't use it no more. You got to be careful with it. It use you like you use it."

"Oh, yes."

"It turn on you, you don't watch out."

"I can imagine."

"Yessuh."

The old man sat back down on the easy chair. "My granddaughter," he said. "She need a job. Can't get no work."

"What does she do?"

"She went to school. She gots some education. College. Scholarship."

"Wonderful."

"She quit. Took up with some friends. They take her out drinkin'. All night sometime. She come home, sleep all day. She say she can't get no work. Ain't nothin' she wanta do anyway, she say. No good jobs for colored girls. Don't wanta make no beds or scrub no floors."

"Can she write?"

"Yes, suh. Has a fine hand."

"Yeah. I didn't mean quite that. There's a position open in one of my companies here in Dutchtown. Importers. They need someone to write brochures and catalogues. A little college is all a person would need."

"These people . . . they colored?"

"Yes."

The old man nodded. "She might like that. She one smart little girl. She could do it."

"She'll have to do her own typing."

"She can do that too."

"Castle Imports, East One Hundred Forty-fifth Street. Tell her to tell them I referred her."

The old man nodded. "Thank you, suh."

Carney took another swig. The stuff was flowing smoother now. "I'm beginning to like this."

"It get better and better."

"I'll bet." Carney set the bottle down. "I have to use your bathroom."

"In the hall."

The bathroom door was ajar. He opened it and stopped. There, on the floor in front of the commode, lay a girl of about nineteen. Her head was wedged between the seat and the wall. She had vomited and missed the bowl.

Carney checked her. Her eyelids fluttered and she moaned.

The woman was standing at the door.

"I don't put her to bed no more. She can stay there all night for all I care. She can live in there."

Carney picked her up. She was light, a soft bundle in a cerise cotton party dress, one shoe dangling.

He carried her into the bedroom and put her on the big bed. There was a quilt at the foot of the bed; he unfolded it and covered her. He looked at her face for a while. The girl was pretty.

Velma was standing behind him. He turned and she gave him his hat. She was holding the bottle.

"Let's get out of here," she said.

He took out a wad of bills and offered it to the woman. She regarded him gravely, looked at the money, then took it.

"Good night," Carney said, putting on his hat. "Say goodbye to Mr. Hamilton for me."

The woman nodded silently.

Tony woke up when the car door opened.

"Have your beauty rest?" Velma asked, sliding in beside him.

"Jeez, musta dozed off." He rubbed his eyes.

Carney got in and shut the door. "Let's get over into Hellgate."

Tony watched Carney drink from the bottle. "You come all the way up here to buy some bootleg hooch?"

"Yeah. Start the car, you dumb guinea jerk."

Chuckling, Tony turned the engine over. He was adjusting the choke when a car went past. Something made him lift his head.

"There's Riordan."

He gunned the motor, pulled out of the parking spot, made a U turn, and raced down the street, making the Leland's engine whine and roar. He tore around the corner, left, raced a block, careened right, and nearly collided with an oncoming cab. A horn blared. He swerved, straightened out and slowed, glancing into the rearview mirror.

"I think we lost 'em."

Tony cruised for a block, then checked the mirror again. His eyes widened.

"Madonn'!"

He floored the accelerator and the straight-eight Leland engine howled.

"Where's the hardware?" Carney asked.

"On the floor in the back!"

Carney got to his knees and reached, couldn't get it, and tumbled into the back seat. He picked up the submachine gun and cocked it. He pushed Velma down in the seat, then rolled down the back side window and stuck the barrel of the gun out.

A green Durant Roadmaster was pulling into the oncoming lane to pass. Carney let it have a few rounds in the general area of its huge shiny grille.

There was an answering shotgun blast that shattered the rear window. Carney ducked, waited, then sat up. He pointed his index finger through the jagged hole in the glass.

Fire left his finger and enveloped the Durant.

The Durant slowed, flames dancing on its shiny paint. But the fire began to dissipate, rolling off and turning to smoke. The flames soon burned out, leaving the car untouched. The big car sped to catch up.

"They got somethin' workin', boss!"

"Yeah, so I noticed."

Tony tore right around a corner.

He slammed on the brakes, and Carney hit the back of the seat. Ahead, a huge truck was angled into the street, unloading, and blocking the way.

"Out!" Carney yelled. "Run for it!"

Tony reached into the back seat for the submachine gun, brought it out, opened the door, raised the gun and got off about twenty rounds before being cut down by a storm of bullets.

While that was happening, Carney opened the back door, rolled onto the pavement, crawled between two parked cars and hid behind one.

He heard advancing footsteps. He summoned power—and was amazed by how much was available.

"Carney!"

He recognized the voice as Seamus Riordan's, who would have been Tweel's *capo de tutti capi* had Tweel been Italian. Since he was not, Riordan was lieutenant hood, first under the demons.

"Come on out, Mr. Carney. You can't win. The deng's got us fixed up so good you can't touch us. Come on out. We won't hurt the dame. She's one of us."

Carney stood up.

Seamus Riordan, tall, tweed-jacketed and red-haired, stopped in his tracks when he saw the strange-looking long tube in Carney's hands.

"Whatcha got?"

"Bazooka," Carney said.

"What's that?"

Carney demonstrated, aiming at the Durant. The missile left the tube with a *whoosh*. By the time Riordan swiveled his head to follow it, the Durant had blossomed into a gorgeous red fireball. The concussion knocked Riordan down.

"They didn't fix you up good enough," Carney said.

Riordan got to his knees, groped for his lozenge-magazined submachine gun, got it and raised it—but by that time Carney was there to kick it away. Carney then kicked Riordan's solar plexus.

"Not quite good enough, Seamus, me boy."

Another kick. Riordan groaned.

"Were you sent to pick me up or kill me?"

"Pick you up."

Carney's foot found a softer spot near Riordan's groin.

Riordan screamed, "Kill you!"

"That answer was extracted under duress, but I believe you."

Carney went to Tony. Most of the bullets had found his legs, but a few had hit his chest. He was still conscious.

"*Madonn'*," Tony said. "I'm hit. It don't hurt, though. Funny. Always wondered."

Velma was on her knees on the front seat, looking down at Tony.

Carney asked her, "You okay?"

She nodded, then reached for something. She handed Carney the bottle. "Saved it."

Carney took it and pulled out the cork. He tipped the open bottle to Tony's lips.

"Drink a little."

Tony drank. He choked. "Boss, that tastes like lighter fluid."

"You get used to it. It might save your life."

The big Durant burned, thick black smoke coiling into the narrow band of sky between the tenements. Out of the sleeping city night, sirens approached.

Voyager

IT WAS A TIGHT FIT FOR TWO BEASTS AND TWO HUMANS inside the tiny craft. There were four seats, but they were small, obviously designed for nonhuman occupants. Ironically, the nonhumans were the most discommoded: Snowclaw spilled out of his chair, and Goofus's sufficed only for his tail and hind legs.

Jeremy's voice came out of the intercom spearker. "Okay, everything seems to check out. We're ready any time you guys are."

"We're ready as hell," Gene said.

"Yeah, whatever that means."

"We're ready, Jeremy," Linda said.

"Okay. Remember, no more voice communications once you get started, but my messages will be on the computer screen. The computer will be doing most of the piloting anyway. If contact is broken for some reason, the craft's automatic systems will kick in. So don't be too worried. I programmed it to do just about everything on its own."

"Reassuring," Gene said. "For some reason Chernobyl comes to mind . . . but, hey, this is an adventure."

Jeremy sounded a bit put out. "A good . . . you know, like, *attitude* would help, Gene. A little respect for technology, maybe."

Gene tugged at his collar. "Hey, it's rough bein' a computer, you know? You don't get no respect."

"Very funny, Gene," Linda said sternly. "Does everything have to be a joke with you? Can't you take one thing seriously? I mean, just for once?"

Gene cringed. *"Eeep."*

"I'm scared! I don't know about you. You always act so goddamned brave and macho. Sometimes . . . Gene, sometimes you really make me mad."

"Sorry," Gene said in a flat voice. "Okay. Jeremy. Let her rip. Don't bother with a countdown or anything. That'll just make it worse."

"Okay. Good luck, you guys. Be careful."

"Yeah, we will."

It was quiet inside the craft except for Goofus's heavy panting.

"I'm sorry I snapped at you, Gene."

"Forget it. We're all under pressure here."

Gene busied himself with checking instruments, most of which he didn't understand. The computer screen was a confusion of numbers and letters decipherable only to those fluent in hieratic computerese.

Gene turned to say something and bumped into Goofus's enormous head. "Get your dog breath out of my face, Goofus."

As if he understood, Goofus scrunched back in his seat.

"Good boy. God, this is nerve-racking, I'll tell you. Maybe we should have had a count—"

A high-pitched whine filled the tiny compartment. Then the craft shuddered slightly.

The view out the view window disappeared, replaced by something difficult to apperceive: a murky, swimming nothingness, inchoate and devoid of feature.

"We're off," Gene said. "We're out in the interuniversal medium, I guess. The non-space between the universes. I hope this scheme works."

"I'm not even sure what the scheme is," Linda said.

"Well, I'm not crystal clear on it either, but somehow Jeremy reduced Melanie's old clothes to data and fed them into the computer."

"How'd he do that?"

"He faxed them. I dunno what he did. I think he just took two video shots of them, getting perspective parallax, combined those two signals into a 3-D image, and fed the results into the mainframe. So now the locater spell has something to work with."

"Okay," Linda said, "I think I understand that."

"You're one up on me. Anyway, what we're going to do is this. We're going to riffle through whole bunches of universes and let the spell sniff at each one. If Melanie shows up in any of them an alarm will sound. When that happens, we enter that universe and Goofus tracks her down. Got that?"

"Got it."

"Simple and straightforward. And highly implausible."

The whine of the craft's engines increased in pitch. The *Sidewise Voyager*'s occupants felt a barely perceptible sensation of thrust.

"Okay, here we go."

There appeared outside the viewport a flickering montage of rapidly changing scenes, similar to the effect produced by a motion picture film in which each frame is a discontinuous and separate image—or by a slide projector gone beserk. Each image appeared only long enough to persist in the human (and probably nonhuman) visual apparatus, a fraction of a second at most.

They sat and watched. Nothing else happened for a good while. At the top of the computer screen an intelligible message appeared—ALL SYSTEMS GO, GUYS.

Gene gave up trying to make sense of the instruments and sat back. "Well, this could go on forever, since there are an infinite number of universes. Or variations on the same universe."

"Which is it?" Linda asked.

"I dunno. I think the latter. Look at this stuff. Each universe has a world, a planet really, in it, right underneath us. There may be universes in which there isn't a planet, or maybe no planets at all. But if that's true, we haven't run into one yet. I guess what we would be seeing would be empty space."

"It's hard to make anything of that jumble out there," Linda said. "It goes by so fast."

"Yeah. It's like we're skipping across the surface of the big pond of spacetime, skipping like a stone, touching but not really entering the water."

"There's not much feeling of motion."

"No. How're you doing, Snowy?"

Snowclaw said, "I'm fine, except I got a cramp in my leg."

Gene shifted a little. "Is that better?"

Snowclaw moved his leg. "Yeah, thanks."

"Well, at least the thing works," Linda said.

"Seems to be working."

Flashing red lights appeared on the control panel.

"What's that?"

Gene peered at the instruments. "I don't know."

More warning lights appeared, flashing ominously. Soon the whole panel looked like an eight-alarm fire.

"Gene, are we in trouble?"

"Uh . . . yeah. Massive systems failure, it looks like. Either that or there's a sale at K-Mart."

"Is Jeremy still in control?"

The computer screen was blank.

"Looks like we lost contact. We're on our own."

Outside the craft, the flickering had stopped. A vast red sky was the main feature. Below was an ocean edged by a thin strip of beach. The whole scene was suffused with red light.

"Are we going to crash?" Linda asked.

The ground was slowly getting closer.

"No, this thing becomes an aircraft when it enters a universe. There's enough left of the control system to land us, it looks like."

The craft settled slowly, but not slowly enough to avoid landing with jarring bump. The whine of the engines died, and there was quiet.

Gene exhaled. "Well. That's that. Unless we can fix this thing, here we stay."

"Where are we?"

They looked out. Something very unusual was in the sky, a great swollen sphere of redness, bathing everything in its dim light.

"A red giant," Gene said.

"What's that?"

"A stage in the evolution of some stars. They get real big, losing brightness and energy. It could be our sun a couple of billion years from now."

"We're billions of years in the future?"

"Some future, somewhere." Gene sat back and folded his arms. "In any event, we're stranded."

"Oh, no."

"Linda?"

"What?"

"I'm scared now."

CASTLE BY THE SEA

"I WAS TALKING TO BARON DELWYN when I heard someone groan behind me," the princess was saying to Tyrene.

"Yes," the baron said. He was a small man in knee breeches and hose. "It was Damik. Actually he was just passing by. I saw him. He walked behind Her Highness, stopped, seemed to be about to go back the way he'd come, then groaned."

"He bumped into me," Dorcas said. "He turned around with this awful look on his face, clutching at his chest. I saw blood where he was touching. Then he collapsed."

"Baron, you saw no one near him?" Tyrene asked.

"Well, there were a dozen people milling about out here after dinner. But I didn't see anyone near him when he fell."

"And you were faced the other way, Your Highness?"

"Yes. I didn't see a thing until Damik backed into me."

"Who was out here at the time?" Tyrene asked the group of lords and ladies in the foyer.

Lord Arl looked around first before answering. "I was one," he volunteered. "Although I went into the library shortly before it happened."

Tyrene said, "My lord, did you see anything suspicious?"

"Such as?"

"Did you see anyone near the count?"

"Well . . . I hesitate to direct suspicion at anyone."

"My lord, there has been a murder committed. Someone stabbed the count. Someone here, in this room."

Trent said, "I was talking to him. Out here in the hall. I suppose there's no denying that he left me just moments before he collapsed."

"And where were you when he did, Your Highness? If I might ask."

Sheila, disturbed and distraught, was standing at Trent's side, her arm in his. He pressed her hand reassuringly. "Right there, near the door to the dining hall. Right where I spoke to Damik."

"And what, sir, were you doing at that exact moment?"

"Just standing there thinking. Thinking about what Damik had just said."

"Sir, which was?"

"That he was going to go to you with the name of the person who owned the dagger."

"He was . . . ?"

"He claimed he saw someone recently purchase a dagger similar to the murder weapon. He told this to Thaxton, Dalton, myself, and my wife."

"I see."

Baron Delwyn said, "He told me as well. In fact, he seems to have told a number of people. Lord Linwold remarked to me just an hour ago that Damik had told him the same thing. Seems he was disturbed about this and didn't know what to do."

Tyrene nodded. "So. This is very interesting. Count Damik was privy to potentially damning information regarding the identity of the murderer, and now he's dead."

Thaxton and Dalton were standing off to one side.

Dalton leaned over and whispered, "They were all in a position to stab him. Trent, Belgard, Rilma . . ."

"And a cloud of witnesses standing about, none of whom saw anything, as usual."

"Well, this murderer seems to have some tricks up his

sleeve. Don't forget your hypothesis about magic. Hypnosis, black magic spells . . ." Dalton thought. "Invisibility?"

"An invisible murderer," Thaxton said. "Now that would explain a lot."

"Yes," Dalton agreed. "It would. If it weren't for the fact that there's no magic in this aspect."

"Who says there isn't?"

Everyone watched silently as Guardsmen bore the body away.

When they were gone, Tyrene turned to face the assembled group. "I will do all further questioning in private, my lords and ladies," he announced. "But in the morning. There is a storm gathering, and it looks to be an ominous night. There is a murderer loose in the castle. I suggest you all retire to your rooms and bolt your doors. Good night to you all, and may your respective deities, whosoever they may be, forfend any harm."

The group broke up and dispersed, almost all ascending the wide staircase that led to the level where most of the bedrooms were.

Tyrene came over to Thaxton and Dalton. "At least there will be no more murders tonight. I'm going to post guards at the doors of all the prime suspects."

"Ah, you have a list," Thaxton observed.

"And a short list it is," Tyrene replied. "Unlike those in mystery romances."

"I should say not," Thaxton said. "Just under a dozen suspects is *de rigueur*."

"Thank the gods that's not our problem here," Tyrene said. "I can't say that I'm close to a solution of these crimes, but things are becoming increasingly clear."

"Such as?" Thaxton asked.

"That this is a relatively simple matter made obscure by deliberate obfuscation, if not outright lying."

"How so?" Dalton asked.

"Gods, man. Can't you see? They're all covering up for someone! Murder's committed under their noses, yet no one sees a thing. A likely story! Oh, they're thick as thieves, this lot. They'd rather see the culprit go scot-free than break their damnable code of 'discretion.' Scandal is the worst thing they can imagine."

Dalton said, "We were discussing the possibility of some supernatural means."

"Don't think it didn't occur to me. I suspected thaumaturgical homicide right off, but have since discounted it. There are a thousand dark spells designed to do a man in, and this lot knows 'em all, I'll wager. But, you see, each is a magician himself, and can employ forfending spells to ward off a hex or a curse or a dozen other eldritch evils. They're all well versed in these matters, let me assure you. Which is why the simplest method is all the more effective. It's unexpected."

Thaxton said, "And you think the murderer is counting on the silence of his peers to keep his identity concealed?"

"Damik did much soul searching about revealing even circumstantial evidence," Dalton pointed out. "Though he decided in the end to do it."

"So Trent says," Tyrene acknowledged. "But he may be lying."

"Wouldn't Trent lie the opposite way?" Thaxton asked, "and say that Damik wasn't going to tell?"

"Possibly," Tyrene said.

"In any case, I find it unlikely that Damik would announce to a group that included the murderer himself that he knew who the murderer was."

"Damik was like that," Tyrene responded. "Very given to subtleties and devious ploys. It may have been his way of giving Trent notice, yet providing witnesses if anything should happen to him, which in fact it did."

"I see," Thaxton said. "But I find it difficult to imagine Trent a murderer."

"You didn't know him in his youth," Tyrene told him. "Admittedly that was quite a spell ago, even as Perilous time is reckoned, but he was one hotheaded young buck, quick to anger, quicker to pick a fight. I'll admit I've seen him change, and he was an exile on Earth for the longest time, which might have worked some ameliorative influence on him—"

"Earth isn't exactly the most peaceful of places," Dalton pointed out.

"Be that as it may. He has changed for the better in some respects, but I'm old enough to know that pards may change their spots yet still be pards."

"Leopards," Dalton supplied to Thaxton. "Poetic usage, as a lot of castle lingo is."

"Yes, leopards, I beg your pardon. But you take my meaning, I'm sure." Tyrene scratched himself, which Thaxton had by then put down to nervous habit. "If only these were a pack of your common cutthroats. I could order a strip search and turn up the second murder weapon in a trice. We weren't so lucky the second time. No one left a knife lying about for us to—"

Tyrene had turned his head as he spoke, and now froze. Thaxton and Dalton followed his astonished gaze. Something was lying near the base of the far wall.

"Ye *gods!*" Tyrene breathed.

They went running to it.

"Damn me!" Tyrene said, kneeling to examine it. He was mortified.

The knife lying on the floor next to the wainscoting was a twin of the first murder weapon.

"That's what you kicked," Dalton said to Thaxton.

"What's that?" Tyrene asked, looking up.

Thaxton told him.

"So it was there all along. But how is it no one saw it before?"

"It was invisible," Thaxton said.

"Damn me." Tyrene clucked and shook his head. "So it *was* magic."

"I think so," Thaxton said. "But we're no closer to finding out who did the magic."

"True," Tyrene conceded, "but the light grows ever brighter."

"Invisibility certainly explains why no one saw anything," Dalton remarked. "There was nothing to see."

"At least not in the murderer's hand," Tyrene said. "You might tend to dismiss or forget seeing someone do this"—he made a fist and brought it up against Dalton's chest—"if it looked like a jape or a friendly tap."

"Again, though, there's a problem," Thaxton insisted.

"What's that?" Tyrene asked.

"Why would the murderer drop his weapon at the scene of the crime? *For the second time?*"

The captain ruminated before answering. "Ordinarily, I would say, simply to get rid of it as quickly as possible so as not to have it turn up in a search. But they all know I wouldn't and couldn't ask them to submit to such an indignity." Tyrene scowled. "I simply haven't a clue as to why the knife was dropped."

"Neither do I," Thaxton said. "As of now, anyway."

Tyrene's brow lifted sardonically. "I trust you'll apprise me of any sudden revelations."

"I'll be sure to," Thaxton said dryly.

Tyrene picked up the knife. "I suppose it won't do any good to test it for prints. I'm not going to get a messenger through that storm out there, anyway. It can wait till the morrow."

"No prints," Dalton said, shaking his head. "I can't recall any of the prime suspects wearing gloves."

"Aye, but I'll wager any purse it'll be clean, as before. Mayhap the trick was done magically," Tyrene declared. "Damn me again. I'm hoist by my own petard."

"Well," Thaxton said. "I suppose there is nothing left to do. Everyone's locked doors by now."

"I suggest you gentlemen do the same," the captain told them. "And I'll take my own advice. I'm fagged out, truth be told. This nasty business has sapped me. My heart aches, and a drowsy numbness pains my sense."

"As though of hemlock you had drunk?" Dalton asked.

"Or emptied some dull opiate to the drains." Tyrene yawned. "I crave your pardon, gentlemen. I must to bed." He turned and walked off, waving. "Until the morrow, then."

"Good night, Captain," Thaxton said.

"These people have such poetic speech," Dalton observed, marveling.

It was a dark night of *Sturm und Drang*.

Lightning split the sky, revealing the desperate sea as it dashed itself against the rocks below. Rain pelted the castle, and wind wailed over the ramparts. Between flashes, the sea was gray-green, suffused with a strange luminescence, boiling and churning.

Dalton came away from the window and sat back in the stuffed chair. He picked up *The Moswell Plan* and resumed reading.

Thaxton lay in bed, absorbed in *Magiekal Divershyns.*

They read as rain spattered the diamond-patterned windows and thunder rolled across the coast.

There came a knock at the door.

"Who the devil could that be?" Thaxton said, making to get up.

"I'll get it," Dalton said, rising.

Dalton turned the huge key in the lock, threw the bolt, and opened the heavy oaken door, its wrought-iron hinges creaking.

"Good evening, Mr. Dalton."

"Princess Dorcas. Your Royal Highness, please come in."

"Thank you. I'm so glad you're still up. I had no wish to disturb you."

"Not at all."

Dorcas came into the room, smiling. Thaxton was already on his feet.

"Your Royal Highness, what a pleasant surprise," he said.

"You're wondering why I'm up and about," Dorcas began.

"Well, ma'am, it's not the wisest thing to be doing with the murderer about."

"The murderer has already tried to kill me," she said, "and failed. There will be no second attempt. That would be too risky. I think the murderer realizes now that I won't reveal what I know."

The two men looked at each other.

Thaxton said, "Ma'am, if I might be so impertinent as to ask, what *do* you know?"

"The identity of the killer."

Dalton coughed, recovered, and said, "Won't you please sit down?"

Dorcas sat in the stuffed chair. "Please, gentlemen, be seated."

Dalton dragged up the hard-backed chair. Thaxton sat on the end of the bed.

"You say you know who the murderer is," Thaxton said. "May I ask how?"

Dorcas smiled. "That will take some explaining." She glanced at the book beside the reading lamp on the table. "Ah, I see you're reading my book."

"Oh, that's your copy?"

"No. I wrote it."

Dalton's eyes went wide. "*You* wrote *The Moswell Plan*? You're Dorcas Bagby?"

"That was the pen name I chose, yes. You see, I really don't have a surname, so I took the name of my landlady. I was living in England at the time. Most of our family have spent a good deal of time there, getting educated. Trent, Incarnadine, all of us. Oh, there is the family name of Haplodie, but that sounds so strange, and in fact it's a gens name, a clan name, not a proper surname. Anyway, writing the novel was something to pass the time while I spent a summer in Kent with friends of the family. It was a short-lived phenomenon. The urge to write never came over me again."

Dalton said, "Well, I can tell you that I'm enjoying it immensely, and it's an especial joy to be actually reading it after so many years of hearing about it."

"It's known?" Dorcas asked.

"Mostly by reputation. But it is known."

"I'm elated. I'd thought the book consigned to obscurity. It's long been out of print. The publisher is no longer in business."

"Are you sure this isn't your copy?"

"No. Where did you find it?"

"In the Peele library."

"I didn't know there was a copy here. Well." Dorcas sat back. "And now, I suppose you want me to explain how I can claim to know who the murderer is? Very well, I'll tell you, though you might not believe me. It's very simple. I saw guilt on the person's face."

A flash of lightning threw diamond patterns across the room, and a loud report shook the windows.

"And the person knew it when I looked. We locked eyes,

both aware of the other's thoughts. It lasted only a second, but it was as if we had spoken for an hour. This happened very shortly after we were informed of the viscount's death. I knew then that I was in danger."

"Sounds as though it was a frightening experience," Dalton said. "Would you explain in more detail how this ability of yours works?"

"It is the Eye of Yahura, the Interior Eye. With it one can look into one's own soul, and into that of others. It's the soul, of course, that radiates from the eyes and communicates emotions to other people. Most people assume it's the face and the facial muscles, but of course the face can move very little. With the Eye of Yahura it's possible to see even deeper, down to the seat of the emotions, and there read the state of the *samra*, or soul-substance, which remains hidden and is not usually revealed by the eyes, except in the case of certain holy persons."

"Were you born with this ability?" Dalton asked.

"No, not at all, though I was a fairly adept castle magician until I gave up that school of magic and adopted another entirely. I learned it partly from my husband, the Diktar of Sagrapore, and partly from a very wise and holy woman by the name of Bassara Ulani. I studied for several decades before becoming proficient."

"Very interesting," Thaxton said. "What do you intend to do with this knowledge . . . of the identity of the murderer, I mean?"

"Nothing."

"Why?"

"My brother Incarnadine is wise. He made a law which prohibits a person from being charged with a crime based on information obtained from divination, necromancy, clairvoyance, or any paranormal means. The law is a very vital protection of human rights. It prevents the abuse of magic and gives jurisprudence an objective basis. Imagine if someone could be charged, tried, convicted, and even executed on the word of some clever and malicious charlatan. Or on the false evidence of a real magician. It is unthinkable. That is why my revealing the murderer's identity would do no good whatsoever. I have no evidence on which to base such an accusation, and nothing but evil would come of it. That is why I must remain silent. I think even the murderer realizes that now."

"You remained silent even though your life was in danger," Thaxton observed. "Remarkable. Tell me this, ma'am, if you please. Count Damik is dead. You're saying that the murderer meant to kill you instead?"

"Yes, that I also read on the murderer's face. I am sure the killing of Damik was somehow a mistake."

"If Damik was stabbed, which looks certain, how could it have been a mistake?"

Dorcas shook her head slowly. "It puzzles me, too. But I am certain the murderer meant to kill me, not Damik. The murderer touched me."

"He—or she—touched you?"

"Yes. On the back. Just one finger, lightly, in passing. I thought the person wanted to speak to me, but no, not even a look. Just a touch. It was the touch of death. I could feel it. It was like the touch of a corpse. Cold, unfeeling."

"How long before Damik's murder did this happen?"

"Just moments. Perhaps forty-five seconds. A minute at the outside."

"And somehow," Thaxton prompted, "Damik got in the way."

"Yes. But I don't understand how. I know it was magical, and that the knife or the dagger was somehow incorporeal, or—"

"Oh, it was corporeal all right," Dalton interjected. "It was just invisible for a little while."

"I see," Dorcas said. "Of course. And the dagger was thrown?"

"Possibly," Thaxton said. "That's what we don't know."

"Your Highness," Dalton said, "why have you come to us?"

Dorcas smiled. "For sympathy. I had no one to share this with. My husband is recuperating from an illness and couldn't come to the fête. I couldn't go to my relatives; they're distrustful and might think me trying to stir up trouble. They'd rather see the whole matter dropped. Murder doesn't disturb them so much as the adverse reflection on the family. Also, I had a feeling about you two gentlemen."

"What sort of feeling?" Thaxton asked.

"That you knew even more than Tyrene. That you were closer to getting to the bottom of this than he was, as good a man as Tyrene is and as good as his intentions are. I wanted to be close to you, to reassure you that you were on the right track, although I can't give you any guidance whatsoever. All I can do is lend you my emotional support. And, finally, you're Guests. Guests seem to have special talents, sometimes. I find that fascinating."

Dalton said, "You're talking to two very untalented Guests, magically speaking. I can levitate about an ounce of weight, if I set my mind to it. Thaxton . . . Thaxton, old boy, exactly what *can* you do?"

"Not a bloody thing, I'm embarrassed to say."

Dorcas said, "Oh, I think you have great untapped potential. You've simply never explored it."

Thaxton was surprised to hear it. "You don't say?"

Dalton yawned. "Excuse me. It's way past my bedtime, I'm afraid."

"Oh, I'm keeping you up. I'm so sorry."

"Let us walk you back to your quarters," Thaxton suggested.

"Would you gentlemen consider letting me stay here for the night? I'd feel much better."

"Of course," Thaxton said. "You'll take the bed, Dalton the cot, and I can curl up in the chair."

"Oh, no, I wouldn't put you out. I intend to go into *bramhara* sleep, and that's usually done in a sitting position." She got up and sat back down with her legs in an improbable knot under her.

"However do you do that?" Dalton wondered.

Dorcas wrapped her arms around her upper body so tightly that she seemed to be trying to touch her hands together behind her back. "This is the position of *bramhara* sleep."

Thaxton said, "Uh . . . which is?"

"An alternative state of consciousness in which being is

contingent upon discretionary choice, not imposed by ontological fiat."

"Oh, that."

"It is a restful state as well as being contemplative and transmaterial. I often go into *bramhara* during times of emotional stress. I'll be fine right here on this chair, gentlemen. Please just ignore me."

Dalton rose and went to the cot. He picked up the nightshirt that Ruford had laid out for him. He held it up. "I ought to have a sleeping cap with this. I'll go into the bathroom to change. But one more question, Your Highness."

"Certainly."

"How do you keep that stone on your forehead?"

"The Eye? Very easily." Dorcas unwrapped her arms. Cupping her hand in front of her face, she tilted her head down. After a second or two, the diamond dropped into her hand. She held it up. "Just a common diamond. I tune my body so that there is a natural affinity between the organic element of which it is composed, carbon, and the carbon which makes up a great deal of my body. The two naturally attract." She tilted her head back so that she was looking directly at the ceiling, then placed the diamond on her forehead. She held this position for about five seconds, then slowly brought her head back to the perpendicular. The stone stayed put.

"Remarkable," Dalton said, shaking his head. "Absolutely remarkable." He went into the bathroom and shut the door.

"If you don't mind, I'm going to stay up a bit longer and read," Thaxton said.

"Please do anything you wish," Dorcas said, and went into position again. Her eyes closed.

Thaxton lay on the bed and picked up the book.

Dalton was dreaming of a woman, a beautiful woman. She wore a white gown, a thin chemise, and was walking barefoot at the surf's edge, the breakers washing up the smooth packed sand to wet her feet. The sky was blue between white puffy clouds. She was coming toward him, sea breeze blowing the thin cloth of the gown tight against her well-formed body. She

*was smiling. This was her kingdom, this kingdom by the
sea. . . .*

"Dalton!"

"Huhhh?"

"Dalton, old boy. Wake up!"

The woman, the sky, the sea—all faded away.

Dalton opened his eyes. Thaxton was bending over him,
hand on his shoulder.

Thaxton shook him again. "Are you awake?"

"Good God, Thaxton, what is it?"

Thaxton was excited. "I've got the solution, old boy. I know
how the murder was done. And if I can get a messenger
through to the castle, we may be able to find out just who the
murderer is."

"God, I hope I see her again," Dalton said.

"Eh? Get up, old boy. We must go see Tyrene."

St. Valentine's Hospital

THEY WOULDN'T LET CARNEY INTO THE EMERGENCY ROOM no matter how much persuasion magic he worked, so he had to be content with word from a sympathetic nurse that Tony's condition was stable. They would operate in the next hour to get the slugs out. Tony had a good chance of pulling through.

He went back to the waiting room, where Velma was smoking and reading a two-year-old copy of *Liberty* magazine. He beckoned and she put out the butt, got up and came to him.

"How is he?" she asked.

"He'll pull through. This stuff"—he patted the neck of the bottle in his coat pocket—"probably helped."

"Is it helping you?"

"I'm as high as a Mass at St. Peter's. Let's get out of here."

"Hey, Carney."

Carney turned. It was Detective Sergeant James "Mack" Duffey of the Necropolis P.D., smiling a coldly cynical smile, thumbs hooked in the pockets of his baggy brown wool pants.

"What can I do you out of, Sergeant?"

"Want to take a look at your future?"

"Sure. Whaddya got?"

"We got Duke Holland for you. Or should I say, somebody got him? Good."

"I thought he was dead."

"He's been on his way to Hell for the past five hours. Thought you might want to pay your respects. After all, he's a colleague of yours."

"Lay on, Mack Duffey."

Duffey led him down the hall. A uniformed cop, standing guard outside a door, let them into small examination room and closed the door. Velma stayed outside.

There were two more cops in the room, along with a plainclothes clerk with a steno pad, scribbling away in shorthand. Holland lay on a gurney, shirtless, his upper body ventilated with bullet holes. Carney wondered how he could still be alive. But he was. He was talking continually in a low, breathy murmur. The stenographer seemed to be trying to take down every word.

"Delirious," Duffey said. "He's been gabbling away like that for hours."

"Can't anything be done?" Carney asked.

"Nah. The docs say it's only a matter of time."

"They came up with that prognosis all by themselves, eh?"

Duffey guffawed. "They didn't need no coachin'."

Carney laughed mirthlessly. "What's with the steno?"

"Evidence."

Carney nodded. "Can I try talking to him?"

"Be my guest. But you'll get nowhere."

Carney approached the gurney. Holland's head shifted slowly from side to side. Dried blood caked his lips. His eyes were glazed, his sight on sights unseen. On and on he droned, the words slurred together, almost unintelligible.

Carney moved closer. He bent over the dying man, turning his ear toward those cracked lips:

". . . Well, you know or don't you kennet or haven't I told you every telling has a taling and that's the he and the she of it. Look, look, the dusk is growing! And my cold cher's gone ashley. Fieluhr? Filou! What age is at? It saon is late. 'Tis endless now senne eye or erewone last saw Waterhouse's clogh. They took it asunder, I hurd thum sigh. When will they

reassemble it? O, my back, my back, my bach! I'd want to go
to Aches-les-Pains. Pingpong. There's the Belle for Sexaloitez!
And Concepta de Send-us-pray! Pang! Wring out the clothes!
Wring in the dew! Godavari, vert the showers! And grant thaya
grace! Aman. Will we spread them here now? Ay, we will. Flip!
Spread on your bank and I'll spread mine on mine. . . ."

Carney straightened, backed off.

"He was a big man," Duffey said, with underlying satisfaction. "Look at him now."

"Don't rejoice so loudly, James."

Duffey opened the door for him.

Velma was engaged in casual flirtation with the door guard. She saw Carney, and rounded it off nicely with a smile and a squeeze of the cop's big biceps. The cop grinned droolingly.

Carney took her arm and guided her down the hall, except she should have been guiding him; he wobbled like a loose wheel.

"How is he doing?" she asked.

"Not bad for a guy with no education," he said.

The Leland had bullet holes in it but still worked. Carney turned east, toward the river. The hole in the back window sucked out all the heat the heater threw at them, but the flow warmed them a little. Carney drank as he drove.

"We'll wreck if you keep doing that," Velma said.

"Possibly."

"You could at least offer me a drink."

"Powerful stuff, Velma, honey."

"I can take it. I can swill any kind of booze."

She took the bottle and had a swig. She choked, and sprayed all over the windshield.

He laughed, taking the bottle.

"What . . . *is* that stuff?"

"A little saint remover, my darling turpentine, eye of newton, denatured spirits, a little o' this an' for a' that."

"It's awful."

"Oh, it be, it be. 'O, for a draught of vintage! that hath been cool'd a long age in the deep-delved earth.' Havin' a good time. Yessuh."

Velma fanned the fumes away from her mouth. "What bathtub did that come out of? That's not liquor, that's poison."

"Why, hell, woman, it's full of the true, the blushful Hippocrene, with beaded bubbles winking all over the bloody brim." He belched. "'Scuse me."

She laughed. "You're drunk."

"Yes, ma'am. Ah is drunker'n a skunk sunk in a sump. Smashed to smithereens, colleen. I gots the spirit!"

"God, are you drunk. You didn't seem so potted in the hospital."

"I was like unto a fern. But I was a-workin' a sober spell. A straightening-up spell. A sorites of sobriety. But now it's gone, gone. Now I drunk, man."

"You sound like that old codger."

"He the man with the power. What power? The power of—"

He had to make a hard right to get onto the bridge. He just made it, swerving the Leland crazily.

"Hey, take it easy," Velma said. "Good gravy!"

"Good night. Good night, good night, Irene, I'll see you in my dreams, wetly."

"Watch it. They're still looking for you."

"Oh, they seek me here, they seek me there. Those demons seek me everywhere."

"They're not through with you yet."

"Am I in heaven, am I in heck? What do I need with all this dreck?"

"You're not drunk. You're looney."

"La lune, la lune, keep a-shinin' in jejune. Oh, they won't bother me again. They know I'm coming to pay a visit. Why waste energy? If the mahatma can't come to the mountain, then the mountain'll come over the moon, and the dish ran away with the spoon."

"I'm cold," Velma said.

"Don't worry. Sumer is icomen in. Lhoude sing couscous, or maybe shishkebab. Hey, what can I do to warm you up, babe?"

"You're one to talk."

"Whaddya mean?"

"I had you pegged as one cold fish."

"You'd rather hot crabs?"

"How come you haven't made a pass at me?"

"Was it expected?"

"You're a guy," she said.

"Oh, we're back to that again, are we? Do the bastards make the passes? I guess, huh, 'cause the simps simper. Or is it the big fish? Oh, such a *beeg feesh*."

"Guys only think of one thing."

"Monists, all. I myself am of that stripe, but a fecal monist. Know what that is?"

"Uh-uh."

"That's the philosophical position that everything is shit."

"That's right. For the birds."

"Turd thou never wert. Okay, I'll make a pass."

They were across the river. He veered right and bumped up onto the curb, bumped down again. The car screeched to a halt. He pulled back the hand brake and shut off the motor.

"I'm a simpering bastard, but I hope I'm acceptable."

He took her in his arms and their mouths met. Her tongue was as quick as Dara Porter's, but smoother, less sharp. His hands went a-roving, and the moon was still as bright. She was soft, yielding, eager, and warm.

"We can go to my place," she said, her breath hot on his face.

"I thought you bunked at the Tweeleries."

"Only sometimes. I have a place in Hellgate. Put your hand there. Right there."

"Ah, 'Come live with me and be my love, and we will all the pleasures pr—' "

She stopped his mouth with hers.

A time later he went on, " '—Ae fond kiss, and then we sever . . . flow gently, sweet Afton, among thy green braes, through caverns measureless to man, down to a sunless . . .' "

He stopped and pulled away. He shook his head and it seemed, to his dismay, to rattle.

"Whoa! Ye gods! This is working up to be one monster of a spell. I've never seen its like. I'd as lief never see it again. But . . . on the other tentacle, a man's gotta do what a man's gotta do, do." He popped the cork and took a drink.

"Give me that," she said, grabbing the bottle away from him. She took a pull, and it went down successfully. Her eyes bulged.

"Smooth, huh?"

She gasped. "Yeah." She took another.

"You got yo' mojo workin' now, babe."

"C'mere, you beeg feesh."

She drew him to her and they sank together into the depths, while the Lethe flowed softly by, dark and deep in the night.

WORLD

THE STAR THAT WAS THE SUN HUNG, bloated and swollen, in a dusk-red sky. A billion years ago it had been small, yellow, and hot. Now it was a ruddy monster giving off little light compared to its former compact self. Nor did it have much heat to give, but its immense size brought its surface closer to the planet. The air was temperate.

The green sea looked as it had looked five billion years ago.

They walked the beach and found something unusual lying in at the edge of the surf. It was large and looked dead. Its shape was indeterminate. It had tentacles on one side, claws or hooks on the other. Its body was flat, except toward what amounted to a head, where it bulged. The skin looked like leather here, blubber there. The color was a mottled blue-green. There were two eyes in the head, and a third, perhaps malformed, on the hump behind the head.

Goofus sniffed at the creature, barked once, and sat in front of it.

"Gene, it's really gross."

"It would probably have thought us pretty damn homely. But that means little to me. I'm no relativist, aesthetic or otherwise. I say that's ugly, and I say to hell with it." Gene walked on up the beach.

"I feel kind of sorry for it," Linda said. "Dying alone in this place, at the end of the world."

"I wonder if it's good to eat," Snowclaw said.

"Snowy! Don't be disgusting."

"Well, I'm hungry."

"You're always hungry."

"And that looks like blubber to me. Parts of it, anyway."

"Yuck. Well, have a nice time. C'mon, Goofus."

Snowclaw stalked the animal's length and breadth, eyeing it.

"Nah." He walked away.

Linda looked back over her shoulder. "Goofus?"

Goofus was still planted in front of the thing. He looked expectant, as if waiting for his master to give a signal.

"What is it, Goofus?" Linda walked back, Snowclaw following.

Goofus barked.

"He must sense something about it," Linda said. "I wonder what."

"Maybe it's still alive."

"Do you think?"

"It looks dead, but you can never tell about big sea critters. I know. I hunt them."

"That looks like a mouth, there. Maybe that slit there is a nose. Sort of. Nothing's moving."

"You know," Snowclaw said, "something tells me it is alive. Just barely."

"Oh. Did you see it move just then?"

Goofus got up on all fours and barked.

"I think it did move," Linda said. "I wonder if we can do anything to help it." She cupped her hands to her mouth and yelled, "Gene!"

Gene had wandered back to the ship, which had come to rest on dry sand a little way up the beach. Gene waved and yelled back, "Just a minute!" He climbed inside the *Voyager*.

"What's that?" Snowclaw said.

Something had extruded from the creature: a metal rod looking not unlike a radio aerial.

Linda put both hands up to her cheeks. "Oh, my! Could this be a machine?"

The end of the rod unfolded into a wire mesh disk. The disk rotated slowly until it was aligned with the *Voyager.*

"God, I hope that's not a weapon," Linda said.

"You want me to rough it up a little?"

"No! Snowy, don't do anything."

Goofus barked and sat on his haunches again, watching the thing intently.

One of the eyes on the creature blinked.

"It *is* alive!" Linda exclaimed. "But I don't understand the aerial. Is this thing animal, vegetable, or mineral?"

"Maybe a little of everything?" Snowclaw ventured.

A high wave came in and washed over Linda's pretty silver boots. They were watertight. "Do you think it's trying to communicate with us?"

Gene came running from the ship.

"Hey, there's something going on with the computer. It's going nuts. . . ." He saw the communications dish. "Now what the hell is that?"

"We were asking the same thing," Linda told him. "I think it wants to establish contact."

"Well, apparently it has, at least with our computer. The screen's jumping with activity and I can't make head or tail of it. And this looks to be the cause of it all."

"What do you think it is, Gene?"

Looking at the thing afresh, Gene gave it a clinical scan. "Some sort of intelligent, seagoing life form. Doesn't look anything like a dolphin, but those flaps back here might be fins of some kind. Lessee—eyes, breather holes, and that's gotta be the mouth, although it's kind of on the small side. Maybe it doesn't eat much. And of course, your basic telecommunications link, standard on any sentient creature."

"Is it sick, in trouble, what?"

"Prolly both. Beached, like a sick whale. Very like a whale, only smaller."

"I wish there was something we could do."

"Like? I wish we could help, too. But . . ." Gene raised his arms in despair.

"Maybe if we pushed it back into the ocean."

"I'd say the thing weighed something on the order of two thousand pounds, advoirdupois. Besides, it's obviously an air breather, or it'd be dead already. Likely has lungs *and* gills."

"I still wish we could do something."

"Aside from comforting it, there's little. But of course, we're assuming—"

The creature emitted a whistling sound. It started in a high pitch, then descended until it became a rush of air.

"That sounded so sad," Linda said.

"Yeah."

"What were you saying?"

"I was going to say that we're only making assumptions here. For all we know, the thing is in the middle of a proper and natural life function, like spawning, or something. Or it's just sunning itself after a swim. Who knows?"

"I think it's sick," Linda said. "Goofus knew right off."

"I'm not going to argue with Goofus. The critter looks terrible enough."

The whistling sound came again, this time varying in pitch. It wandered up and down the chromatic scale, then settled in the middle registers. The creature started to modulate the sound, and something like a voice began to emerge from all the piping. It was doglike at first, which elicited another woof from Goofus, but then it became less feral and, while not exactly human, began to sound like something that could form words, though none came.

This went on for a long time. Snowclaw grew bored and strolled up the beach, sniffing for quarry. Gene left the strand and went to examine the strange trees that grew inland. They were gnarled bonsai-like little things with pink leaves.

Linda sat and listened. Every once in a while she thought she heard something that sounded like an effort to speak.

Finally, after about a half-hour, she heard, quite clearly, "Ablomabel."

She stood up. "Excuse me?" she said.

"Ablomabel."

"Could you say that again?"

"Ablomabel?"

"Oh. Okay." Linda touched her chest. "Linda."

"Vinah."

"Linda."

"Vin-dah."

"No, Lin-da . . . *Linda*. Linda Barclay."

"Lin-dah-baleee."

"Yeah, sort of. Pleased to meet you."

She coached it along, and at the end of a few minutes she was rewarded with, "Lin-DAH bar-CLEE."

"Right. But it's more Lin-da BAR-clee. Never mind how it's spelled. Okay, your name is Ablomabel. What are you?"

"What . . . are . . . you?"

"Oh. Are you asking me a question?"

"Ask-ing you a ques-tion."

"Gee, you're coming along fine. That was a good sentence."

"Thank you."

The voice was almost human.

"You want to know about me," Linda said. "I'm a human being. I'm from the planet Earth."

"Ear-r-th."

"Yes."

"Ear-r-th. Yes."

"And I and my friends came here in that craft over there. The one you're communicating with. But I guess you know that."

The creature said, "I know. I know. I know everything in computer. I am of it with."

"Then you know pretty much all there is to know about us. There's a lot of information in that computer."

"Much data is giving."

Gene had returned in the middle of the conversation.

"Linda, are you giving bootleg Berlitz courses again?"

"Ablomabel, this is Gene. Gene, Ablomabel."

"So I am pleased meeting, Gene, you," the creature said.

"The pleasure is all mine. Tell me, does 'Ablomabel' have any meaning in your language?" Gene asked.

"Yes, meaning title of leader of . . . thought-process-change group?"

"Ah. A scientist? Philosopher?"

"Yes!" the Ablomabel said. "Meaning much the same, yet different, I am thinking about."

Linda said, "Ablomabel, are you feeling ill? What are you doing here?"

The Ablomabel answered, "There is an ending. I am coming to shore, to home, once again, last time. Then ceasing to function. Ending. Death."

"That's terrible. Is there anything we can do?"

"There is an ending to all," the Ablomabel said. "I am fatigued, weary. Long time with sickness. And old, very old. There is no one left, I fear that. No one reports. I am last, I think. Then, I die, I think. I came here to see again the sun, which dies."

"That's so awful," Linda said. "Are you sure there's nothing we can do?"

"I am sure, thank you, please. But glad is in my mind for meeting my new friends. I will stay longer, not die yet."

"Oh, please don't die. You must have a lot to tell. Can you tell me, do you live in the sea?"

"Yes, my kind is sea-living."

"How long has your kind lived in the ocean?"

"Very long time, since when the Yvlem decreed there should be living in the sea again after long time deadness in the sea. Many . . . years ago, eons, long time."

Gene asked, "You obviously have technology, and it seems to be part of you. Are you part machine?"

The Ablomabel answered, "All living who does, are parts of machines, in part machine, and machine parts. Comprehend this?"

"I think I understand. Cyborgs."

"Indeed, there are machines who are living as well."

"So you have robots, cyborgs, but no living things that aren't either one of those?"

"Small organisms, some plants, yes."

"How long has civilization been on this planet?"

"Many long time. Cannot say with exacting. Since the sun was young."

"Billions of years," Gene said. "That's incredible."

"Permitted asking you questions?" the Ablomabel said.

"Shoot. I mean, of course. Go ahead."

"Where is it you are coming from?"

"I think you'll be able to understand this. From another universe."

"Yes, that has been thought, but nothing done in this matter. Another universe. Your machine. You built it?"

"No," Gene said. "I found it. A long-forgotten race of beings built it."

"They were indeed great beings, I think."

"They were pretty remarkable. Unfortunately, their machine doesn't work very well. It ceased to function. That's why we are here. We can't leave. We're stranded."

"This is very unfortunate in the way of bad luck," the Ablomabel said. "Have been attempting to repair the craft?"

"Have been attempting," Gene said, "but no luck so far. Our resources are limited. Tell me, can you possibly help?"

"Gene," Linda scolded. "Ablomabel's dying."

"Already have sent message to machine city not far from this place," the Ablomabel said. "Alerted to the possible trouble and help to be lending."

"That's decent of you," Gene said. "Machines, you say?"

"Yes, they still live and are active. They say they will come to help. But do not hope this much. Your machine in the nature of strangeness is great, I think."

"Yeah, you can't get parts. A real lemon. The warranty expired, and everything went."

"Detecting irony."

"You're detecting it. I mean to say that the craft has never lived up to expectations as far as successful operation is concerned. It was an experimental design. Do you understand? All the harder to fix, consequently."

"Understand. But is it permitted to attempt?"

Gene nodded. "It is permitted, and thank you very much."

The Ablomabel said, "I am fatigued. Conversation has depleted my energy reserves. I will, permission granting, rest awhile and not speak, until the machines arrive."

Linda said, "By all means. Take a nice nap. Don't tire yourself."

The wire mesh communications dish folded up, and the rod retracted into the creature's skin. The opening that received the whole affair closed up.

They had a picnic lunch on the beach. Snowclaw had collected an assortment of shellfish. Finding none edible he complained of hunger.

"Try this," Gene said, handing him a ham salad sandwich.

Snowclaw took it and popped it into his mouth, chewed twice, and swallowed. "Great," he said. "Now what else can I breathe?"

"Sorry, Snowy. But you ate all the stuff we brought for you."

"Canned fish. Great, but I need fresh stuff or my fur starts to fall out."

"There's the ocean," Gene said. He handed Snowclaw his gun. "Go out and shoot some fish."

Linda said, "Gene, there may be sentient creatures out there. Shellfish are one thing, but Snowy eats whales and like that. But he can't do it here. It wouldn't be ethical."

"She's right," Snowclaw said. "I'd probably get sick eating this stuff. I'm tired. I'm going to sack out."

Snowclaw stretched out on the sand, crossed his ankles, and closed his eyes.

The long red afternoon wore on. The green sea went on rolling in and out. All was still. No birds flew, no insects buzzed. Nothing crawled on the beach. For the most part, it was a dead world. Yet, in its way, it was beautiful.

"Gene, how come the sun's not going down?"

"The planet's tidally locked. No rotation."

"You mean it's always like this?"

"Yeah."

"How sad. How sad to see a world end."

"Yeah. I think I'll take a nap, too."

Linda rested her head on Gene's shoulder.

"Gene, do you think we'll ever get back?"

"I don't know. It doesn't look like it."

She watched a high thin cloud drift toward the sun.

"Gene, I'm glad we're together."

"Yeah."

Linda stared at the watercolor sky. Presently, she closed her eyes.

PEELE—DINING HALL

THE LORDS AND LADIES HAD GRUDGINGLY ASSEMBLED, rousted out of their beds in the early morning hours. Vehement protest was still being voiced when Tyrene arrived with Thaxton, Dalton, and Dorcas.

"We've not had our breakfast yet," complained a bewhiskered and indignant baronet.

"My lords and ladies," Tyrene announced, "I humbly beg forgiveness for this inconvenience, but we have arrived at what we think is a solution to the murder of the viscount Oren, and, perforce, to that of Count Damik."

A hush fell over the assembled nobility.

Tyrene continued: "We have been up all night with the working out of this solution. Much traffic has passed between the two castles, Perilous and Peele, and between the raindrops, as 'twere. What we would ask you to witness is in the nature of a demonstration. Ordinarily, for any other criminal case, we would hold off presenting this evidence until the preliminary hearing. But the nature of this evidence is so extraordinary and of such subtlety that I wish to reveal it here this morning. My reasons are twofold. One, a person of quality is involved. It has been so long since a scion of a noble house has been brought up on capital charges that I wish this individual's peers to be impressed with the strength of the prima-facie case, so that there is no feeling that we are merely casting about for a suspect, hauling in the first hapless fish to be netted. Two, I believe the evidence to be forceful enough to dissuade a lord magistrate from releasing this individual on his own cognizance after arraignment but prior to a hearing, as is the custom when the defendant is of high noble station. I have no doubt that, were this custom followed, the suspect would flee through a well-chosen castle aspect, where decades might go by before justice prevailed. I hope I have made myself clear."

Tyrene surveyed the room, as if to acknowledge anyone who would pose a question. No one did.

"Very well, my lords and ladies. I shall now turn these proceedings over to the individual by dint of whose unflagging determination and incisive intellect the case was cracked. I am speaking of Mr. Thaxton of the castle."

A murmur went up, borne on a note of surprise mixed with no little displeasure.

Thaxton strode forward. "My lords and ladies. What you are about to see is a demonstration of magic. Now, I well realize that, as castle inhabitants, you regard magic as a commonplace on the order of toast and tea or the Monday wash. But this magic is unusual in that the feats we will perform here this morning are among the few that are known to be possible in this aspect, this world. And they are, at first, not very impressive as magical tricks go. But bear with us, please. I should like at this time to beg the assistance of one of the castle's leading adepts, a person whom you all know, Her Royal Highness, the princess."

Dorcas stepped forward.

Thaxton held up something shiny. "I have here in my hand a coin, a shilling, which I've been carrying in my pocket for a good while now, not having any place to spend it. I'm going to ask Her Highness to make this coin invisible."

Thaxton gave Dorcas the coin. Dorcas held her right hand palm up and placed the coin in it. She brought her other hand down on top of it and stretched her arms out. Then she began to speak some strange words, a few sentences. When she was done, she held her stance for a moment longer, eyes shut.

She took her left hand away. The right was, apparently, empty.

No one seemed impressed.

"Mere legerdemain," someone said.

Dalton came to her, bearing a small cast-iron pot with a metal handle such as would be found in the castle kitchens. He held it below the princess's outstretched hand.

Dorcas slowly tilted her right hand. Something in the bucket clinked.

Mild surprise was evinced. Dalton shook the pot and it rattled dutifully. Thaxton reached his hand and seemed to pick something up. He held his hand up.

"As you can see . . . rather, as you cannot see, the coin is invisible." He poised his hand over the pot, and the pot clinked again. Thaxton repeated the action. He then picked the invisible object out of the pot again.

"My lord, if you would be so kind?"

Uncertain, Lord Arl looked around, touched his chest and said, "Are you addressing me?"

"Yes, my lord. Please take this coin so that everyone knows no sleight-of-hand was involved."

Reluctantly, Lord Arl came forward. Thaxton handed him nothing.

Arl took the non-thing and hefted it. He nodded. "I feel it. It's invisible all right." He handed it back to Thaxton.

"Thank you, my lord. Now, Her Royal Highness has told me that she did not put so great a charge on the coin as the instructions call for. Consequently, it should become visible very shortly."

Thaxton knelt, tilted his hand. There came the unmistakable sound of a coin tinking against the stone floor and settling into a spin. The sound eventually stopped.

Thaxton rose and stepped back, his eyes on the floor. The crowd edged closer.

It took about a minute. Suddenly, the shilling appeared on the floor.

Thaxton picked it up and pocketed it. He looked over heads and made a motion.

Two servants moved a table to the back of the room, and the crowd shifted, clearing a way to it.

Thaxton took a handful of something from another servant. "I have here about half a dozen common tavern darts," he said, holding them up, "borrowed from the Peele Castle recreation room. On the far wall—there, in front—we have placed a target such as could be found in any pub in half a hundred worlds."

Dorcas approached the circular target, reached out, and touched the center ring with her right index finger. Then she accompanied Thaxton to the table, which stood about forty feet away.

Dorcas took a seat at the table. Thaxton handed her a dart. She took it and laid it on the table in front of her. She then began to trace complex patterns above it with both hands. This done, she picked it up with her left hand and gently stroked it with her right.

"I bid thee fly, and strike where I laid my touch."

She handed it to Thaxton. He took it, faced the target, made a few peremptory motions, and threw.

Forty feet away, the dart struck the target dead center.

Dorcas was already working on a second dart. Her preparations done, she gave it over to Thaxton. This time Thaxton faced in the opposite direction and threw the dart over his shoulder.

The dart flew with amazing and quite unjustifiable speed toward the round corkboard target, thunking squarely into the inner ring, tight against its mate.

The crowd by this time was quite impressed.

Thaxton took another prepared dart. He faced the target this time, and simply held the dart between thumb and forefinger. He relaxed the pressure of his fingers and the dart jumped from his hand, streaking to the target with astonishing speed.

Thaxton threw the fourth dart toward the left wall. The dart's curving trajectory led it inevitably toward the front of the room and the target. It struck the bull's-eye with a solid thud.

Thaxton said, "My lords and ladies, what you have seen is

simple parlor magic. Real magic, to be sure, not sleight-of-hand or illusion, but—nevertheless—quite trivial. The spells employed came from a book."

Dalton handed it to him.

"They come, in fact, from this arcane tome, my lords and ladies. *The Book of Magical Diversions* by Baldor of the Cairn. This copy comes from the Peele Library, and I'm told it's been there for generations, quite conceivably dating to the time when the castle was occupied by the aboriginals of this aspect. I am also informed, by qualified scholars, that the book originated in this world, and is in fact the only volume extant dealing in the magic here. As you have no doubt by now guessed, these two spells—the Coin Invisible and the Charmed Dart, could be combined into something quite deadly."

A wave of murmuring realization spread through the assembled nobility.

"Yes, I think you all see what I'm driving at. Some adaptation would be necessary, but the two innocuous spells you have just seen could be cobbled together into an effective assassination spell. A malevolent spell of black magic."

Thaxton set the book on the table. "Of course, the question is, who did the thing? Let's tick off a list of qualifications which any suspect must have. First, he or she must be an adept magician. That would include a large portion of the population of Castle Perilous. But the degree of skill would have to be rather high. High enough to exclude the average magician, which would eliminate most of the castle's Guest population except for a very few, but would include most if not all the castle nobility. And as no Guests were present at the princess's fête, we must cross them off the list entirely. No, only members of the castle's noble families would qualify."

Thaxton began walking the perimeter of the circle of noble men and women who had gathered round.

"It's clear we're still not very near the point where the identity of the murderer becomes obvious, for this book has been sitting on the shelf in the Peele library for centuries. Anyone could have read it, anyone here. But perhaps it would be helpful to find out who read it *recently*, or who could have 'read it recently. And for that we need another book. Peele Castle's guest book."

Bearing a folio* volume, Ruford pardoned his way past his betters. He handed Thaxton the book.

"As you know," Thaxton continued, "it's customary for Peele guests to sign in and check out, hotel-style, so that charges for food, servant wages, and overhead can be assessed. Let's take a look at those who recently stayed at Peele, shall we?"

Thaxton opened the book. "And we find something very remarkable. The half-dozen most recent quests include three individuals who have or had a motive to commit the murder. Lady Rilma, for one." Thaxton stopped in front of her. "It that not true, my lady?"

Lady Rilma drew herself up. "This is an outrage." She glowered at Tyrene. "I will not be browbeaten by this barbarian upstart."

"But you did read the book, my lady, did you not?"

"I certainly don't remember."

"We have testimony from one of the chambermaids. She remembers seeing the Baldor book lying on your night table."

"The word of an illiterate chambermaid—!"

"Who happens to be doing graduate work in magic at the University of Thule. Shall I have the young lady come down and give oral testimony? Tyrene has her deposition already."

Lady Rilma seemed about to explode. "All right! Yes, I read the book. Of what significance is that?"

"None, my lady, except that you hated your husband. He was malicious, boorish, ruthless, and cruel beyond belief, in addition to being an incorrigible philanderer."

"How dare you!"

"True or not?"

"Gods!" Rilma's gaze fell to the floor. "How can I deny it? It's true, all too true. Yes. There is not a person in this room who does not know that I hated Oren. Enough to kill him? Yes! Gods, yes. On one occasion I even tried. He laughed at me when I picked up the scissors. He turned away . . . and I

---

*Up yours, Osmirik.

struck. Had he not been wearing that thick leather hunting waistcoat, I would have stabbed him in the back. But all that was exposed was his arm. If I'd had the presence of mind, I would have opened the scissors and slit his jugular."

"Yes," Thaxton said. "And the fête, when you said you heard your husband grunt with pain and surprise, could the reason really have been because at that moment you plunged an invisible dagger into his back?"

"I did not do it."

"You had a dagger in your possession. True?"

"Yes, concealed in my bodice."

"You saw Oren make improper advances—however acceptable to or even encouraged by the recipient—improper advances to Lady Rowena. You knew this would happen at the fête, because it always did when your husband and the lady met at any gathering. It happened again. You then prepared the dagger, made it invisible—"

"Yes, I did. Yes! I was going to use the spell. But not for him! I didn't kill him!"

"No? Then who was the spell intended for?"

Lady Rilma pointed across the room. "Her! That woman!"

Lady Rowena paled, her hand going to her throat.

"Yes, her! She was just as responsible for my constant humiliation. Even more, because she could have protested, and he would have listened to her. But she had to play the hussy in front of her husband! That vile vixen! It was she I wanted to kill."

"But you didn't."

"No."

"You didn't take the spell any further. Why?"

Lady Rilma wobbled. One of the lords assisted her to a nearby dining chair, into which she slumped.

Her voice was low. "Because the monster would have succeeded in corrupting me completely. He was vile, he was bestial. But if he had driven me to kill, he would have won over me. His victory would have been complete. Through the grace of the merciful gods, I realized this, and I did not go up to Lady Rowena and lay the targeting touch on her. I put the dagger away. Not even when Oren threw the capon wing at me did I take it out again, though anger flashed through me, as it did whenever he struck me."

Thaxton walked away from her, turned. "But the spell would not have worked, my lady."

Rilma was slow in answering. "No?"

"No. There was no way to work the flying-dart spell using a dagger instead of the dart, as it is written in this book. Your Highness, would you explain why?"

"Yes," Dorcas said. "An assassination spell is malevolent magic, sometimes called black, but of course color has nothing to do with it. These parlor tricks are innocuous magic, sometimes called white magic. The latter employs the cooperation of playful spirits, benevolent spirits. Sprites, pixies, wraiths, call them what you will. They will do the bidding of any magician who has the skill to guide and direct them. But a black spell requires the command of a malevolent spirit. The spells in this book are not of this variety. You can render a dagger invisible, but you cannot do harm with it. The flying-dart trick will not work if the dart is directed at a human being."

"Thank you, ma'am," Thaxton said. "So you see, Lady Rilma, you were in no danger of committing murder, unless you had actually attacked Rowena or your husband in the old-fashioned way."

Thaxton continued walking the grim circle of suspects, witnesses, and innocents.

"So, it would take quite a good magician to work up a new spell, in an aspect that didn't admit of much magic. This would take a bit of research. Research that you were in the habit of doing . . . Lord Belgard."

Belgard took out his monocle, rubbed it on the sleeve of his morning coat, and fit it back in. "I won't stand for this."

"You do a lot of reading in magic, don't you, my lord?"

"And what of it?"

"Very dangerous magic."

"Sometimes. Purely a scholarly interest."

"Oh? Then why did you purchase a Helvian dagger? You needn't deny it. Tyrene's plainclothesmen traced the knife by the tiny initials of the smith carved into the boxwood handle.

Not usual in a cheap item, but some craftsmen have pride all the same. The vendor sold that particular type of dagger to several people, but he remembered your monocle. Again I ask you, my lord, why did you purchase the weapon?"

Belgard looked around, huffed, and said, "I simply bought one, that's all."

"So it was you Count Damik saw buying the dagger."

Belgard's shoulders fell. "Yes."

"And he, being a knife fancier, asked you why you wasted your money on such inferior merchandise."

"Yes. He did say that."

"And what was your answer, my lord?"

Belgard summoned his ruffled pride. "I didn't owe him an answer, and I'm damned if I owe you one."

"Could it have been because you were contemplating just such a spell as Her Highness described, an assassination spell to do Oren in at the fête, and you wanted to do it with a common knife that would be hard to trace, a cutlery version of what is known in my world as a Saturday night special?"

"No! I had no such intention."

"You could have read the Baldor book."

"Never clapped eyes on it."

"And there are no witnesses to your having done so, my lord. In that you're quite safe. But the Perilous library has records of dozens of books on magic which you took out on loan."

"What of it? Lots of people do research on magic." Belgard sneered. "Even chambermaids."

"Yes, but not everyone has a motive for killing. You did. You've been stewing in hatred for years. And Oren was eminently detestable. He was a rotter, a scoundrel, and a villain. To say nothing about tupping your wife—"

"You bastard!" Belgard swung his Malacca cane, which Thaxton neatly sidestepped. Belgard lost his grip and the cane went clattering across the flagstone floor.

"So sorry," Thaxton said calmly.

"Yes!" Belgard screamed. "Yes, I hated him, and I would have killed him, once I perfected my spell. And it *is* a guided dagger spell, but nothing like the child's play you seem to think

I'd toy with. No, I've been working on mine for years. It was designed to foil all his protections, all his defenses. It's effective over great distances. I can even cast the spell in my home aspect and have the dagger travel—*invisibly*—through the castle and into Oren's aspect. It's a masterpiece, and it would have worked, if I'd had the time to perfect it. But cast it here? In this aspect? Nonsense! Why? I never saw that book of yours. I don't care how long it's been in the Peele library. I never set eyes on it!"

Thaxton walked away. "No, I don't think you did, my lord."

Thaxton kept stalking. He stopped in front of Trent, who was standing hand-in-hand with his wife.

Trent grinned. "And this is the point in the scene in which the murderer blurts out a confession, right? All right. Means? You're looking at one of the best magicians in the omniverse, if I do say so myself. Motive? I would have killed the son of a bitch eventually, either in a duel or some other way, for molesting my wife and attempting to sodomize her. The man was a mad dog and should have been put out of his misery years ago. There is no end of victimized servants—he had a taste for teenage upstairs maids especially—who can attest to that. And he wasn't content with just rape and 'involuntary deviant intercourse' as the statutes put it. He usually added beating as a lovely little fillip. Opportunity? I could have thrown demons at him at any time, defenses or none, and Tyrene's men would have found his body parts artfully arranged around his billiard room. But Inky would have gotten wind of it and would have been pissed off at me. So, as far as the murderer is concerned, whoever he may be—all I can say is, there but for the grace of the gods go I. Yeah, I confess to intent. But I didn't kill him. Somebody beat me to it."

Thaxton strolled on. "Be that as it may. There is another name in the Peele guest registry. And the name is one that hasn't been bandied about very much, if it was on the suspect list at all. Why do you think that is . . . Lord Arl?"

"Because there's nothing to connect me with the crime," Arl said mildly.

"Oh, but I beg to differ, my lord. You have a reputation as a competent magician."

"Hardly in Trent's league."

"No, but a good one. And you have been known to research in the library."

Arl laughed. "I must say, this is turning into quite a charming little witch hunt. Am I suspect merely because of my bookish ways? Have something against intellectuals, do you?"

"Very clever ploy, my lord, turning the tables like that. Admirable. But it so happens this matter has much to do with reading habits. You did a lot of browsing in the Closed Stacks, where the 'eldritch and pernicious tomes,' as Osmirik likes to call them, are kept. Isn't that true?"

"As did Belgard, Trent at one time or another, and any number of other people. Dangerous books are fun, after all."

"Jolly good fun, but you happened to give close attention to a particular book of black magic, the ironically titled *Flowers of Forgetfulness*. It is in fact a book of spells to do people in, isn't it? A book of assassination spells."

"Never chanced across it, so I can't say."

"Never read it?"

"Can't say that I have."

"I see. Isn't it interesting, though, that this book contains a Flying Dagger spell that is similar in form to the Charmed Dart spell."

"Does it? How interesting indeed."

"Yes, quite. And one very amenable to adaptation. It could easily—given that the practitioner was skillful enough—easily be combined with the dart spell and made to work in the Garden aspect."

"Really."

"Yes. And the spell in the *Flowers* book explains another puzzling aspect of this case. Namely, who pulled the knife out and dropped it? The answer is: it pulled itself out. Would you like to know how, my lord?"

"I'll bite."

"Because the Flying Dagger spell is designed to return the dagger to the assailant after the deed is done. Neat trick, that. No murder weapon to trace. The dagger travels stealthily to the target, strikes, wiggles some to cause more damage—twistin' the knife, don't you know—yanks itself out, and returns as sneakily as it came. But in the viscount's case, that part of the trick didn't work, not completely. Your Highness, would you be good enough to explain to his lordship?"

"Certainly, Mr. Thaxton," Dorcas said. "When spells are combined, as they often are, there is always some difficulty with parts of the component spells canceling each other out. That is probably what happened in this case. The dagger succeeded in extricating itself from the body of the victim, but at that point the spell misfired, and the dagger fell to the ground, inert, the spirit freed from the task of returning it to the assailant."

Arl regarded Thaxton frostily. "Why did you think I wouldn't know about spell misfires?"

"I beg your pardon, my lord. Just trying to be thorough."

"In any event, it makes no difference," Arl said, "because I neither read the book nor cast the spell."

"Let's return to that in a minute, my lord. When I happened to find the dagger, just before I did, I almost ran into you. Could you have been looking for it?"

"Hardly."

"You thought the spell had failed when you didn't get the knife back. It should have dropped harmlessly at your feet. Even though the dagger could not easily be traced, you would have felt safer finding it before the invisibility part of the spell failed as well. Isn't that right?"

"No."

"But you were unable to find it. It was invisible. You couldn't understand what happened at first. In fact, when you followed Oren out, you were wondering if the spell had worked at all, weren't you?"

"I was leaving the party. That's all."

"You saw Oren get up and leave, and you couldn't see the dagger or what it had done, so, beside yourself with anxiety and curiosity, you followed your brother and discovered me with him in the alcove. You knew you had succeeded, but you still didn't understand about the dagger not being in him. At some point you must have realized that the knife had worked its way out but dropped, and when I nearly bumped into you, you were searching for it. And would have found it, were it not for the bad luck of my seeing it first. Perhaps you did see it first, but decided not to be the one to turn it up. Does any of this strike your fancy, my lord?"

"None of it. None of it's true."

"Then why, my lord, did you touch your brother on the back?"

"When?"

"Why, shortly before the dagger struck."

"I don't remember."

"Lady Rilma remembers it quite distinctly."

"She's balmy. Always has been."

"I believe her. And you also touched Princess Dorcas on the back, shortly before you let a second dagger fly, at her. Is that not correct, my lord?"

"No! It's a lie!"

Thaxton turned to Dorcas. "Your Highness, have you any objection to swearing before a court of law that Lord Arl touched you on the back shortly before Count Damik was murdered?"

"None whatsoever," Dorcas answered. "It would only be the truth."

" 'Laying the touch,' " Thaxton said. "Part of the spell. Part of the killing spell. I have the feeling that Lord Belgard's spell is a tad more sophisticated. No need for the touch. Different targeting apparatus entirely. Right, my lord?"

"Entirely!" Belgard answered.

"Yes. Yours, Lord Arl, was a bit technologically backward, taken from a very old book. Your spell was effective up to a radius of no more than fifty yards. But in the Garden aspect that wasn't a problem. Plenty of hiding places. In the lilacs on the other side of the pond, for instance."

"A lie. Lies! Fabrications!"

"Anyway," Thaxton went on, "you tried to murder the princess for the simple reason that she knew that you were the murderer. We won't go into how she knew. Let's say she had a strong suspicion, which you knew about. You had to eliminate her, but, again bad luck. Damik just happened to walk behind her at the crucial instant, and he took the knife. He was a friend of yours, too."

"Yes, he was."

"And you killed him—quite accidental, this killing."

"You're insane. Tyrene, I've had enough of this!"

"Let's get back to the book for a moment. You were less adept than Belgard magically, but quite the cagey plotter. Belgard took his books out on loan. You didn't. You didn't want anything in the library records. So you did all your reading in the library."

"To coin a phrase, so what?"

"But the books were in the closed stacks, and to get to them you had to fill out a call-slip, including the title, author, and call number. We have such a call-slip for the *Flowers* book, in your handwriting."

"Nonsense. I throw those things away. They come back with the book. They're not kept."

"True. But you slipped up. You used one as a bookmark and left it in the book when it was returned. We have it, my lord."

"Which proves nothing! You have nothing but circumstantial evidence! This is an outrage and I won't tolerate it a moment longer."

"But there's a witness."

"What?" Arl's voice went cold. "What did you say?"

"An eyewitness . . . or in this case an *ear*witness, who, among the lilacs and forsythia, heard you chant, 'I bid thee fly, and strike where I laid my touch,' the exact incantation of the Charmed Dart spell. It was a young servant who was in there sneaking a smoke. Naturally, the boy didn't make his presence known. He was, as my American friends put it, goofing off. When you left the lilac grove, the boy saw you. He has so testified."

Arl's face had grown pale. Gradually, the color returned. He took a vast, despairing breath. "I suppose it's no use. Yes, I did it. I cobbled up the spell. It went wrong, I followed Oren out to see what the deuce had happened, saw you, saw that I had succeeded."

"And you were appalled by what you'd done, weren't you?"

"Yes, at first. The sight of him, actually dead by my hand—it shook me. But he deserved to die. Everyone knows that."

"But why did you kill him, my lord? Mind telling us? That we didn't know, and still don't. Namely, the motive."

Arl smiled. "I did it for my son."

"Your son?"

"Yes. Oren was childless, no descendant to take the peerage. But I heard that lately he'd been grumbling about having a barren wife and no offspring. What with Rilma having attacked him, he had legal cause to divorce her. I was afraid of just such a development. In fact, I'd always wondered why he hadn't got rid of her sooner. Finally, after years of agonizing deliberation, I resolved to act before it was too late, before he sired a legitimate son. With Oren dead, the viscountcy would devolve to me, and thence to my firstborn male offspring when I die. It was the only thing I could have given my son. As everyone here knows, I lost most of what little I had to harebrained business investments in partnership with Damik. The peerage was to be my only bequest to my son. To give him a starting point a notch above the crowd. That's all. That is why I did what I did. My motive was unselfish."

Thaxton said, "But you were quite prepared to kill, and in fact did attempt to murder, an innocent person—the princess."

"Yes. I was convinced she knew what I'd done. Were I caught out, the peerage would of course not be transferred to me or to my son. No peerage can be passed by dint of assassination."

"I see."

Tyrene was there with two Guardsmen.

"I'm afraid you'll have to come with us, my lord," Tyrene said.

"Yes, of course."

Thaxton stopped Arl with a touch. "Pardon, my lord. One more thing. You know, you were quite right. The case against you was purely circumstantial. With a good barrister you might have gotten off."

"What hanged me?"

"Your own admission, my lord."

"Eh? What about the young servant?"

Thaxton shrugged, deeply apologetic. "A bluff, my lord. A mere bluff. In fact, this whole proceeding was a bluff. We had no ironclad case against anyone. The case against you was strongest, but still completely circumstantial. We concocted this little melodrama purely in the hope that someone would blurt out a confession. For no other reason would we have put Trent, Belgard, and especially Lady Rilma through this agony."

"And I blurted," Arl said with a wry smile. "Very clever, Mr. Thaxton. Very clever indeed. You are to be congratulated."

Thaxton bowed his head. "Thank you, my lord."

They led him away.

Chastened and silent, the assembly of noble men and women left the hall.

Dalton wore a look of utmost awe. He came up to Thaxton.

"Thaxton, old boy, I'll never insist that you play golf with me again. Tennis from now."

THE TWEELERIES

CLARE TWEEL WAS A BIG, WELL-PROPORTIONED MAN who wore suits tailored to every bulging muscle—the one he was wearing now being no exception. Of a tasteful gray tweed, it was stitched and tucked to accentuate the V-shape of his body. He stood by the fireplace sipping sherry and watching Helen Dardanian put another record on the phonograph.

"You seem to like string quartets," he said.

"When they're not quintets or trios," she said, setting the cactus-needle stylus down on the shellac record. An *adagio* movement began, dark and sombre.

"Not exactly romantic," he said.

"I don't feel very romantic," she said, "prisoner that I am."

"It's temporary."

"You only have twenty minutes left."

"I'll think of something at the last minute. I usually do. Come sit by the fire."

She came over and sat on the Louis XIV settee. She wore a knee-length wine-colored frock with a fashionably low waistline. Her hair was blond and unfashionably longish, eyes a robin's-egg blue. Her face had a lofty, classic beauty, and her legs were long and shapely, turned on the lathe of a master craftsman.

He sat beside her and handed her a glass of wine. She took it. He raised his glass.

"Let's drink to my damnation."

She raised hers. "Damn you, anyway."

He chuckled and drank.

She took a sip. "I must say, you're taking it rather well."

"If you gotta go, you should go with style. No screaming. Don't let them drag you. Walk tall."

"Think you can do that?"

He shrugged. "Maybe. We'll see."

"Is there any way of getting out of it?"

"Demons don't renegotiate contracts."

"I think it's appalling. I can't imagine you feeling anything but a numbing terror."

"Oh, it's scary to contemplate. But I signed the agreement. There were certain terms, certain conditions and obligations. And now, it's time to fulfill my part of the bargain. Can't say that I haven't had fun while it lasted."

"But the price . . . it's awful."

"That comes with the territory."

"Speaking of which, they'll pretty much have your territory when you're gone."

"Yes, they will. But that won't be my problem."

"Their territory will be most of Necropolis, if not all of it."

"John Carney can probably hold them off. For a while at least." He sat back. "But let's not talk about him. Let's talk about us. There's not much time left."

"What about us?"

"Is there any future?"

"But you have exactly . . . nineteen minutes of future left."

"As said, I usually think of solutions at the last minute. We had something going once. I wanted to see if there was any chance of picking it up."

She shook her head. "Whatever could you be thinking of?"

"Of us. Together. As we once were, in love."

"I liked you, Clare. Admired you. Very much. You have it

all, you know. Good looks, riches, intelligence, power. You even have a sense of humor. At times, you've shown tenderness. There's not much more a woman could ask for."

"And yet . . . ?"

She stared into the fire. "There's something missing."

"Nobody's perfect."

She laughed. "Sounds ridiculous the way I put it, doesn't it? I suppose it doesn't make any sense. I suppose I should love you."

His eyes were serious. "Did you once, Helen? A year ago?"

"I suppose . . . Clare, these *words*. Admire, like, love. I can never get the meanings crisp and sharp. They seem to smear over into one another."

"Love is special. A unique entity. Discrete and indivisible. Monadic. It has some special properties, philosophically speaking."

"It's an intellectual thing?"

"No, of course not, but the mind is engaged in some way."

"What is it, Clare? Do you think love can redeem you? Save you?"

"Possibly. Maybe not. But what could make Hell a heaven? Not to reign, but to love. What are hellfire and brimstone to the flames of passion?"

"You really mean it, don't you?"

"Of course. Physical pain? That means nothing. It can be ignored. But an eternity of regretting that I never loved, was never loved? That's unendurable torment."

She looked at him for a long moment. "Clare, I don't know what to say."

He put down his glass, took hers, set it down, and took her in his strong arms. Their kiss was long and involved.

She broke it off and caught her breath. "Clare, I don't think I can help you."

"Don't fell obligated. Doesn't work like that."

"Clare, I do. I do feel obligated somehow."

"Marry me, Helen."

"Marry you?"

"Yes. Be my wife. Be with me forever."

"Clare, I won't go to Hell with you."

"You couldn't. They wouldn't take you. Your beauty would be an affront to them. Not just your face—your soul."

"Clare, this is . . ."

"Say yes, darling."

"Darling . . . seventeen minutes."

"Forget about that. The J.P. is just down the road. He can be here in ten minutes. Besides, the dengs'll grant me a grace period."

"Odd way to put it."

"They will. They like gestures. They'll enjoy stoking a bridegroom into the coals, fresh-plucked from his bride's tender embraces."

"God, Clare, that's awful."

He kissed her again. This time their embrace lasted longer. Her body aligned with his and pressed against him, her right leg up over both his. He stroked her thigh lovingly, longingly.

"I'll marry you, Clare, if you think it'll help. God, it's the least I can do."

"Don't do it for that reason."

"What do my reasons matter?"

He gently pushed her off and got up.

"It's him, isn't it?"

"Who?" she asked.

"Carney. You still love him."

She frowned. "I wasn't even thinking of him."

"I'm not blaming you, Helen. But it has to be full and free, without let or hindrance. No encumbrances."

"I said I'll marry you, Clare. I meant it."

"I believe you. But—"

A resounding crash came from the far part of the mansion. The floor shook momentarily. Shouts and exclamations outside.

"God, what was that?"

"Stay here," he said, striding out of the room.

Once out the door, he ran down the wide hallway, and took the steps three at a time.

On the ground floor he followed his ears through the immense house until he found the source of the commotion in the ballroom.

A gray Leland sedan had crashed through the big French windows, taking a part of the wall with it. The crumpled hood was inside the room, as was the driver's door. John Carney was struggling out. There seemed to be a shimmering aura surrounding him. It was prismatic, colorful, but faint.

Tweel was astounded. "John! Nice of you to drop by."

"Happy New Year! Merry Martinmas! The blessings of Bran be on you."

Tweel threw his head back and laughed.

Carney found the bottle under the front seat and upended it in his mouth. He drained it and looked forlornly upon its emptiness. "To the lees. Finished. No more. Nevermore. The nectar of the dogs."

"Of the dogs?"

"Tastes like dog urine. But smooth." He threw the bottle to shatter against the wall. "*Frater ave atque vale*. Give my regards to olive-silvery Sirmio."

Tweel chuckled. "John, you're polluted."

"Aye, that I be. But do I wake or sleep? That is the question."

"You look wide-awake to me. To what do I owe this unexpected pleasure?"

"I gotta take a piss. I mean my wisdom teeth are doing the backstroke. You got a facility?"

"Yeah. Indoors, too. Down the hall—"

"Wait a minute. Help me with her, will you?"

"Who you got in there?"

"Boss!"

A man with a submachine gun poked his head through the hole in the wall.

"Boss, he crashed the gate! Like a maniac! He tore through the garden, ripped up the lawn—we couldn't stop him. Our damn guns wouldn't fire for some reason!"

Tweel said, "You think he'd come here with his hand inside his fly?"

"The damn car had sparks and stuff comin' off it! You want I should let him have it, boss?"

"Heel, boy. I'll handle this."

"Okay, boss."

Carney was struggling with the not-quite-conscious Velma, trying to lift her out of the car. Tweel helped. They got her upright, and Tweel stooped, letting her fall over his back, and picked her up in a fireman's carry.

Tweel patted a well-rounded buttock. "Nice to see you, Velma."

Carney said, "You told me, 'I wanchu to find Velma for me,' so I did."

"You found her all right. Come on upstairs. Helen's here. We can have a party."

"I always hew to the party line. Where're the dengs, by the way?"

"They're around somewhere. What's going on, John? Is this a social call, business, you selling insurance, what?"

"The time has come, old Walrus-breath, to speak of many things. Like, what the hell is going on with you and the dengs?"

"Oh, they're calling in my marker."

"Yeah? I thought so. When?"

"Midnight. It was twenty-four years ago tonight."

Carney looked at his watch. "Stopped. What's the time?"

"Not too frigging much. Come on, we have time for one drink."

Tweel walked, Carney weaved, out of the ballroom.

In the hall they ran into Fioretto Roberto "Bobby" Speranza, spat-shoed and dapper as ever. His ski-jump nose was a little red, but he was essentially sober.

"Your Honor!" Carney said.

"I wanna tell ya, these dengs are murder," Bobby said. "You go to one of their parties, and you're so happy to get home you're glad you went. Ba-boom. Rimshot. But seriously, folks."

Carney said thickly, "Hell of way to treat a mayor of a great metrotopil . . . metropopol . . . a big town."

"Oh, you're pumpin' ethyl tonight, boy," Mayor Speranza said. "Did you drive here or wash in with the tide? You're sloshed."

"And I intend . . . excuse me . . . to get a lot sloshter."

"Whew, that breath is dynamite! I'd buy you a drink, but it's a clip joint and you'd only disappear at closing time."

"I'm not that kind of girl."

"Speaking of cured ham," Bobby said, gently poking Velma's rear with his cane. "Velma?"

"She has a wooden leg, only it's solid," Carney said.

"Clare, seriously now," Bobby said, "when the hell are they going to let me out of this upholstered cesspool?"

"Bobby, you got me," Tweel said, shrugging Velma. "No, actually, the dengs got me. For keeps."

"They really going to cash in your chips, huh? Well, take plenty of weenies to roast."

"I think they roast other stuff down there," Tweel said. "What can I say, Bobby? There's nothing I can do."

"They got half of the city council here. Any more and we'll have a quorum and send out for pizza."

"It never was your town, Bobby."

"Shit, I know that. But damn it, being the mayor should count for something."

"Didn't you get to cut the ribbon when they opened the sewage treatment plant?"

"Oh, and I still have wet dreams about it, but I mean, *seriously* . . ."

"It's their town now, Bobby," Tweel said, moving on.

"They can have it! Just let me go home and get a shower, f'crissakc!" Bobby watched them walk away. "I'm tellin' ya, it's murder. I'm going to refer the whole thing to my lawyer. He needs a good laugh."

Whistling, twirling the cane, Speranza strolled off down the resplendent mirrored hallway.

"How'd he get elected, anyway?" Tweel said. "I can't figure it."

"Didn't you buy that last election?"

"Yeah, and I can't for the life of me figure out why."

As they rounded a corner, a deng leaning against the damask wall straightened up and took a toothpick from his mouth.

"The Boss wants to see youse."

"Tell Ashtaroth I have a date with him at midnight, not before."

The deng smiled toothily. "You don't got much time." The smile drooped. "Now. Drop the broad."

"Drop dead," Tweel said.

The deng looked at Carney. "You too."

"I'm otherwise engaged, thank you."

"Come on. I wanchu to meet a guy."

"Well, if youse insist. Who's this Ashtaroth anyway?"

"The Boss."

"Come on," Tweel said. "He's commandeered my office."

Tweel's office was an expanse of blue-and-gold deep-pile carpeting and red leather furniture. A well-dressed deng sat behind the polished walnut desk. His eyes were soot-black, his tie whiter than a sacramental host.

"Come in, boys," Ashtaroth said, cigarette in hand.

Tweel laid Velma down on the couch.

"John, nice to see you," the demon said, smiling.

Carney approached the desk. "Have we met?"

The deng said, "We have mutual friends. Can I get you a drink?"

"Yeah, as a matter of fact, before I stuff you back into the stinking hole you came from."

"Is that any way to respond to an offer of hospitality?"

"Deng, your leathery ass is heather, and I got Heathcliffe revving up the combine."

Ashtaroth puffed impassively. "Really. You're pretty drunk."

"Things are not what they seem. I want you and your minions out of here in one minute, starting now."

Ashtaroth plucked the cigarette from his bloodless lips. "Hey, who do you think you're talking to?"

Carney reached across the desk and grabbed a lapel, pulled the huge body forward and took the other lapel, brought the deng's face close to his. Sparks flew from the points of contact.

"WHO THE FUCK D'YOU THINK I'M TALKING TO, FUCK FACE? THE FUCKING WINDOW?"

Astonished at Carney's strength, the deng desperately tried to detach himself. Carney pushed him away and sent him tumbling over the executive leather chair.

The deng rose, slapping at the tiny flames that had sprung up on the lapels of his shiny gabardine suit. "You're dead. I don't care what kinda hocus-pocus you got working, you are one dead cookie, pal."

Carney lanced a finger at him. "I want you out of here, out of this town, and down your hellhole, *pronto,* or you're going to regret it."

The deng came around the desk and strode toward the door. "Get bent. I take no orders from you. Okay, so we can't get no leverage this time, but we're taking him—and there's nothing you can do about that. *We got a contract!"*

Ashtaroth left, slamming the door.

"You guys didn't seem to hit it off," Tweel said.

"Chemistry, you know."

"Yeah. Shit, what am I gonna do?" Tweel sat and passed a meaty hand through his shiny black hair.

"*Now* you worry. Twenty-four years ago you didn't worry so much."

"What can I say? I was a fool. The power, the glory, the shining chrome on the pussywagons, it blinds you."

"Oh, don't make me puke. You got a brain, why didn't you use it? You knew you couldn't win."

Tweel held his head in his hands. "I know, I know. Jesus Christ Almighty."

"Too late for that stuff. Boy, you really got your tit caught in a wringer this time."

"What can I say, Inky? I'm basically an asshole."

"I'd say you were an anal opening of the first magnitude. An asshole's asshole. Not only that, you didn't R.S.V.P. Dorcas's invitation."

"Shit, I forgot. Tell Mom I'm sorry, okay?"

"You tell her when you get back to Perilous."

"That's a laugh."

"Don't worry about it. They're only local demons."

"Their Hell is one of the best in the omniverse, I hear. Exquisite refinements. Really, they are very good at what they do."

"Hooray for them."

"Uncle Inky, what the hell am I going to do?"

"I dunno. I gotta take a piss first, then . . ."

"Ah, enough of this puling," Tweel rose. "I want to see Helen before they take me." He picked up Velma again easily.

Carney said, "Is there a bathroom on the way?"

Helen was staring into the fire, empty wineglass in hand, when she heard the door open.

"John!"

"Hi, Helen. I need a drink or a place to pee, or both, in any order."

She got up and hugged him. "It's so good to see you."

"Nice to see you. They drag you here?"

"Sort of. I wanted to come. I knew he was in trouble."

"He's in a pile of trouble."

"Is Velma okay?"

"Yeah, one ruby grape of Proserpine and she was out like a light."

"Why are you here, John?"

"To save this jerk's butt."

"Oh, John, can you do it?"

"I dunno. I feel it's possible."

She looked up. "John, there's something like faint flame dancing around your head." She drew back from him. "In fact, around your whole body."

"Aura. You read auras?"

"Nope. What's it mean?"

"It means I'm cooking with gas. I don't know what the hell it means, but I feel good. I feel positive. I sense the vibrations. I've been getting more fiber in my diet. Got that drink?"

"There's wine."

Carney reached for the bottle and took a drink. "Excuse me," he said, wiping his mouth on his sleeve, "but I have to keep a certain blood-level up."

"John, you've been drinking. You never drink, very much."

"Dutch courage."

"There's going to be a fight?"

"There's gonna be a battle of epic proportions. Dionysus meets Godzilla, plus selected foreshortened subjects. I wish I could get you out of here."

"Three minutes," Tweel said, staring up at the clock. He looked extremely worried.

"You have to do something, John," Helen said.

"Take it easy. Want a drink?"

"No." She sat on the settee. "He asked me to marry him."

"What was your answer."

"I said yes. It was a qualified yes, though."

"Do you love him?"

"That's always the question, isn't it? It's a question I can never answer. I wonder if I can love anybody."

"You can if you love life. Existence."

"Maybe I don't," she said. "I'm frightened of life sometimes."

"Aren't we all, sometimes. *Videlicet*, the present moment."

"Maybe I don't love life."

"Well, you can learn. But this is hardly the time for deep discussion." Carney took another drink, then looked at her. "What are you thinking of?"

"Being back home, in Illinois. Sometimes I get homesick."

"What did you do to support yourself back there?"

"I worked in a cracker factory. Nights, I sang in speaks. Real dives. In one of them the dancers went bare-breasted."

"Cracker factory?"

"Yes, snack foods, that sort of thing."

"What did you do?"

"I was a taste tester. But I quit to come here."

He took her chin. "Was this the face that munched a thousand chips and spurned the topless bars of Illinois?"

"That's me."

"All is gross that ain't you, Helen."

"John." She kissed him tenderly.

He said, "One kiss from you and I'll be Methuselah."

"Two minutes," Tweel said, his eyes still on the clock. Beads of sweat had appeared on his brow, tiny drops, a film of worry and fear.

The house began perceptibly to shake.

Carney said, "Sit tight and try not to be scared." He patted her hand.

He got up and paced the room, now and then lifting the

bottle to his lips. He examined the paintings, the expensive vases, statuary, and other objets d'art.

"One minute. One minute to live. O gods. Uncle Incarnadine, save me!"

"Stay calm, kid."

Earthquake tremors shook the house. Paintings fell from the wall, vases toppled, and shelving collapsed, spilling fine limited editions all over the floor. Furniture began an eerie dance, shifting positions.

Carney lifted Velma off the couch and brought her to a corner of the room near Helen. He beckoned to Helen and had her sit in the corner, holding on to Velma. He moved a heavy Chippendale highboy in front of them.

"Thirty seconds! Gods save me! I don't want to die! I don't want to burn in Hell forever!"

Tweel was on his knees before the clock, fists at the sides of his head, his eyes shut against the terrible moment about to come.

To the sounds of cracking boards and splintering wood, the floor split down the middle, creating a wide chasm into which rugs, furniture, and lamps plunged. Flames leaped from the abyss. The hole went down to the basement and farther, into a deep pit that was the source of the searing fire. Smoke and sulfurous fumes rose.

Carney threw the wine bottle into the hole. He stood at the edge and unzipped his fly.

Tweel was still on his knees, staring with horror into the Avernean depths, mouth agape. The flames lit his terrified eyes, but he could not avert his gaze from what was in the pit.

"Oh! Is it ugly! Oh, close it up, close it up!"

The smoke and fire coalesced into a form hideous beyond description, but its human lineaments were discernible.

The ugly thing jabbed a taloned finger at Tweel.

"You, shit-breath! Get your ass down here, now!"

A pale yellow stream arched past the thing's face.

"Hey . . . what the bleeding blazes . . . ?"

Carney stood in blissful relief, emptying his bladder into the internal conflagration.

"You, there! Just what in Hades do you think you're doing?"

Carney said. "When you gotta go . . ."

Thick clouds of steam began to rise from the hellflame below. They billowed to the crumbling ceiling and filled the room.

"Now, just a damned minute. You just can't go whipping it out and whizzing wherever your fancy pleases. People live down here!"

"Yeah, they're going to be all upset about a little pee water. Spoil their day, it will."

"That's not the point. The point is you don't casually piss on somebody's property. What if I came over to your game room and took a dump on your pool table?"

Carney grunted pleasurably. "You know, when it's like this, after holding off so long, it's almost as good as an orgasm. Know what I mean?"

The steam roiled up in puffy white clouds, obscuring the fiendish apparition. Carney continued his evacuation, playing the stream in fancy filigrees across the chasm.

At length, he was drained to the dregs. A few last spasmodic spurts, and he was done. He repacked himself and zipped up.

It took a while for the steam to clear. The flames were gone. Nothing was in the pit but sooty, steaming rock, reeking acridly.

The apparition was partially dispersed, but still had voice.

"Son of a bitch! It'll take a thousand years to restart those furnaces! If they start at all! We might have to replace them!"

"Easy installments, no payments till spring."

"Okay, pal, we got your name, and we know where you live. You think you're big stuff? Well, think again. This won't be the last time this abyss gapes before you."

"Abyssinia."

The infernal specter vanished. Faint smoke rose from the pit, carrying a smell like a four-mile-wide kitty-litter box.

Tweel staggered to his feet. He came to the edge of the abyss and looked down. "They're gone. They're really gone." He looked up. "You did it, John. You pissed on the flames of Hell. It was epic. Homeric!"

"Have any more wine?"

CITY AT THE END OF TIME

A GARGANTUAN CATERPILLAR-LIKE MACHINE HAD ARRIVED and disgorged from its hatches hundreds of lesser machines: robots, drones, and automatons of every description. Big and small, they converged on the *Sidewise Voyager,* invading its interior, crawling on the hull, attaching probes and contacts, and generally taking its measure. Then, having reached a consensus on what was ailing the craft, the visitors set about trying to fix it. Tool attachments spun on the ends of mechanical arms, and busy sounds came from within and underneath the crippled ship. The area around the *Voyager* swarmed with antlike metallic workers engaged in countless auxiliary tasks, moving to the music of beeping diagnostic instruments.

Gene, Linda, and Snowclaw had wakened to Goofus's barking and the sounds of the commotion. Fascinated, they watched the goings-on.

The Ablomabel had returned also. Antenna up, the dying being monitored the progress of the robot work force.

"They are saying there is chance of success," the sea-creature said.

"Encouraging," Gene said. "Have they ever worked on anything like the *Voyager* before?"

"All machines are alike in certain respects, perhaps," the Ablomabel said. "Being that they are of the same class."

"If you've seen one you've seen them all. Well, as far as road service goes, these guys sure beat most service stations. They looked very organized. What do they do when they're not helping strangers from another dimension?"

"They do not do much," the Ablomabel said. "The time is long past when they were needed. Now, just maintenance every few centuries."

The work continued. An occasional flash lit up the undercarriage of the ship.

To pass the time, the Ablomabel related the story of his life, describing the seagoing civilization of which he was the last representative. He outlined the history of his race and its cultural, social, and technical development, and tried to fill his visitors in on the last days of the breakup of that culture and its eventual lapse into a moribund state. He also tried to give them some idea of the history and fate of other varieties of intelligent life on the planet. At one time there were thousands, if not tens of thousands, of different but peacefully coexisting races and subraces—all, it seems, the product of technologies that abetted the proliferation of artificial and semiartificial life forms. This glorious pluralism was in the past, however. Now the world was depopulated, almost lifeless.

The trouble for Gene, Linda, and Snowclaw (and perhaps for Goofus, for he seemed to find the narration interesting as well) was that most of the Ablomabel's story was hard to understand in detail.

". . . it was then that the Yvlem decreed the laws of Nyah Lyeh, and the Weem protested, yet they were not so much uncooperative as shifting paradigms in the manner of Gel Minap-Tev, yet they eventually achieved Yow-Negarah. At the same time, factions within the Humenathylathuiopuhthem demurred, wishing to curry favor with the Yvlem, yet not wanting to assume the onus of Slagg-Gefeen. . . ."

At the end of it, the Ablomabel heaved a sigh, and fell silent.

"That was interesting," Linda said. "Thank you, Ablomabel."

"I am only too happy to have obliged," replied the Ablomabel, whose English had improved markedly in just the last half-hour.

"Is there any chance that your race can get reestablished some way?" Linda asked.

"I am afraid that the reproductive machines of the Hblutmen are not capable of being re-*vohm*ed easily, and the task is beyond my poor powers."

"What about the machines helping?"

"Ah, but their doing so would precipitate an ethico-philosophical quincunx. Such a step would invoke the Imperative of Nexial Periphrasis, if I am transliterating correctly."

"Oh. Uh-huh. I see."

They all waited silently, watching the sea roll in and roll out under the huge red sun.

At last the machines made their report.

"They say that the craft is now functioning," the Ablomabel announced, relaying the message. "They estimate the chances of further malfunction to be within the parameters of acceptable risk."

"Meaning it's damned dangerous," Gene said. "But that's okay. We'll be going now."

"Oh, Ablomabel," Linda said.

"Yes," the Ablomabel returned, "sadness is in my primary pumping unit as well."

"But we can't just leave you here. You helped us. You saved our lives."

"What else could an intelligent being have done under the circumstances?"

"A lot of nasty, heartless stuff. But you didn't. You helped."

"Only too happy. Only too happy," was all the Ablomabel could say.

Linda hugged the creature's massive head.

"Goodbye, Ablomabel."

"Goodbye, Linda Barclay. Goodbye, Gene Ferraro, Snowclaw, and Goofus. May you live to see the cosmos reborn in the coming time of the holy Bunya Vree-Gel."

"You too," Gene said. "So long. Thank the machines for us."

"They, also, are glad to have been of service."

They left the Ablomabel to his long, peaceful dying at the edge of the sea.

The lights on the control panel were all green. The craft hummed reassuringly.

Gene snapped switches, pressed buttons. The lights on the panel reconfigured. The engines began to whine and whir.

The flickering montage began again. Thousands of universes flashed momentarily into being, then were gone. Gene darkened the viewport somewhat to make the flickering less hard on the eyes.

Time passed inside the tiny craft. Goofus stood watch while Snowclaw slept snoringly. Gene and Linda played tic-tac-toe on the computer screen, then chess, then Nintendo Super Mario Brothers (Jeremy's doing).

"This is fun," Gene said, "but that music can drive you nuts."

"Watch out for those crawly things. They're . . . whoops! You're dead."

"Damn it. You know—"

Goofus began to howl.

"Goof? What's the matter?"

A high-pitched beeping sounded.

"Hey, that's the alarm!" Gene yelled. "The locater spell."

Outside, the flickering had stopped. Below was a green, forested world.

"She's in this universe," Linda said.

"Yeah, but *where* is the question."

Goofus was barking excitedly, thrusting his head between Linda's and Gene's shoulders.

"Hey, Goof? Take it easy, okay?"

Goofus seemed to want to jump through the viewport.

"I guess we're on the right track," Gene said.

The craft cruised at an altitude of about a hundred meters,

following a winding stream below. Here and there, verdant early summer wheat fields showed evidence of intelligent and probably human habitation.

Goofus turned his head to the right and barked. Gene banked the craft accordingly and came about to the new heading.

"See anything?" Gene asked.

"No. Wait a minute! There are some guys . . . There she is! Gene, I see her! Uh-oh."

"What?"

"She may be in trouble. Gene, land quick."

"Okay, but I'm not good at this."

Gene sent the *Voyager* into a power dive and leveled off at the last moment. The craft settled gently in the middle of a clearing.

"Hey, not bad for a tenderfoot pilot."

"Let's get to her quick!"

With difficulty, they all spilled out of the craft.

"Which way?" Gene said. "I lost my bearings."

"Follow Goofus!"

"Oh, yeah."

Goofus led them a merry chase through woods, down an incline and up a hill, following a beaten path. Eventually Goofus lost his pursuers and disappeared into the brush.

"Gene, hurry!"

"I'm coming, I'm coming."

They came out of the woods onto a rutted road, where they beheld a strange sight. Goofus was trying to chew the sword arm off a chain-mailed knight. The man was writhing on the ground near a naked Melanie, who just sat there watching. Nearby, two other knights lay bloodily dead, while a third man, sword in hand, stood idly by, observing the scene with detached curiosity.

Linda dragged Goofus off his victim. The man groaned, holding his mangled arm.

"Phasers on stun," Gene said, pointing his futuristic weapon at the man. The gun went *voomp* and the man fell over unconscious. A green cross was emblazoned on the white tunic that covered his suit of mail.

"Just for insurance until we find out what's going on," Gene said. "Shoot first and ask Christians later is my motto."

Linda brought Melanie her clothes.

"Hi, there!" Gene said to the man who was watching. "There's a Federation law against interference, but, hey, screw it!"

"He saved my life," Melanie said, pulling on tights. "Or tried to, anyway. And he doesn't know me from Adam."

"Is that why he's eavesdropping?"

"Melanie, what happened?" Linda said.

"Oh, these are the days when knights were bold, I guess. They were going to rape me and this one tried to kill me. Who's the dog belong to?"

"That's Goofus, and he found you," Linda said.

"Thanks, Goofus."

"Whoorrrrff!"

"I thought I'd never see you again," Melanie said.

"You thought! My God, I was sick with worry. You were my responsibility."

"I guess stepping into that aspect was dumb, huh?"

"You couldn't have known, and I should have kept my eye on you till you did know."

"Hey, this guy's head is split like a melon," Snowclaw said.

"I did that," Melanie said soberly.

"You?" Linda was amazed.

"Never in a million years did I think I could ever kill anyone. But I did."

"Well, you did a pretty good job," Snowclaw assured her.

"I'll have to live with it for the rest of my life."

Decent again, Melanie went up to the stranger who had come back for her.

"You didn't have to come back. You risked your life for me."

He had no trouble understanding. "Aye. I've been known to do stupider things." He sheathed his sword. "But all's well that ends well. I'll trust your friends to take you home. I'll not ask what far country you or they come from. 'Tis all been passing strange."

She kissed him on the cheek. "Thank you."

He smiled. "Be well, girl. And don't leave home again without a husband or some man to look after you."

He turned and walked back up the hill. Melanie watched him go. Then she called out to him. "What's your name?"

"I'm called Baldor. Baldor of the clan Cayrn. Fare thee well, pretty maid!"

Linda found Gene pointing his gun at a tree. He fiddled with the setting and aimed again.

"Gene," Linda said, "what are you up to?"

"I gotta see what 'vaporize' does."

"Don't destroy a tree just to—"

A plume of wispy smoke wafted out of the barrel of the weapon. It billowed into a faint cloud and dissipated quickly.

"What the shit is this nonsense?"

"You wanted vapor, you got vapor," Linda said, laughing.

"Probably hair spray. Or deodorant." He holstered his weapon. "Let's beam the hell offa this jerkwater planet."

"Right, Captain."

"We need an ending, here. Where's Gene Roddenberry when you need him?"

CASTLE PERILOUS—APOTHECARY

IN RUMPLED EVENING SUIT WITH BLACK TIE UNDONE and hanging, the King of the Realms Perilous came walking in, holding an ice bag to his head.

"Ramon!"

No answer. He bellowed again, wincing. "Ramon!"

Ramon the apothecary came out of the back room. "What's the big emergency?—Oh. Your Majesty. What can I do for you?"

"You can shoot me or give me something for this headache. It's killing me."

"Can't you whip up a spell?"

"If I had any pharmaceutical spells handy I'd whip one up, but as you can see, I'm dying. Besides, what I'm hung over with, magic can't touch. Now, can you get cracking?"

Ramon raised his pale eyebrows. "Well, you don't have to shout."

"Move, Ramon."

"Yes, Your Kingship." Ramon went back into his cubicle. There he rattled bottles and retorts, put pestle into mortar and pestled something, then poured something which bubbled and fizzed. He came out carrying a beaker of fizzing, bubbling stuff.

"Drink this off," he said.

The king took it and downed it.

"Gods, that's awful."

"It'll work."

The king gave back the beaker. "Thanks, Ramon. See you later."

"I'll put it on your bill."

"Yeah."

He held the ice to his head all the way up to the castle's Administrative Offices.

He came through the door to find his secretary typing away. The secretary jumped to his feet.

"Sire, you're back! There are a hundred matters . . ."

"Just the important stuff, Tremaine. I'm dyin'."

"What's amiss, Sire?"

The king went through to his office. "My frigging head, that's what. What have you got?"

"We must review the case of the Advocate General against Lord Arl. That is the most important. Then there is . . ."

"Wait a minute."

The king took a seat at his desk. Behind him, a cinquefoil window opened onto an aerial aspect of a huge modern city.

"First things first. Draft a letter of commendation to Tyrene and his detectives. They did a good job of basic legwork. And, let's see . . . oh, yeah. Thaxton."

"He cracked the case, Sire."

"So I was told. I was suspicious of Arl, but I wasn't sure, because when I scanned the scene of the crime I couldn't see a thing. I knew magic was afoot, but I wasn't sure Arl was up to it. Anyway, Thaxton really surprised me. Let's give him a peerage."

"What? I mean, Sire, we can't—"

"Why not? Make him a duke."

"Duke?"

"Duke."

"Duke of what?"

"Duke . . . duke . . . Duke of Earl."

Tremaine sputtered, "Duke . . . Duke—?"

"Duke of Earl," the king repeated.

"Sire, I really don't think we have a slot available for a duke."

"No? Okay. Forget the peerage, just give him a fancy title. Uh . . . make him a lord."

"Very good, Sire."

The king swiveled around to look out the window. "Gods, my head. Leave me alone for a minute." He watched the clot of traffic on the streets below. "Oh, Tremaine?"

At the door, Tremaine said, "Sire?"

"Dorcas's boy Clare? He's back. Send him down to the stables for six months. Punishment detail."

"Yes, Sire."

"Half a year of shoveling shit ought to straighten that foul ball out. *Uhhh,* my head."

"Very good, Sire."

Tremaine shut the door, silently mouthing, *"Duke of Earl?"*

GAMING ROOM

THE WHOLE GANG WAS ON HAND, talking, laughing, gaming.

The windows opened to the castle's "real" world, and mullioned glass doors led out to a balcony that provided a spectacular view of the Plains of Baranthe, now steeped in the light of a full moon.

Thaxton and Dalton were playing chess. So were Gene and Goofus. The chess pieces were big enough for Goofus to get a good but delicate grip on them with his teeth.

Gene castled. Goofus moved his queen's bishop up for a daring gambit.

M. DuQuesne looked on with amazement. "That is one intelligent animal."

"I dunno about that," Gene said. "He's only beat me once."

Dalton looked up at his partner. "You suspected Arl from the very first, didn't you?"

"Yes. The first thing he said when he saw the body was, 'What do you know of this?' Not 'What happened?' or 'How did he die?' Subtle difference, there, and at first I thought I might be imaginin' things, but I got the feeling he knew more than he was telling."

"Remarkable. I wonder what his fate will be."

"The rope, I suspect."

"You think?"

"If they don't give him a bloody medal. Oren was a monster. No one's going to be mournin' the blighter."

"Still, murder is murder."

"And murder will out. 'Out, damned spot' and all that sort of rot. And a bit of 'O they're hangin' Danny Deever in the mornin'.'"

"I must say, you've a cheery outlook on this sort of thing."

"Oh, well, it was a bit of fun, and we all had a jolly good laugh. Actually, old boy, I owe it all to you."

"Eh? How's that?"

"Well, if it hadn't been for Dorcas Bagby, I wouldn't have found Baldor of the Cairn next to her in the B's."

"Message for Mr. Thaxton!"

A young page rushed to Thaxton had handed him a wax-sealed envelope.

"Thanks, m'lad." Thaxton looked at the seal. "The king's signet. Well, I wonder what—"

Everyone crowded around as Thaxton read the note.

Dalton drummed the table with his fingers. "Well? For pity's sake, Thaxton."

Thaxton said, "Seems I'm bein' elevated to the peerage."

"Really!"

"That's wonderful," Linda said, pecking his cheek.

"Congratulations," Gene said. "What rank?"

"Lord."

"Is that high?"

"Oh, I don't really know. It's not a rank in itself, I don't think. It's a rather general title. It comes with no estate, so it's nothin' more than an honorific."

"You mean I'll have to call you 'Lord Thaxton' from now on?" Dalton said.

"Well, as there's no hereditary title or estate, the usual custom is to use the given name."

"You know," Dalton said, "this is extremely odd, but I don't know your given name. If you've told me, I've forgotten."

"It's Peter."

"So your title would be 'Lord Peter'?"

"That's right, old man. But don't feel obligated to use it. I'm not one for puttin' on airs."

Dalton eyed him at an angle. "Any reason why you're suddenly dropping your *g*'s?"

"Am I?"

Dalton moved his knight. "Check. And, I believe, mate."

Thaxton surveyed the board. "So it is. Good game, old man."

"Really. Now, usually you get good and mad."

"Do I? Sorry. Well, I need a bit of air."

Out on the balcony, Thaxton breathed deeply. The air was cool, fresh, unpolluted. It was a balmy spring night. The moon—bigger and with different markings than Earth's—hung like a beneficent smiling face in the sky. The castle was spread out below, vast and mysterious in the moonglow.

Leaning against the balustrade, Thaxton laughed into the night.

"Bloody marvelous."

ADMINISTRATIVE OFFICES

IN THE STREETS BELOW, traffic was approaching gridlock. It was a typical day in the big city. Strangely enough, in all the days since he'd moved into this office, he'd never bothered to find out what city it was, though it had always seemed to him that it looked a lot like . . .

The intercom buzzed.

"Yeah?"

"Call on line one."

"Who?"

"A man who says he's the Land Surveyor?"

"Rats. Okay, I'll take it."

He picked up the phone.

"Hello? . . . Yeah, this is the castle . . . yeah . . . uh-huh . . . uh-huh . . . no. No, I'm sorry. Look . . . yeah . . . yeah . . . Look, Franz, can you? . . . Yeah . . . yeah . . . yeah . . . Hold it a minute . . . Wait, let me give you some advice."

He glanced down at the hopelessly clogged traffic, then leaned back in the swivel chair.

"Franz? Get a life."